ADVANCE PRAISE FOR MENDEL:

"A fantastic read! This fictional story gives insight into what some young student-athletes dealt with on a regular basis growing up on the South Side of Chicago."
—Howard Griffith, two-time NFL Super Bowl Champion of the Denver Broncos

"'Love is sacrificial.' The central theme of this book resonates with me most. I saw firsthand the sacrifices made for me being raised by a single mother. This story depicts perfectly how one's high school experience can shape one's future."
—Ernie Young, former Major Leaguer, Olympic Gold Medalist in 2000 Sydney Olympics, and Coach of USA Baseball National Team

"*Mendel*, the story, pays tribute to the Catholic institution, on the South Side of Chicago that impacted the lives of tens of thousands of melanated youths of the inner-city and forever changed their lives, as indicated by the character, BJ in the story. Read it! You won't be disappointed."
—Nolan Lane, former professional baseball player for 13 years drafted by Cleveland Indians

"Mendel is a gritty urban story with heart."
—Jenna Mattison, direc⸺ ⸺⸺⸺ ⸺⸺⸺⸺ ⸺⸺⸺ ⸺, and producer

"*Mendel* by Damone Bester is an absolute must read. Though a fictional story, the main character, BJ's interactions with classmates, teammates on the track team and home life is relatable for many inner-city youths today."
—Ed Adams, Hall of Fame track coach, six-time track state championships, nine-time Indoor/Outdoor Catholic League Championships, nine-time Chicago Coach of the Year

"The very first chapter took me back to my freshman year working hard to avoid being tossed in that huge "P-shaped" pond during Homecoming Week. I graduated from Mendel in 1976 and BJ's character is so real, he could have been any number of classmates I had there. Mendel was a life-changing experience, and so will this book be to anyone who opens their heart to it."
—The Honorable Judge George Stephenson (Minnesota, Second Judicial District)

"An extremely powerful story of a young black man, from his high school days at the prestigious Mendel Catholic Prep, where I also had the privilege to attend. Brandon -aka- BJ and I would have definitely been Homies." —Dr. Ramel Werner, Educator Chicago Public Schools

"A profoundly impactful literary work of art that moves your spirit to pursue its highest dreams. Damone Bester's creative style masterfully conveys what makes Brandon tick. Mendel is a precious jewel for your reading collection."
—Dineaux Hanson, actor, voiceover artist and sports announcer.

MENDEL

DAMONE BESTER

THE
STORY
PLANT

The Story Plant
Studio Digital CT, LLC
P.O. Box 4331
Stamford, CT 06907

Story Plant trade paperback ISBN-13: 978-1-61188-326-8
Fiction Studio Books e-book ISBN-13: 978-1-945839-63-4

Visit our website at www.TheStoryPlant.com

First Story Plant Paperback Printing: April 2022
Printed in The United States of America

To Geno. This book would not exist if it wasn't for two old friends reminiscing.

And to all the Mendel and St. Martin De Porres track teams. Blue Smoke, baby!

Acknowledgements: Darell Bester, Karla Bester, Mark Bester, Eugene Billings, Anthony Brown, Jerome Brown, Jason Davis, Ron Dubin, Isaiah "Zeke" Johnson, Dr. Allan Joseph, Tim Levy, Mark Malatesta, Jenna Mattison, Dr. Ramel Werner, and special acknowledgement to Coach Ed Adams who taught us to "reach back" and "dig deep."

CHAPTER 1

A BRIEF HISTORY

/

Love is sacrificial and often comes at great cost. My parents taught me that through their own sacrifices. It took me a while to learn it, but once I did, it was a lesson I have never forgotten. One doesn't simply *live* in my hood; you *survive*.

Yet not everyone can survive growing up the Chicago way. It takes a certain kind of toughness, tenacity, grit. Some people fold, others break; few survive. Survival looks different to many people. For a young Black male living on the South Side of Chicago, survival isn't guaranteed. That's why my story's atypical, and maybe by sharing my story I can help other kids my age too.

My life in Chicago was—I loved Chicago. I still do. The neighborhoods, the parties, the music, my family, friends, enemies, even the gangs, all had a part in raising me. Everything about Chicago—especially my old high school, Mendel—shaped me into the person I am today.

Founded back in the fall of 1951, Mendel was run by the Augustinians. It was named after Gregor Mendel, who was called the Father of Genetics. My old high school sat on a luxurious plot of land nearing forty acres. During the spring and summertime, Mendel looked like it had been plopped down in the middle of a plush forest. Green was everywhere. Huge shrubs and sky-scraping evergreens stretched for blocks, encircling the monstrous campus.

Bordering the prickly pines was a continuous chain-linked fence topped with barbwire that surrounded the entire school. The never-ending fence was about eight feet tall and was so close to the trees that the brush needles protruded out the mesh gate. This made Mendel look more like an impenetrable fortress than an inner-city high school.

People constantly joked that I attended high school on a college campus. Mendel even had a pond smack dab in front of the school's main building. It was rumored the pond was originally made to look like the capital letter *P* for Pullman. That was the name of the school before it was Mendel, Pullman Tech. I believed the rumors were true because there was an old, corroded patch of land at the north end of the pond. It was clear to me that this "island" probably served as the hollowed-out portion of the capital letter *P*. Over the years, the apparently once beautiful pond morphed into the shimmering gray puddle that we were stuck with.

During my tenure at Mendel, many freshmen got dumped into the school's pond. It was almost like a rite of passage for seniors to dunk the freshman. Thankfully, I never had the privilege of being dunked. Neither did I attempt to drown any freshman. Although, there were a couple that I wanted to humiliate in the waters of "Lake Mendel," like when Prince embarrassed Apollonia in *Purple Rain*. But I didn't want to get suspended.

On either side of the main building, where most of the classes were held, were two other buildings. The tan brick building to the left was Mendel's gymnasium and cafeteria. That's where all the good grub, exciting hoop squad games, and after parties went down.

The one on the right was the school's monastery. That's where the chemistry lab, the art classes, and the band practices were held. Not to mention where we would congregate for Mass every week like clockwork.

Mendel was a Catholic college preparatory school situated in the Roseland community on the city's South Side. Unfortunately, my neighborhood gained the notoriety of being called the Wild-Wild or as others called it The Wild Hundreds. Not the kind of monikers you want your community to be known for, being wild.

Yet on Mendel's campus, my crew and I always felt safe. We were a city unto ourselves, the students, faculty, and staff. Within Mendel's "city" gates, both the teachers and students strived for excellence. That was their reputation way before I got there. In fact, many of the teachers at Mendel were once students. That showed how special of a place Mendel really was to have former students come back there to teach. The Mendel community had always been a close-knit family. And in every family, there's a history that laid the foundation for the future.

One of the things I loved about Mendel was they didn't have the same old classes that every other school had: English 101, Intermediate Algebra, Geography. Boring! We had classes like Life Skills, the private school's version of Home Economics. Life Skills was taught by Brother Tyler. In that class, we learned how to balance a checkbook, create a budget, shop for groceries, even change a tire.

In Mrs. Epps class, My Own Biz, for juniors and seniors, we learned how to set up a business plan, learned whether to become a sole proprietor or an LLC, learned how to invest in real estate, and learned how to gauge if a business would turn a profit or fold in the first two years.

But my all-time favorite class was Morality & Ethics, taught, oddly enough by Mrs. Morales. Mrs. Morales was a gorgeous, fiery Latina. My boys and I loved Morality & Ethics class because we could argue at the top of our lungs when debating our point.

The way Mrs. Morales' class worked was she would introduce a topic at the beginning of class. Then we had ten minutes to come up with our arguments as to why the topic was or was not morally ethical and we'd discuss the topic for the majority of the class. During the last five to ten minutes, Mrs. Morales would give her supposition of the topic. It was great. Sometimes she would break us up into teams, other times, she'd have us fend for ourselves, individually.

But it was midterms; that meant we had to write out our answers in essay form. I had already zipped through my exam and was daydreaming about how horrible

Christmas break was going to be when the school bell rudely interrupted.

I whipped my head around. A parade of classmates passed my desk donning their mandatory private-school dress code attire. The girls in their white, pink, or pastel blue blouses with black or gray skirts. Guys with our gray, black, or navy-blue slacks and cardigans along with white or pastel button-down shirts. We were already looked at a bit differently by our public-school friends for going to private school so, most of us felt that we were branded by having to wear uniforms on top of it.

Since Mendel's inception, we had been an all-boy's school. Yet due to increasing financial woes, we turned co-ed that semester to expand admissions, which made for a pleasant experience.

The hallways suddenly smelled fresh and perfumy.

Guys didn't beef as much anymore because they wanted to show how popular and cool they were. The girls at Mendel were attracted to a smidgen of *bad boy*. No one really wanted an outright hoodlum.

And for some reason, even most of the teachers seemed nicer once the girls arrived.

We descended upon Mrs. Morales' desk like a gaggle of geese being fed Ritz crackers. I was last in line to hand in my exam. I placed my test on the desk and turned to leave. Mrs. Morales' accented shriek stopped me dead in my tracks. I looked back over my shoulder.

Mrs. Morales waved me over.

I huffed out a sigh and obeyed her command. Her eyes peered at me over the top of her wire rimmed glasses as I approached. She waited patiently for the last student to exit.

"Thought about what we discussed?"

"Some," I answered respectfully unenthused.

"Well?"

"I. . .I don't know."

Mrs. Morales sighed a deep sigh and leaned back in her chair, "See the nine o'clock news last night?"

"No."

"There was a student, graduated from Julian last year," she sat up again. "He wasn't working. Didn't go to college. Just hanging around taking the year to decide what he wanted to do with his life, family says. He was shot in the head yesterday, died on the spot. You know why?"

"Any number of reasons. Owed somebody money, disrespected someone, um—"

"No. He didn't have a plan. You only have one semester left, BJ. What's your plan?"

"I don't know Mrs. Morales."

"Armed forces?"

"No."

"College?"

"No."

"Why not?"

"Who has the money for that?"

"Get a scholarship."

"A scholarship? Doing what?"

"I don't care. Anything Brandon."

Mrs. Morales took a deep breath turning her head slightly. She removed her glasses. Looking up at me genuinely, calmly, she said, "You need to come up with a plan for your life, BJ, or you'll be the next person shot 'for any number of reasons.' Comprende?"

I nodded.

"Now, go on. You don't want to be late picking up Monica."

Even though she dismissed me, I knew she wasn't finished with this discussion by a long shot.

"Have a good Christmas," I said softly.

"Mm-Hmm, you too," Mrs. Morales replied scooping up the test papers. I could tell by the way she banged the exams on the desk straightening them into a pile she was slightly annoyed with me. I wish I cared more than I did. Truth was, I didn't know what the future held for me. I didn't care whether I lived or died.

CHAPTER 2

OUT WITH THE OLD

/

As soon as my baby sister and I entered the house we were attacked by the sound of screeching furniture being dragged across a hardwood floor. This caused the "Junior Detective" of the house to sprint off to find the source.

"Spud, get out of that wet Gi," I yelled after her. As usual, she ignored me.

Mr. James thought it would be a good idea to put Monica into martial arts to help burn off her endless supply of energy. In theory it was a good idea, not in practice. Spud came home even more wound up, eager to try all her wrist-grab locks on me.

I picked up Monica from day care after being scolded by Mrs. Morales and took her to kid's class at Master Miller's Academy on the South Side, a Dojo for this Korean martial art called Kuk Sool Won.

I locked the front door behind me and that's when it hit me. My olfactory senses were accosted by the overpowering smell of Pine-Sol, or Lysol, or some other kind of Sol. I began choking to the point of gagging.

It quickly dawned on me; it was the day that Auntie Emma and Mr. James wanted to clean the entire house from attic to basement. In addition to cleaning, there was some nonsense about downsizing and packing up the rest of Mom's belongings. To me, that was just a nice way of saying "out with the old," meaning my mother, and "in with the new," meaning Mr. James. But I wasn't having it.

The transition of having an unwanted house guest may have been a little easier to deal with if Mom were still around. Even though Keko and I shared the same gene pool, it felt like there was a total stranger living in my house. He had only been gone for eight years or so, but still, I didn't know him at all any anymore.

Of course, Auntie Emma felt comfortable; she had her baby brother back. But how he conned Monica to fall head over heels for him in a few months, I have no idea. My mother was still pregnant with Monica when Keko went to jail, yet she was calling him Daddy like she'd known him her whole brief existence.

Not me. There was no way in the world Daddy was rolling off these lips. Matter of fact, I didn't call him Daddy, Pops, Dad, Father, Papa, or even Keko for very long. I was cursed with being a "junior," but I never called him Brandon Sr. either. Mr. James was the name I finally settled on, "Mr. James."

The ear-aching noise shrieked again. I fought my way through the invisible cloud of cleanser fumes to my mother's old bedroom. I stepped into the open doorway. There was a whirlwind of clutter. Mama's shiny blue footlocker was in the center of the floor. A carved trail etched in the hardwood floor revealed that the footlocker was either pushed or dragged from the closet to its present spot. The floor's surface was ruined.

Ordinarily, the likely culprit would have been the sweaty little girl, who was still in her Gi, sitting in the middle of Mom's queen-sized bed amongst a pile of clothes. There was a slight beauty to Monica's annoying defiance. I affectionately referred to my mother and Monica as my "heart." Well, Mom was the "heart." Monica, the "heartbeat," always running, jumping, bumbling around. That girl could never keep still. Even if we managed to corral her, we couldn't keep her mouth closed. Inquisitive described most six-year-olds, relentless described my baby sister.

Monica had Mom's jewelry box open on her lap, and appeared to be wearing every bracelet, ring, watch, and necklace she could find. Quite a phenomenal feat considering it only takes about eight seconds to walk from the front door to Mom's bedroom.

"Monica, what are you doing? Thought I told you to get out of that Gi."

Hmph, ignored again.

Finally, Auntie Emma surfaced from the walk-in closet with arms full of Mom's clothes still on their hangers. "Emily" was her real name, but we called her "Auntie Emma" or "Auntie Em" for short. She flung the clothes onto the bed almost drowning Monica, who just giggled, and punched her way through the jeans, blouses, skirts, and dresses.

"Hey, baby."

"Hey, Auntie. What's going on in here?"

Auntie Emma sighed, "Downsizing Kathy's stuff."

"Downsizing?"

"Yeah, shipping some stuff off to a few of your mom's kinfolk in Detroit and Texas."

"Detroit and Texas?"

"Are you a parrot? Quit repeating everything I say. She has a few cousins around her size. The shoes? I'm taking the ones that I like that I can fit. The rest of the stuff will either go to the Salvation Army, Goodwill, somewhere."

It really didn't matter what she told me. I wasn't going to like her answer anyway. Auntie Emma disappeared again into the wardrobe.

"To the same cousins who couldn't even make the funeral?"

"BJ, not everybody has money to travel at the drop of a dime."

She reemerged flinging another pile of clothes onto the bed. Then immediately buried herself back in the closet.

"Why do we have to get rid of any of it?"

"What, baby?" she said popping her head out.

"It just seems. . .all of this stuff is a part of her, you know? I don't understand why y'all trying to erase all traces of her."

Auntie Emma walked over to me and placed her hand on my shoulder. She looked me square in the eyes and told me in only the way that Auntie Emma could, "Boy, get out of here with all that sulking, you giving me a headache."

Before shooing me out of the room, Auntie Em hugged me, and told me that I had such strong feelings because it was the first time I'd lost someone really close to me. I guess when you've lost as many friends as Auntie Emma has you become a little numb to death. Not me. It's been seven months and I still haven't gotten used to her being gone. I mean, I was never going to see my mother again. Why didn't anybody get that?

Auntie Emma experienced a lot of death because of the old gang ties she and my father had when they were younger. She use to tell me all about their gang fights and drive-by shootings. She'd get so into the story; it was like watching a post-traumatic stress disorder victim reliving an attack. Her voice cracked, and her body shook as if she had the chills. She'd stare off deep into space as she slowly talked. At times, tears would roll down her face, tear after tear in a constant flow as she reminisced. Then she would suddenly snap out of it and glare at me. I would be totally engrossed by the story, of course, not so much in admiration, but rather in shock or sometimes disdain.

I think she knew I was somewhat affected by these stories, so she slowly, but surely stopped telling me of her wild days with my dad. He was often jailed for those wild days.

Besides, I didn't have to hear tales about my father from my mom or his big sister. My dad was a thug legend on both the West and South Side. I heard story after story from the older guys in the hood about Dad stealing cars, fighting, selling drugs, bullying people. I've even witnessed his hoodlum lifestyle myself, firsthand.

I moseyed out of my mother's old bedroom into the living room. Before I knew it, a single tear was on my cheek followed by a wave of emotions that I hadn't felt since the funeral. Seeing the pile of clothes and shoes and jewelry that screamed "Kathryn James was here," all being prepared to ship off to relatives I barely knew was extremely difficult for me.

I could still see her lounging in certain outfits that were strewn across the bed. Like her favorite purple sweater that had the Tabasco sauce stain that wouldn't come out even after several washes. And those faded Jordache jeans that were so old that she threw patches over the knees. Mom always preferred comfort over the latest fashions. She use to always tell me, "BJ, it's too cold outside for you to be trying to look cute." We disagreed often on that point. It was never too cold to look "fly."

I grabbed the family photo album off the coffee table and plopped on the couch. Thumbing through those forgotten pictures was enough to bring a smile to my face. There were so many happy memories that included my mom: backyard barbecues, birthday parties, Thanksgivings, Christmases.

As I reminisced, one picture came to life. I took the picture from underneath the thin plastic covering to examine it more closely. It was a picture of Mom and me racing each other in front of the house. I grinned even harder. I had to be only about nine years old in that picture. *Man, she loved to run.* I often wondered why she never played sports in school. That's when it hit me. I had been robbed of the opportunity to know more about her, to make new inquiries, to make additional memories.

I wouldn't be able to share the best moments of my life with her. She would never see me graduate from Mendel or meet my future wife or kids. She would never see Monica grow up and have a family. She never got to see Mr. James come back. Even though I had beef with him, she still loved him, and wanted to be with my dad again. I guess I should be grateful for such a positive example. My parents were still married when Mom. . .well, it just wasn't the norm in our neighborhood.

A sorrowful dread settled within me as I remembered her. I tried to think about something different, something pleasant but I couldn't. I was heartbroken. My body began to tremble as I was on the very brink of an emotional breakdown right there on the family sofa. That was until a thunderous bang that seemed to shake the entire house saved me.

"What was that?" I yelled to Auntie Emma, fighting back tears.

"Your daddy's in the attic clearing out some of Kathy's old stuff," she shouted back. It was bad enough that Auntie Emma was getting rid of my mom's belongings, but I couldn't let Mr. James throw away memorabilia too.

"Here," she yelped again. "Come take this footlocker up to him."

I shut the picture album and sprang to my feet.

/

THE SECRET PLACE

We lived in a modest two-flat home on 114th Street between State and Perry. My dad got the house after I was only a few months old. We lived on the first floor; Auntie Em had the entire second level to herself.

The back stairs ran the entire length of the house connecting the first and second floor back porches. Many houses on the South Side had similar setups, but with the staircases on the outside. We were fortunate enough to have our stairs inside the house, which made it a lot easier to run up, and down to see Auntie Emma, especially during the winter.

I lugged the weighty footlocker through the kitchen to our back porch. Taking a second to catch my breath, I climbed the mountain of steps all the way up to the attic.

The structure of our attic always intrigued me. The only way in or out was through the back stairway I had just entered. It was essentially one gigantic room that ran the full length of the house. The side walls were shaped like an upside-down letter *V* because of the roof's incline. Anyone my height, five ten or taller, needed to walk down the center of the attic or run the risk of smacking their head on the pyramid-shaped ceiling.

And for some reason there was no overhead lighting in the attic, so we rarely went up there at night. Yet on a bright sunny day, like that day was, sunbeams would break through the two-toned windows to fill every crack, and crevice of the upstairs dungeon with light. It ever amazed me that the sun could illuminate the attic so brightly despite the years of caked-up dust, and filth covering those windows.

I busted through the attic door with the footlocker and there he was, my dad, Mr. James pacing in circles by the dust-stained windows, casting a shadowy silhouette of what I believed the Loch Ness Monster would probably look like, if it were real. Though it was winter, he had nothing on except a pair of cut off jean shorts, a raggedy T-shirt, and a beat-up pair of low-top Nike's with no socks. Steam rose off his body like an outdoor sauna in the dead of winter.

"You bring me some water?" He inquired kneeling down to sift through the footlocker at his feet.

I shook my head *no*.

"Where you want this?" I asked, gesturing at the footlocker I just lugged upstairs.

"Another one? How many footlockers did this woman have?"

I shrugged my shoulders in response.

"Just leave it there. I'll sort through it later."

I pushed the footlocker across the floor over to the side wall careful not to crack my noggin on the low ceiling. I began to feel a bit nostalgic perusing around the dusty attic. With each step the floorboards moaned like they would give way beneath me at any moment. I couldn't remember the last time I had been up there. No wonder Mr. James and Auntie Emma wanted to clean and downsize.

There were boxes upon boxes of moldy clothing with moth balls sprinkled on top as if they were decorations. There wasn't anything in the world that my mother didn't feel could be preserved with a few moth balls. She had them everywhere—under our beds, in the back of dresser drawers, inside every coat closet. It's a miracle I never found any inside my book bag on the way to school.

Deep in the back corner were even more boxes containing random items like toys, old nursery books, bowling balls, and roller skates. The oldest, most familiar box of them all was used for storing our plastic Christmas tree and lights each year.

I laughed to myself as I saw my old, rickety dresser from when I was a kid in the corner behind Mr. James. Two of the dresser drawers didn't open, and the other three couldn't fully shut. I went over and gave one of the stubborn drawers a tug for old-time sake. It still wouldn't budge.

Next, I visited the makeshift laundry lines Mom, and Auntie made from old jump ropes. The thin, frayed ropes coiled, and zigzagged about the attic like a giant cobweb. Clothes, guaranteed to be from the sixties and seventies, still hung on the droopy clothes lines.

The last attic attraction was the footlockers. The shiny blue one that I brought upstairs made five altogether. There were two black ones, a red one, my shiny blue one, and a green one. With Mom being gone, I guess we will never know if the different colors had any significance.

Mr. James knelt and sifted through the contents of one of the black footlockers. As I watched him working tirelessly, I still couldn't help but think that maybe Mom's things should just be sorted and placed safely to the side as mementos instead of discarded like unwanted trash. Besides, it was my mother's stuff. Shouldn't I have had a say in what happened to it?

"You sticking around to help?" Mr. James asked me.

"Nah, just looking."

I hovered over Mr. James, inspecting his every move as he rambled through the locker.

"Yeah, we can probably throw most of this stuff out. It's junk anyway."

"None of it is junk! What makes you think you can just come up in here and change everything?"

I still don't know what made me snap that way. Maybe it was all the memories that came flooding back when I thumbed through the photo album. Or maybe the fact I wouldn't be able to create any new memories with my mother. Whatever the reason, my comment came out a bit more raw than intended.

Mr. James glared up at me with a menaced look I hadn't seen before nor ever wanted to see again. Then he stood. Beads of sweat rolled down his prison yard muscles and tattoos. But scarier than the image of him putting me in a headlock with those cinder blocks he called arms was the silence. He stood there without saying a single, solitary word. He just stared at me. I couldn't help but think, *Was this it*? *Was I going be killed in my own home by my psychotic, ex-con father?*

I didn't dare take my eyes from him. If he would have lifted even a pinky finger, I was out of there. But he didn't bum-rush me. Instead, the Herculean specimen just stood, motionless, like a statue waiting to be admired. And I did just that. I sized him up from head to toe just in case I did have to fight for my life.

But the more I looked, the more intimidated I became. Not only did he have traps on top of his traps, biceps on top of his biceps, pecs on top of his pecs, but also there were scattered bullet wounds, and old knife scars covering his body from narrowly escaping battles on the West and South Side. I think I even saw a cigarette burn. I was pretty nifty with my hands and gained enough of a rep that people didn't really bother me. But Mr. James had been in actual street wars.

At that very moment, something horrific swept over me. I acknowledged there was an unseen force inside the attic with us—among us. The hairs on the back of my neck stood. Goosebumps formed on my face and arms. Instantly, I knew the invisible entity was fear. That reverential fear a son was supposed to naturally have of his father. I hadn't a clue what Mr. James was going to do to me, but my body instinctively knew that it should be frightened.

"BJ," his voice rumbled. "You've been testing me ever since I've got out. And it ends today."

Mr. James stepped from behind the footlocker. *Oh no, he is gonna kill me,* I thought. He grabbed me by the shoulder, almost immediately his grip softened.

"Look, Brandon, I miss Kathy too. I imagine it was tough without me all those years."

"We managed," I squeaked out trying to sound less frightened than I was.

"Well. . .good. But I'm back now and there can only be one head of this household. Know who that is, right?"

"You."

"Me. Now, since you're so concerned about what stays and goes from up here, the attic is yours. I want it swept. I want it mopped. I want all this stuff downsized. Anything we don't need, pitch it."

"Like what?" I asked in a softer, milder tone. But by that time, Mr. James' button had already been pushed.

He snarled back, "Like this raggedy dresser. Like them old bowling balls over there, all them toys piled up in boxes, and old baby clothes of y'all's your mama kept. If we don't need it, toss it."

"That'll take me forever."

"I didn't say it had to be done today. Take all the time you want. Just get it done."

And with that, the true master of 51 West 114th Street threw down his gauntlet establishing his decree. I watched as the satisfied Mr. James walked away.

CHAPTER 3

CHRISTMAS BREAK

/

Christmastime in Chicago was about the hustle and bustle. Even the poorest of the poor would try to save, scrape, or rob to bring Christmas cheer to their own loved ones.

I had just gotten back from Christmas shopping with Auntie Emma. We went over to River Oaks to pick up some things because Auntie Emma didn't like shopping in the city. One would never find her at any of the local shops or even downtown looking for her presents. Nope, Auntie Emma was a suburban snob. She loved going to the suburbs because she swore, to get the best deals, we had to go where the White people shopped.

Our original plan was to go shopping, get back home, wrap all the presents and hide them before Mr. James and Monica returned from their shopping trip. We were cutting it kind of close as Auntie Emma was forced to drive slower than usual because it began snowing on our way back. Well, "snow" is an understatement. The word "blizzard" is closer to the truth. Snowflakes the size of flapjacks blanketed our windshield.

Monica was like a bloodhound when it came to snooping out hidden presents. Like many Black kids in my neighborhood, Monica quickly figured out that Santa Claus doesn't come to the ghetto. But even if Spud didn't surmise there wasn't a Santa Claus, I'm sure Mama would have told her. Mom burst my bubble pretty early from believing some cheery, white-haired, fat Caucasian man snuck presents into our home while we slept. She told me, "I worked hard to buy you these toys and you better not break them. Oh, you ain't know? Mama is Santa Claus."

But Monica, she just reasoned it out one day, being her naturally inquisitive self. "How could Santa come here when we don't have a chimney? How does Santa know if I'm naughty? If Santa got me these toys, why does Mama get so upset when I break them?"

Auntie Emma and I scrambled to wrap our gifts. We rushed to the dining room spreading all our purchases over the table and began wrapping. If Santa did exist, he would have promoted me and Auntie Emma head of his gift-wrapping department. We passed scissors, tape, and glittery reindeer designed wrapping paper back and forth like a two-person assembly line. Present after present was neatly wrapped, taped, slapped with a name tag, and placed on the floor. Next!

There was a slight pause in production when I noticed Auntie Emma looking at the items I'd bought.

"Busted!" I yelped. "I wrapped your gift last week, nosey lady."

"Oh, I wasn't looking for my present," she laughed. "I was just wondering what you got Keko."

The assembly line came to a complete halt. My first instinct was to say, "Same thing I did last year, 'Nathan.'" But I couldn't say that without getting a backhand across the mouth. I looked at Auntie Emma blankly as her eyes filled with hopeful curiosity. She waited for the answer which never came. She then angrily gathered the rest of her gifts, some wrapping paper, some tape, and went to the kitchen.

I guess I could understand why it was so important to her that Mr. James and I got along. After all, he was her baby brother. I knew she was proud of him for keeping his nose clean for so long, getting a job, and taking care of Monica.

Honestly, I kept waiting for the other shoe to drop. Maybe the whole family reunion thing was just too sudden for me. Mom hadn't talked about him in such a long time. Auntie Emma brought him up every now and then, but after a few years, we all just went on with our lives without him. Maybe Mom felt it would have been too much for me to handle if she spoke about him all the time. I would have never guessed that Mom was keeping in touch with him and planned all along to have him back in our lives. I guess I got used to life without him.

I followed her into the kitchen to explain, "Auntie? This is kiddy stuff anyway. He won't care."

She sat at the kitchen table with a disapproving look plastered on her face.

"It's the thought that. . .wouldn't you want a gift from your kids if you were gone all this time?"

"It's not my fault he was gone."

"BJ, you'll never understand the sacrifices your father made for this family."

"Like what?"

Just then, I heard the front door open, and the patter of little feet came running into the kitchen.

"BJ, BJ, guess what Daddy got you for Christmas?"

If my Auntie's looks could kill, I would have been chilling right next to Mom. Mr. James roared from the living room, "Monica, it's a surprise!" Monica pouted and stomped her foot. "You all come here," Mr. James continued. "BJ come help me with this tree."

We all went to the living room. I stepped outside onto the front porch with Mr. James to help drag the artificial Christmas tree that he just bought into the house. I didn't understand why he needed my help. Obviously, he had lugged the heavy tree up the stairs successfully. What's a few more feet? I guess it was another "bonding" moment for him.

Ever since I could remember, we've used a fake tree for Christmas. Mama didn't like the messy pine needles left over from real evergreens. Apparently, neither did Mr. James. I felt our old tree was fine, but Mr. James didn't like the fact that we were still using the same old tree that we had before he went to jail, so he bought us a new one. Monica was so excited that she had to see the new tree right away.

Auntie Emma told me to get the scissors. I quickly went to the kitchen and grabbed the scissors from off the table and hurried back. I handed the scissors to Mr. James since he was hovering over the box.

"Thanks Beej. So...I'm just saying, Emily, be careful."

"Ya know I heard about that on the news. They're calling him the 'Bump and Jump Burglar' or the 'Thump and Bump Thief' or something like that."

"What y'all talking about?" I finally asked.

"A rash of muggings in Roseland," Auntie Emma began. "All the victims have been older women."

"Yeah, they haven't caught this fool yet, so I was telling your Auntie to be extra careful when she's out."

"OK, OK, Auntie, stay away from strangers," Monica blurted out. "Daddy, open the tree."

"Little girl, go over there and sit yourself in that chair," Auntie Emma scolded through a chuckle.

But once Mr. James sliced open the box, Monica hopped right back up anyway. She skirted over to the box and began yanking branches out.

"I got an idea," stated Mr. James. "Why don't we put on some Christmas music, make some hot chocolate, and put up the tree and lights tonight?"

"That's OK with me," agreed Auntie Emma.

Monica jumped up and down, "Yea, yea, hot chocolate with marshmallows, too, Daddy."

"Yes, with marshmallows."

Suddenly, everyone looked at me. I didn't know I was expected to participate in the family-fun day.

"Nah, I think I'm gonna do some work in the attic. You guys have fun though."

"You sure, BJ?" Mr. James asked.

I nodded.

"OK, bye, BJ. Stay warm up there," Monica said nudging me aside to make room for the mess she was creating.

I went to my room to grab a pullover and skull cap. As I came out of my room to head upstairs, I took another glace at my family in the living room. Nat King Cole's silky voice crooned, filling every room with "Chestnuts roasting on an open fire." Everyone was laughing and having a good time, except me. No one seemed to notice or care that there was someone missing. *The Christmas Song* was Mom's favorite too.

/

CHRISTMAS DAY

On Christmas morning, I laid awake in bed watching the sun pierce through my bedroom blinds. I hadn't slept much the last few days. Truth was I'd been haunted by the fact that Mom was gone, and this was the second major holiday I'd have to spend without her. Thanksgiving was a complete blur.

I conjured up just enough energy to scoot myself to the edge of the bed. After a few yawns and stretches I got up and threw on my robe. I knew that Monica would be awake soon to open her presents. This would be her first Christmas without Mom too, and I needed to put on a happy face.

I opened my door and clomped into the kitchen delirious from lack of sleep.

Auntie Emma was already there sitting at the table drinking a cup of Mr. James' coffee, apparently trying to wake up herself. She looked like the Living Dead, bags under her eyes, rollers in her hair—a hot mess.

"Morning baby."

"Hey Auntie. Wow, Monica's not up yet? What time did y'all go to bed last night?"

"About two o'clock," Auntie Emma chuckled through a long yawn. "That girl had us up all night playing that noisy Hungry, Hungry Hippos game. I don't know why your mama started that tradition of opening one gift at midnight Christmas Eve."

I smiled with a sigh. Although Auntie Em didn't have children of her own, she still had those maternal instincts. She walked over to me and gave me a long hug.

"We all miss her, honey. Let's just try to make it through today for Monica's sake, OK?"

"All right," I said, nodding in confirmation.

"I guess I better get breakfast started."

Auntie Em began gathering skillets and pots.

About a half an hour later Monica and Mr. James both dragged themselves out of bed. The smell of good grub could do that. I suppose no one would ever need an alarm clock if there were always someone's big mama or mom or auntie cooking breakfast in the kitchen every morning. Monica woke up around nine o'clock, Mr. James about ten minutes after that. Auntie Emma didn't let any one of us open presents until we had breakfast.

I loved it when Auntie Emma came downstairs to cook us breakfast. I did my best to play it off as if Monica was the only one who enjoyed it. Although, she was the one who always wanted pancakes—pancakes, pancakes, pancakes. I liked pancakes too, but other than tacos, I think pancakes were Spud's favorite.

Yet that morning, I was spoiled with my favorite breakfast. Mama used to cook these smoked sausages from Prairie Belt. They looked like regular Vienna sausages, but in my opinion, they tasted way better. They were about the size of a hotdog and were packaged in a huge yellow can that had a little dark-haired, rosy-cheeked White boy on the front. They were called oil sausages, but I remember as a kid calling them "ore" sausage because I couldn't pronounce the word "oil." Pretty gutsy of a company to name their product oil sausage. To say it, even sounds disgusting. Yet they were anything but. They were made of chicken and pork and were absolutely amazing with rice, scrambled eggs, and biscuits with Alaga syrup. I was on cloud nine when Auntie Emma sat a plate in front of me with that exact combination of edible greasy goodness. Merry Christmas to me.

/

SANTA CLAUS IN THE GHETTO

The whole family was in a good mood after breakfast. Auntie Emma may have even planned it that way to help ease the pain of it being the first Christmas without Mom. Now was the moment of truth for kids both young and old, it was present time. Auntie Emma and I joined Monica and her dad in the living room. Monica was snooping under the tree, crawling from present to present, trying to peek through the wrapping paper. It didn't matter if the present was for her or not, she'd try to look inside. She strongly believed that it was her job in life to tell everyone what they were getting for Christmas. This was her second job next to answering the phone, of course. Monica has ruined many-a-surprises in her short six years of life.

Mr. James relaxed in the recliner, reading the paper with his coffee on the end table. Mr. James didn't join us for that awesome breakfast. He hardly ever ate breakfast; I don't remember why. But he did love his Maxwell House instant coffee. It was like he was addicted to that stuff. There were worse things to be addicted to than coffee, I suppose. He could drink caffeinated coffee day and night, but it never kept him from getting to sleep at bedtime. Weird.

"Who's playing Santa Claus?" Auntie Emma bellowed.

"Not me," Monica quickly rattled back. "BJ can do it."

I must admit; my baby sister was a quick study. Last year she was eager to play Santa, but what she didn't realize was that in addition to handing everyone their gifts "Santa" had the responsibility to clean up all the wrapping paper afterwards.

"Nah, that's OK," I replied.

So, Auntie Emma made Mr. James do it. He pulled the paper from his face, folded it up and sat it on the floor next to his chair. He moseyed on over to the tree, struggling as he got on his hands and knees. Monica was jumping up and down ranting like a complete lunatic, so Mr. James gave her the first present.

Monica snatched it rudely managing to say "thank you" through her spastic shrieks. She ran off to the nearest corner of the living room to tear into the package.

Next, he gave me one.

"Here, this is from your Auntie." I thanked him, then turned to Auntie Emma and thanked her.

Mr. James continued his task of handing out gift after gift, saying who the present was from and handing it to the appropriate recipient.

As the gifts dwindled down, Monica played contently with her presents and Mr. James resumed his place back in his recliner with his paper.

"Enjoying your Christmas, baby?" Auntie Emma asked gently placing her hand on my knee.

"As much as I could. Feels weird without her, you know?"

"Yeah, but she's here, watching us right now," Auntie Em said looking up at the ceiling, smiling, as if to imagine heaven.

"Hey, what's that?" Monica blurted out, pointing to a huge box tilting against the windowsill, poorly hidden behind the curtain. Spud crawled over to investigate.

"That's for BJ. Oh baby, be careful," said Mr. James.

Monica tried to move it.

"Umph, it is heavy. BJ come open it."

I looked at Mr. James. He smiled, "I'll grab it."

He bounced over to the huge box like a big kid in a candy shop.

Auntie Emma leaned over and whispered meanly into my ear, "He wouldn't care about this kiddy stuff, huh?"

She shot me an evil glare before getting up and moving to Keko's recliner.

Whatever was in the box must've weighed a ton because even Mr. James had to re-grip it a couple of times before he could carry it over to the couch. He plopped it down right in front of me.

"Open it. Baby girl, come help your brother."

He didn't have to ask Monica twice. She started ripping and tearing at the wrapping paper covering the box. I reluctantly joined in. I didn't even have to look to know Auntie Emma's eyes were piercing the back of my dome. I turned and gave her a sheepish smile anyway and continued opening the gift. She rolled her eyes in response. Which, at that moment I was grateful for because a few years ago she would have cursed me out. But since Auntie Em doesn't curse anymore, she adopted the habit of rolling her eyes at anything she doesn't approve of.

"What's inside?" Monica asked.

"I thought you knew what it was," I quipped back.

"No, she was just worrying me to death, guessing." Keko chimed in. "Here, BJ, hold the bottom."

We all studied the rough cardboard box wondering what could be inside that was so heavy. Mr. James hoisted the heavy box toward me. I clutched the bottom, so he could muscle out the large slab of whatever it was.

"Here, let me flip it over so you can see it," Mr. James said. "Monica honey, step back."

I placed the empty box on the couch. Monica came over and stood next to me. Mr. James struggled to turn around the massive, polished rock. But when he did, and I finally saw what it was, chills ran through my entire body.

Auntie Emma rose to her feet, covering her mouth, overcome with emotion as tears welled up in her eyes.

"Yeah, I got a great deal on it too," Mr. James said.

"It's pretty, Daddy," Monica added.

She went closer slowly running her petite hand across the marble tombstone.

"Is it for Mama?"

"Yup, baby girl," Mr. James answered. "Well, it's BJ's gift, but, yes, it's for your mom. Can you read it to us?"

Monica's squeaky voice broadcasted the inscription:

Here lies:
Kathryn Jean James
Feb 9, 1951 – May 24, 1985
Loving Mother & Loyal Wife
You Are Missed Every Day

"I like it, Daddy. Look Auntie Em."

"I see it, sweetheart. It's pretty," Auntie Emma said, voice quivering.

I felt like I should say something, but I didn't know what to say. I felt horrible that I didn't have enough money to buy a headstone myself. It was my greatest regret. And there was no way I could have afforded to get something as nice as what he got.

"How did you. . .when did you do this?" I asked.

"I've been saving money ever since I got the CTA job. I remember how sad you were that we didn't have a gravestone for Kathy."

"Wow, I. . .I don't know what to say."

"Nah, you were right, son. She deserves it. We can have it put in once the ground thaws in spring."

I wanted to hate my father so badly for the struggles my mother had because he couldn't control his temper. The result of his actions was that he wasn't there for me, Monica, or our mother.

However, he was back now and had been every day since his release from jail. I considered myself to be an excellent judge of character, so in my stubbornness, I refused to believe I'd been wrong about him all along.

My mind was reeling. I felt like I was in the *Twilight Zone*. It felt as if everyone was staring at me and that's when Monica asked the most hurtful question she could have ever asked.

"BJ, what you get Daddy for Christmas?"

Mortified doesn't begin to explain how I felt. Instant dread consumed me like a cumulus cloud descending on a mountain top. I tried to moisten my mouth by swallowing but couldn't. My throat felt like I guzzled a two-liter bottle of soda pop made of wet beach sand. I stuttered and stammered a few unintelligible syllables and that's when the sweat began to form on my head like teardrops. I couldn't take it anymore.

I looked over at Auntie Emma, who scowled back through angry tears.

I looked at Monica and tried to answer her innocent question, "Well, Spud. . .I, uh—"

"Monica, sweetheart, BJ doesn't have to get me anything," Mr. James interrupted, scooping her up into his arms. "Just being here with you guys is present enough for me."

Monica hugged his neck.

Auntie Em got one last glare at me before storming off to the kitchen.

"I'll go check on the turkey," is what she said. But her eyes informed me that she had taken up swearing again.

I excused myself as well and went to my room. I stayed in there for hours arbitrating the disagreement between my head and heart on whether to forgive the dad who was back in my life as abruptly as he'd left. I had so many friends who were upset about the dads who left their families. And here I was being upset because my dad was back.

Uncharacteristically, we didn't eat Christmas dinner as a family that night. I didn't dare step foot out my room. I didn't want to be responsible for tempting Auntie Emma's mouth to say what her eyes couldn't. Instead, I just laid in my bed going back and forth between staring at the ceiling and walls replaying in my memory how my life changed forever the last day of school my junior year.

/

LAST DAY OF SCHOOL

I had studied hard for all my finals and was ready to cruise through the day on my way to summer break.

The hall was already packed with exuberant students, celebrating the day's end. I strolled the hall laughing to myself at the freshmen who were at their lockers desperately trying to clear out a year's worth of junk. Rookie mistake—we juniors had our lockers cleared out weeks ago. The last month of school was like juniors were the real seniors anyway because they were barely around.

They had senior trips, prom, and no final exams. We juniors were happy running the school in their absence. But ever since that final bell buzzed, our interim reign was over. It was the last time I roamed Mendel's halls as an underclassman. It was me and my boys' school now and just in time. We would be the senior welcoming committee to the fairer sex when Mendel turned co-ed in the fall.

I had more energy than usual for my jog up the hill to Roseland Community Hospital. It wouldn't surprise me if every kid in America could lift the backside of a pickup truck on the last day of school. Typically, my jog from Mendel to the hospital would get me a little winded, but it didn't that day.

Mom had been in and out of the hospital because of a rare form of cancer in her stomach called desmoplastic. The doctors insisted on an aggressive treatment plan, which involved chemo, surgery, and then, radiation, if necessary. But Mom had other plans. She demanded that they just did the surgery with the radiation afterwards.

I knew the only reason Mom went against the doctors' recommendations so strongly was because of Monica and me. Mama knew that chemo would wipe her out physically, keeping her away from us and work longer. Even though my Auntie Emma was around to help, Mom didn't want to be away from us any longer than she had to be.

After several weeks of prepping, testing, and retesting, Mom had the procedure to remove the tumor from her stomach. The surgery was a success, according to the nurse I had spoken with over the phone. She was finally ready to be discharged and that good news made the last day of school that much sweeter.

That death trap known as the elevator ejected me out onto the third floor. Lined against the wall were several wheelchairs for patient use. I nabbed one and made the familiar trek down the hall with more bounce than usual; *Mom was coming home.*

I stopped at the entrance of room 302. Something wasn't right. It just wasn't right. What were they doing to her? My mother's face was blue. How can a Black woman's face look blue?

"Mom. Mom?"

The nurses and orderlies continued yanking hoses and tubes from my mother's lifeless body, business as usual. All except one nurse, Sharon Kimble, who was leaning against the wall with a watchful eye. Her face, tender. Eyes present. Instantly, I could tell the enormity of this moment wasn't wrapped up in a paycheck to her.

The wheelchair I was manning somehow came to life and rolled slowly away from me. Until then I hadn't realized it was the only thing holding me up. My knees wobbled and Nurse Sharon sprang into action, grabbing me before I collapsed to the floor.

She placed her arm around me and walked me down the hall.

As Nurse Sharon led me toward the family and visitors lounge, an uneasiness began to grip me like being caught in the wrong neighborhood. *My mother passed away only minutes before I got here.* Every cell, every fiber within me wanted to scream, but I guess I was in too much shock.

Nurse Sharon was spewing something about "internal bleeding" and "doctors did all they could."

I mean, I heard the words. I saw Nurse Sharon's mouth moving. Still, I didn't understand. I had just visited my mother the day before on my way to school. Nurse Sharon's lips kept moving, but I was certain nothing was coming out. As a matter of fact, I couldn't hear anything at all. No overhead pages. No blaring telephones. No buzzing call lights. The only thing I could hear was my heart beating erratically and stronger than ever. Then, I heard a thud. That's when I realized my rump had smacked the thinly carpeted floor in the hall.

I sat there wringing my hands staring straight into the dimly lit family and visitors lounge across from me. I couldn't believe it. *Is that it?* I thought. *Is death that swift?* One moment we're laughing at *Sanford & Son* reruns together. The next, she's a cold slab of used to be human.

Nurse Sharon placed her hand on my shoulder. That's when it happened. More bad news. A voice thundered, "BJ."

My heart was no longer erratic. It sank, slowly settling at the bottom of my stomach like the phony snowflakes inside those stupid snow globes. I felt myself becoming physically ill.

Out of the shadows of the lounge steps a bald, burly, no-nonsense looking man. His face was chiseled concrete and barely recognizable to me. The last time I saw this man, I was around nine years old.

Finally, he stepped into the hallway. His dark eyes pierced right through me.

I told myself to *get up, get up!*

Somehow my legs strengthened beneath me, and I struggled to my feet like a newborn calf. We stood a foot apart, studying each other's unfamiliar faces.

"Hey son," he said to me.

"When did you get out?" I scowled.

"This morning, I—"

"Why is he here?" I snipped toward Nurse Sharon.

It wasn't her fault that my ex-con dad showed up on the very day God shattered my world.

I couldn't do it. I couldn't confront the very reason my family had struggled for several years, all by myself. I couldn't face this mountain of a man at my weakest moment. I couldn't stand up to the man who was absent from me and Monica's life without my "heart." As much as I wanted to see my mother one last time, touch her cheek, hold her hand, I couldn't stay. My hatred for Brandon "Keko" James significantly outweighed the love I had for dear, sweet Kathy.

"Honey, what's the matter?" Nurse Sharon asked kindly. "It's your father."

"I don't have a father," I barked, then ran down the hall.

I could hear his unfamiliar voice calling out for me.

"Brandon? Brandon Junior wait!"

Out of the corner of my eye, I saw him running after me, but there was no way he was going to catch me. My dad grew smaller and smaller the farther I sprinted down the hall.

/

STRANGER IN MY HOUSE

Silence. No more Christmas music. No more shuffling about. I had a peaceful feeling that everyone had finally went to sleep. My stomach rudely reminded me that in my embarrassment of not getting Mr. James a present, I hadn't eaten any of the Christmas dinner Auntie Emma prepared.

I crept out of my bedroom into the pitch blackness. I eased my way to the kitchen to find all the food had been removed from the stove and counter tops. I rushed to the fridge desperate to devour something. My lips curled into a wicked smile. Wrapped in airtight aluminum foil was a plate of yummy goodness with "BJ" written in black magic marker. I could have cried.

I wasted no time. I tore into the belated Christmas gift of mac-n-cheese, green beans, mashed potatoes and gravy, rolls, turkey, and honey roasted ham. I pinched off a piece of cold ham as I walked to the microwave, balling up the foil and throwing it aside. *Beep, beep-beep.* I punched the numbers to warm my personal edible entrée. I circled the kitchen floor impatiently. *Two minutes don't take this dang long!*

That's when I saw the Christmas tree lights glistening in the distance. I was drawn to the dancing lights on the other side of the house illuminating Mr. James' Christmas gift. I walked slowly from the kitchen, through the dining room into the living room. I plopped on the floor and just stared at the tombstone reminding me how permanent this new norm was.

I allowed my fingertips to trail over the etched lettering on the ice-cold brick. The day of Mom's funeral, every part of my body ached: my head, stomach, arms, legs, even my toes. The only thing that didn't hurt was my heart because it was gone, surgically removed, who knew, maybe by aliens. At that point, anything was possible, I imagined because nothing felt normal to me that day.

Even the interactions with my mom's friends felt other worldly. "She's beyond suffering now, BJ."

"Don't fret, son. She's gone to a better place."

"BJ, you'll be spiritually connected to her forever in your heart."

They didn't understand. Someone even called my mother's passing a "Home-going celebration." Funny, I didn't feel much like celebrating.

I remember sitting on the couch, sulking as I watched Auntie Emma bounce back and forth between guests like a pinball, playing hostess. I didn't know half the people standing in my living room. I thought the point of a repast was to help console those closest to the deceased. Who was closer to my mother than me? Apparently Keko was closer because everyone seemed to know him. It was more like a welcome home party for him than a farewell for my mom.

Everybody was laughing, eating red velvet cake and Harold's Chicken, drinking up all the Kool-Aid; having a good old time. And Keko was right in the middle of it. He was the life of the party, cracking jokes and talking about "the good ole days." Conveniently, they had all forgotten that two hours prior, grave diggers were slathering dirt over my best friend's coffin.

I protested. I debated. I argued and lost. As much as I didn't want my ex-convict father to move in with us, he did anyway. Auntie Emma wanted him to. Monica wanted him to. Heck, even Mom wanted him to move back in. Keko was able to produce more than one letter in my mother's handwriting post marked several months before she died. The correspondence detailed about how she was excited for him to come home and if anything happened to her, he was to move in and take care of both Monica and me.

I loathed the idea. But I couldn't go against my mother's last wishes. What burned me most was that he knew her real condition while I was left in the dark. Even the Roseland doctors and nurses were in on it. Nurse Sharon said Mom didn't want me to know that the surgery was a high-risk procedure. The hospital staff agreed to keep this information from me since I was still a minor.

Before the three-way vote that placed Mr. James on the first floor with me and Monica, he used to bunk upstairs with Auntie Emma. I never understood why those living arrangements had to change. It wasn't like Auntie Em ever had a man up there. Frankly, she scared off most suitable, hardworking, blue-collared brothers. Thank goodness she didn't want the thugs anymore though.

I tried, more than once, to convince Auntie Emma to take on her little brother as a permanent roommate. That was until she kindly reminded me that Mr. James' name was on the mortgage. She said it was very convenient of me to forget that he lived there before being locked up. Technicalities, I mean, I understood the logic of him being back home. I just thought he'd be more comfortable on the second floor with her.

Even though Mr. James contributed to the household right away by getting that city bus driving job with the Chicago Transit Authority (CTA), I still wasn't ready to trust him yet. That was the dilemma my head and heart were having until the microwave's beeping and the smell of scrumptious food startled me out of my daydream.

/

ATTIC

Over the next few nights, we all kept a close eye on the news because the guy who was mugging middle-aged women was still at large and the Chicago PD was absolutely clueless. Auntie Emma told us not to worry about her. But it was hard not to be concerned with this maniac still on the prowl.

I pulled myself from watching the evening news with the rest of the family and headed upstairs. As time went on, I didn't mind going to the pitch-black attic to do my chore. I cherished my alone time in the attic yet, to me, it was useless going up there to clean. I'd spent most of the Christmas break slaving away and felt it was as clean as it was going to get. Besides it's an attic, how *spic & span* did Mr. James want it anyway? But the warden wanted me to do a better job, so it was back to the grind.

I began rambling through Mom's footlockers again to see if there was anything more that I could downsize. I had already gone through her things once and there was nothing left that I wanted to throw away, except some disgusting love letters between Mom and Mr. James that I found inside an old shoebox.

I had separated the good memorabilia from the stuff that wasn't too sentimental. I completed the footlockers and decided to go back over the boxes. The problem was, every time I sorted through a box, I'd get this nudge in my gut telling me not to throw any of it away because it's all a part of Mom. But I knew that wasn't going to fly anymore, so I began taking piece by piece downstairs to the garbage can in the alley.

Each item I took downstairs had a different memory attached to it, like my first bowling ball Mom bought me for league at Palisade Bowl. The old roller skates Mom bought for us. I remember how we use to race in our skates in front of the house. My old Hot Wheels racetrack that doubled as a belt when Mom needed something quick to give me a whoopin'.

Without warning a wave of emotions came over me. I missed her so much. Although I wasn't a blubbering mess, the tears wouldn't stop flowing. I grabbed a broken folding chair and sat down. Why I hadn't thrown that chair away yet was beyond me.

It was a bit shocking that I could get overwhelmed to the point of tears considering it had been several months since Mom died. I guess it was just like that. Maybe what I felt was normal. Then it hit me, if I was still struggling so badly, what about Monica? Was she still hurting over Mom's death in her own little way? I felt horrible. What kind of big brother was I? I hadn't checked in with her once since the funeral.

At that point, I didn't know if the tears would ever stop. I cleared my throat and wiped my wet eyes and got back to work sifting through boxes. There was nothing in the box I was working on that I considered junk, so I decided to go to the next.

I scooted the raggedy chair back to stand up and it hit a shopping bag that was directly behind me. I hadn't really noticed the tattered bag before.

I knelt to rifle through it. The crusty bag was full of old notebooks. I pulled one out and looked inside. It was in my mother's handwriting. *I never knew Mom kept a journal.* I grabbed another notebook then another; they were all journals. I thumbed carefully through the delicate pages of a random notebook and saw an entry dated just a couple of days after my birth.

May 19, 1969

Dear Diary,

> *Precious isn't the first word that comes to mind when I look at this child. . .regret, mistake, confusion are better words.*

Deg Mama, I laughed to myself wiping leftover tears from my face. No one ever accused my mother of mincing words. I forgot how blunt she could be. That made me a little frightened to read her diary because I knew nothing would be sugar coated in there. *Good!*

> *Why did this "incident" happen to me? What did I do to deserve this?*

I grabbed another notebook, a purple one and began reading.

> *I was shocked that Keko wanted to keep this baby, let alone name him Brandon Junior. Now that I'm pregnant, there goes my dreams of going to college and running track.*

I sat there, heartbroken. *My mother blamed me for not fulfilling her dreams.* I often wondered why Mom pressured me to run track. The answer was staring up at me in faded blue BIC ink. I dumped the grocery bag on the floor, got down on all fours, and carefully sifted through all the diaries. It took me a while, but as best I could tell, I successfully organized them chronologically and dove in.

March 21, 1967

Dear Diary,

I wish Allison Marsh would get struck by a truck and die, but not right away, hours later from the excruciating pain. OK, I don't really wish that. But I wouldn't cry if it happened. Today was the day, my day, to join the track team. Little did I know I would be the butt of Allie's jokes whenever the coach turned her back. What if we both make the team? Will I have to deal with her picking on me every day?

March 29, 1967

Dear Diary,

I knew that fat cow was gonna jump me after practice today. I KNEW IT! I should have just let her win all the sprints. I HATE HER! My eye looks like a raccoon's. Mother's gonna kill me when she finds out I got suspended for fighting. And I know she's gonna blame me for not saying anything earlier

*about being picked on. It's not like she can
come up to the school and fight Allie for me. I
just want all of this to be over.*

Mom was bullied! I stared at the journal in disbelief.
What I had in my possession was a slew of answers to
questions I would have never known to ask. *Who thinks of
asking their own mother if she was ever bullied in high school?*
I closed the journal and put them all back inside the grocery bag. I had already been in the attic a few hours, so
to avoid being questioned by the fam, I decided to come
back to the journals later.

/

BOXING 101

That night at the dinner table I sat in complete silence.
My mind was on one thing, my mom. Not only did I de-
rail her collegiate goal, but also her track dreams never
even started because of one *Allie Marsh*. I felt helpless.
There was nothing I could do about the past. At that
moment, I was thankful that I never had to go through
any of that. *How horrible that must have been!* There was a
specific reason why I wasn't a victim of bullying, not that
there weren't many who've tried. But I had a particular
skill set that was taught to me at a very young age.

I was about six or seven years old my mother thought
it would be a great idea to put me in a children's Christmas pageant in one of her friend's church on the West

Side. Mr. James was supposed to go with us to the holiday festivities, but Mom said he was out gallivanting with friends instead. I can hear his many warnings to my mother to never go to the West Side without him. But Mom was so upset with him, she dressed me up in that burgundy monkey suit and off we went to the West Side of Chicago in a snow storm.

Though we got about ten inches of snow that night it didn't keep those church folks from coming out in droves. The church parking lot was so packed we had to park on the side of the building. Mom had me wait in the car while she carried in a cake that she made for the bake sale. She made cookies and muffins too, but nothing tasted as good as her three-layered German chocolate cake.

"OK, BJ, stay here," she said. "Watch Mama's purse while I see if there's somebody inside to help us carry all this stuff."

Mom hopped out the car, shutting the door behind her then quickly opened the back door carefully grabbing her chocolate creation from the back seat. I watched her like a hawk from the front. She reached over and tapped me on the tip of my nose with her index finger and off she went.

I laughed to myself as she walked away. She always tapped me on the nose with her index finger when she felt I needed comforting. Ever since I could remember, whenever I felt down or was crying or anxious about something—*boop*, she'd tap my nose and smile at me then I knew everything would be all right.

I stared out the window watching Mom's blurred body disappear behind the foggy, snowy window. Moments later, I saw another figure quickly approaching from the same direction. I knew right away it wasn't my mother. The figure moved way too lunky to be my mom. Kathy James was the image of grace and elegance even during a blizzard.

An open hand smacked on my passenger side window. I took my winter glove and wiped the window only to see that the fog remained, and I still couldn't see out of it. I had no choice but to roll down the window.

A man stood there shivering in a flimsy jacket, no hat, no gloves, hands shoved inside his pockets to the knees.

"Hey little man," he said, trying to smile through chattering teeth. "Your mom sent me out here for her purse."

I was confused. Mom told me she would find someone to help with the treats. Why was he asking for her purse?

The young man waited semi-patiently for me to respond. I felt bad for him, I knew he had to be freezing, so I picked up Mom's purse that was sitting in the driver's seat.

"Yeah, that's it. Give it here."

His overanxious words felt wrong to me. Something churned in my chest, like a signal, a warning. I didn't know if I should trust this guy. Then the question popped into my mind, *Why would Mom tell me to watch her purse then send someone out here to grab it?*

And that's what he did; he grabbed the purse.

"No, she told me to watch it," I screamed, trying to yank it back from him but he was too strong.

He took my mother's bag and my heart along with it. I thought of chasing after him, but he was way bigger than I was, maybe nineteen or twenty years old. All I could do was watch him slip and slide away attempting to sprint on the icy ground.

My mistake caused a raucous back at home. Mr. James yelled at Mom for going to the West Side without him. Mom snapped back at him for being late. I listened from underneath the covers, curled up in my bed.

My door slowly opened.

I peeked out and saw my dad staring at me, but he no longer seemed upset.

"C'mon, BJ. Get up," Keko said waving me out of bed.

I flung my covers aside and followed him.

When I got to the basement, he was in the back of the room clipping a huge black punching bag to a large hook hanging from the ceiling. I'd often seen that hook but never knew what it was for.

The punching bag looked old and ratty.

"Come here, son."

I walked over and looked up at him all doe eyed.

"How did it feel when that man took Mom's purse away from you?"

I put my head down and thought for a moment. I looked at him and said, "Helpless."

Keko nodded in affirmation. He took two boxing gloves that were as worn out as the heavy bag and slid them onto my tiny fists. He took the long strings and tied them as tight as he could. The gloves felt heavy and still too loose. The same way my feet felt whenever I'd tried on Dad's boots. I remember thinking I could pull my hands right out of them if I wanted to.

"Make a tight fist, son."

I did.

"Now hit the bag."

I went over and took the biggest swing I could, *poof*. The bag barely moved.

"Hit it again. Again."

So, I did. I hit it over and over and over while my dad kept cheering me on.

"That's it. That's it, son. Hit it. Hit it!"

Umph, umph. I swung with everything I had—left, right, left again. It didn't take long for beads of sweat to congregate on my forehead.

"We're going to do this every day until you never feel helpless again."

I boxed in that basement every day, even after Keko got carted off to jail. My boxing excelled from feeling comfortable, to confident, to competent.

CHAPTER 4

SPRING SEMESTER

/

Per usual, Christmas break zipped by and before I knew it, I was one semester away from being a high school graduate. It was weird entering the new year without Mom, but I was determined to make 1986 a great year.

Ever since I found Mom's journals, I'd been a man possessed. Every day I snuck off to the attic under the guise of cleaning up just so I could be near Mom, to see what she saw, to feel what she felt. The more I read, the more I was sucked into her life. Maybe it was because it was the first Christmas without her. Or was it the fresh reminder of the permanency of death in the form of a chiseled gray rock Keko put under our Christmas tree? However it happened, finding those journals sparked a motivation in me that I hadn't had in months.

My mother was the reason I even attended Mendel. My high school was well known for their students' academic prowess, and hyped parties. We embodied the work hard, play hard mantra. The motivation behind the high academic achievement, I believed, was that the faculty had no problem embarrassing the crap out of us at the blackboard if they felt students weren't giving maximum effort.

What was my least favorite form of academic embarrassment? Swats. Now, swats were mostly performed by the coaches on their student-athletes who disrupted the classroom. But it wasn't unheard of for a nonathlete to get swatted too.

There was a coach who drilled several holes in his paddle so when he swatted someone's backside, there was a slow-dragging-like suction that made the paddle stick a few seconds longer to the person's rear end when coach pulled the paddle back. Coaches weren't the only ones who got in on the action, our principal was known for handing out a swat, or two, and the dean of students got his licks in also.

The first time I got paddled, I hurried home to rat on my teacher. Little did I know the principal had already called to report that I had been disciplined. My mom, just like many parents back then, always took the adult's word over the kid's. When I got home, I ran to the kitchen, "Mama, a teacher hit me."

Her response, "What'd you do?"

But I would be remiss if I didn't mention the nuns. After all, what would a Catholic school be without the rap across the knuckles from a Sister Agnus or a Sister Mary-Catherine? Most of my crew preferred swats from the coaches than getting smacked on the hand with that thick ruler the sisters used. Now were these methods unethical? Maybe. Effective? Most definitely. Personally, the threat of academic embarrassment highly motivated me to hit the books and to leave goofing off for outside the classroom.

That kind of in-your-face, tough love was the way it was done at Mendel. And parents couldn't deny the results. Kids were graduating and going to college. As a matter of fact, an article from the *Chicago Defender* ranked Mendel as one of the top ten schools in the country. I believe that's one of the reasons why Mom wanted me to go there. She had heard about the tradition and pride that was instilled into the young men at Mendel. So after she read that article, I was going to Mendel whether I wanted to or not.

/

C-LUNCH

Kevin and I both had C-Lunch together after trigonometry class. He told me to go on ahead of him because he had to make a quick stop by his locker then hit the restroom. Kevin Williams was my best friend. We've been *boys* for almost our whole lives. We went to grade school together back in the day at All Saints on 117th and State. We both grew up on 114th until he moved when we were in the seventh grade. He transferred to Mendel our sophomore year after attending freshman year at Corliss.

The school cafeteria was situated directly underneath our gymnasium. The concession stand inside the café made it awfully convenient for snacks during halftime of a basketball game, or refreshments for one of our many weekend school jams. We had a *set*, another word for "party" (or a "gang," depending on how you used it), once a month like clockwork.

At Mendel we didn't need a specific reason to throw a good party. That's how we got a rep for being a party school. Not only locals from the neighborhood, but people from other schools, and other hoods would take the CTA just to come to a Mendel set. And the café was always open for business.

Our entire student body was convinced that we had the best cooks in the world. They weren't the friendliest bunch, but man, they could throw down on the grub. They cooked stuff like turkey with mashed potatoes and gravy, meatloaf, Salisbury steak, burgers, fried chicken, and a slew of other mouthwatering delights.

That day they were serving a choice of burgers, and my favorite pepperoni pizza, which one of the cooks made from scratch. I said what's up to a few people as I grabbed a tray and hopped in the long serving line. In my opinion, there was something for everyone at lunchtime. But even if some picky person didn't like what was prepared, they could mosey on over to the other side of the cafeteria where the concession stand was set up.

There was any type of junk food a kid could want, like, or need at the concession stand. We had Snickers, Twix bars, Reese's Peanut Butter Cups, Whatchamacallits, M&Ms—plain and peanut, Doritos, Cheetos, O-ke-Dokes, and Hot Stuff. Or if something more sugary was being craved, there was a plethora of candies known for getting stuck between the cracks and crevices of teeth. Tangy treats like Mike and Ikes, Alexander Grapes, Skittles, Boston Baked Beans, Now & Laters, Starbursts, Jolly Ranchers—we called them wine candy, and last but not least, Chews, grape or red. Yet the ultimate sweet of all sweets was Ms. Waters' homemade chocolate chip cookies.

After getting my pizza, and some fries, I veered straight to the concession to get my chocolate fix. Whenever Ms. Waters made her famous cookies, we were like Pavlov's poochies, lining up with our tongues wagging from side to side. Even the kids with diabetes ignored their doctor's orders when it came to the ooey, gooey, goodness of Ms. Waters' cookies.

Box had C-Lunch along with Kevin and me. His real name was Samuel Hughs. I met Sam the summer before our freshman year at Mendel in summer school. If a student missed the entrance exam or scored poorly on it, that person could still be accepted into Mendel provided they passed summer school. I missed the entrance exam because I was in Texas visiting relatives on Mom's side of the family. We called Sam "Box" because he was one of the coldest beatboxers on the entire South Side. Cats from other hoods were always coming to Roseland just to battle my boy in beatboxing. He's beaten down so many people that he barely beatboxes anymore unless it's someone he thinks could really challenge him.

At Mendel there were three different lunchtimes: A-Lunch was from 11:15 a.m. to noon; B-Lunch from 12:10 p.m. to 12:55 p.m. and C-Lunch lunch was from 1:05 p.m. to 1:50 p.m.

Our lunchtime was a little later in the day, but we didn't mind that because it made the rest of the day zoom by. After lunch there were only two more classes then school was out. We loved it.

By the time I got my cookies, Box was already holding down the fort. We didn't have assigned seating or anything, but even when I was a dumb-clumsy freshman, seniors sat in the back half of the cafeteria. So now that was our area. Our own little domain where no one could sit unless they were granted permission by another senior classman. The most feared words to an underclassman trying to enter our territory were, "I don't know him." In other words, "Be gone, peasant!" The converse was true of another saying, "Oh, he straight," which meant, "You may enter."

There were a few exceptions to the underclassmen no-trespassing rule. Bribery with food was accepted if not encouraged. We also welcomed kids who could make us laugh. Every year there was at least one or two freshmen who were just naturally funny without even trying to be. They were welcomed. After all, every kingdom must have its court jesters.

We happily accepted other forms of entertainment from the underclassman: break dancing, or b-boying as it was called, up-rocking, poppin' and lockin', rapping, or my favorite, beatboxing. But nobody could beat *Box*.

If Buff, himself, from the hip-hip group the Fat Boys ever visited Mendel, he'd have to say, "Deg, Box, you're pretty dope!" My man had mad skills. As a matter of fact, Box was the only regular out of our crew who was allowed to sit in the senior section all four years just because he could bust a beat.

On my way to join Box at our regular table, the very last table in back, a group of people began to form. I nudged my way through to see what the ruckus was about. I quickly discovered that, once again, someone was calling Box out.

Ed saw me approaching and smiled, "BJ, why your boy keep dodging me?"

"Name's Paul, that's between y'all," I said as I squeezed into a spot next to Box.

Eddie Edwards was a pimply-faced, annoying freshman. He had been trying to battle Box ever since he stepped foot on Mendel's campus.

"Fool, you ain't nobody to dodge," Box fired back.

"I can't tell. You supposed to be the beatbox king of Mendel, right?"

"Oh, no doubt."

"How, you ain't battled me yet?"

Box just chuckled, slathering ketchup on his fries.

Eddie turned to the crowd behind him. "Y'all wanna see me battle Box, right?"

The boys and girls behind Ed began to cheer, which started a buzz throughout the rest of the lunchroom.

More people began to venture over to the kingdom, curious as to what was happening. At that time, Kevin finally made his way over as well. He squeezed in a spot across from us between two football players.

"Beej, what's going on?" Kev asked plopping his tray down.

"Eddie-Ed challenged Box," I replied.

"Again? Box, please, serve this fool, for me."

Box didn't respond. He removed the bun from his cheeseburger and drowned it in ketchup as well.

More and more people were cramming into our section expecting a beatboxing showdown. Eddie continued to rev up the crowd but got a little too excited while taunting my man.

"What's the matter Samuel, you scared?"

A soft hush began to sweep over the lunchroom. Obviously, several other underclassmen knew the significance of the line Ed just crossed. There were a few things as a freshman you just didn't do.

One was never attempt to embarrass a senior, especially in a room full of people. Two, was never call a senior by his first name when he already has an established nickname. I mean, calling someone by their given name instead of their preferred nickname was a surefire way to catch a beatdown with the quickness or at the very least muffed in the face. So with one comment, Eddie-Ed had broken two high school, cardinal rule no-noes.

Several seniors rose from their seats, prepared to give Ed that beatdown. The familiar chant of "Whaaat . . . whaaat . . . whaaat?" echoed throughout the lunchroom. That was the inner-city high school howl to indicate a fight was moments from happening. This, thankfully, replaced the seventies rudimentary chant of "Fight, fight, fight."

Little Eddie began to quiver. He knew he had gone too far.

Box finally stopped committing foodicide to his burger and fries and rose to address the issue at hand. He stepped over the lunchroom table bench to face Ed who was standing directly behind him.

"Yo," he began calmly, "before you even think about getting at me, freshman, try beating some real comp first."

"I beat Jacob and Cedric," Ed fired back.

"Fool, I could smoke Jacob and Ced beatboxing with one lip."

"Ohhh. . .danger. . .tell 'em, Box," rained scattered responses from the crowd.

"Go battle J-wan, Paul, Dizzy-D, or Caesar," Box continued. "Get some legit wins under your belt then come see me. Until then, beat it, freshman."

Box politely took the open chocolate milk carton from my hand just as I was about to drink it. He slowly drizzled it on top of Eddie-Ed's head. The crowd laughed and slowly began to disperse. But me, I was pissed; I wanted that chocolate milk.

One of the football players at the table grabbed Ed by the arm and escorted him away from the kingdom.

"My dog," Kevin said, reaching across the table to give Box a high five as he sat back down.

"Everybody wants to be the king," Box replied.

Box wasn't a bully or anything, none of us were, but sometimes freshmen had to know their place in the hierarchy of high school.

Our lunch break was coming to an end. Yet the cafeteria was still packed because no one wanted to go back to class early. While the fellas and I were still talking, an open carton of milk dropped from the air, splashing all over the table and soaking nearly every one of us.

We all turned to see where it came from.

Ed leaped on top of his table, fist full of fries in one hand and a burger patty in the other.

"Food fight!" he yelled flinging the flimsy fries in our direction, followed by the burger turned Frisbee.

That's all we needed to hear. The guys and girls in our area scattered for cover. When the coast was clear my crew and I armed ourselves with pizza crusts, half-eaten burgers and donuts, half-empty milk cartons, anything we could grab that wasn't already devoured. The peasants had started an uprising in our peaceful kingdom, and it was up to us to squelch it.

Armed with only the remaining rations of our food and drink, me, Kev, Box, and several other seniors grabbed our shields—cafeteria trays—and charged into battle. It was the first food rebellion under our reign and as the school's senior royalty, we had to fight until victory was ours. Onward!

/

COACH ABRAMS

At last, the school day was over. Words could not describe the embarrassing experience of sitting in class with smelly, stinky, sticky, food-fighting attire. Every inch of me begged for a shower. I would have settled for a backyard and a garden hose. Yet before I could go home and sneak into Mr. James' Old Spice, I had to make one quick stop.

I hung out in the boy's restroom until I felt most kids left for the day. I was able to rinse out the remaining residue of ketchup, mustard, and milk from my high-top fade. After drying my hair under the dryer, I eased downstairs to the lower level of the main building to see if I could talk privately to Mendel's track coach, Alexander Abrams.

I meandered the desolate hallway a bit not really knowing how to engage in the upcoming conversation. It was the last decision I ever wanted to make, but I had been tormented with the idea of accomplishing what my mother couldn't. I needed to do this for her.

While procrastinating in the hall, I moseyed over to Mendel's famed athletic trophy cases. I carefully browsed the shiny plastic and bronze plaques, pictures, trophies, and medals with faded ribbons. The long glass casing housed our respective sports teams' accomplishments throughout Mendel's history: football, hoops, baseball, even bowling.

When I came to the cross-country/track and field section, I stopped to get a closer view. Warm mist from my nostrils steamed the glass for a moment. It wasn't long before I saw several pictures of a young, physically fit Coach Abrams, Principal Cooper, and other members of the track teams of the sixties.

Just then, out the corner of my eye, I saw Coach Abrams come down the stairs and head for his office.

Coach was tall, sleek but not skinny with a mini afro. Confidence oozed off him like high-priced cologne. I approached him with purpose, "Coach Abrams?"

He turned and looked at me, keys dangling from the doorknob. His head tilted, nose crinkled upon getting a generous whiff of sour milk and assorted condiments.

"Shouldn't you be heading home? I'm sure there's a shower somewhere with your name on it."

I chuckled at his attempt to be humorous. "Funny Coach. Nah, there was a food fight in the cafeteria today—"

"I heard. Obviously, you got the worst of it. C'mon in."

Coach completed the task of unlocking his door and we went inside his office.

It looked the same from the last time I was in his office. Plain. Functional. Cold. Coach removed a small box from his office chair and sat down letting out a huge sigh.

"I would invite you to sit, but. . .you know," he points at the obvious.

"Nah, I understand." I chuckled, looking around the room at the blank walls and huge bookshelf.

"What can I do for you, BJ?"

"So Coach, I was thinking. Well, I wanted to ask you if it was all right if I rejoined the team."

Coach observed me in silence. And just before the awkwardness became too unbearable, he said, almost as if asking, "You quit."

"Yeah, yeah, I know, Coach. It was a mistake. I shouldn't have quit. I was going through a lot, you know and—"

"Let me stop you right there. BJ, we had a long conversation about this last year and you said that you never really wanted to run. It was your mom's idea. So when she passed, God bless her soul, you didn't want to do it anymore cuz it reminded you too much of her. Now, you're in my office asking to join the team again? Explain this to me."

"What do you mean?"

"What do you mean, 'what do I mean'? What is it that you really want, BJ?"

"I. . .I was talking to Mrs. Morales before break. . ."

"Yeah, and?"

"We were talking about how I needed a plan. A plan to get out of the hood. So she mentioned something about a scholarship—"

"I had several college coaches, personal friends of mine who expressed interest in you last year, but you quit. BJ, I'm sorry; there are no scholarships left, not from any reputable schools."

"But can't you—"

"BJ, it's too late. Scholarships have already gone out for the year."

I was shocked. I didn't know what else to say. So I said nothing.

"Knowing all of this. . .if you still want to join?"

Too late, indeed. After discovering what I did about my mother, I had to go through with it. I couldn't turn back now. I could still finish out my senior year in honor of Kathy James.

"Yeah," I whimpered. I was sure Coach felt the uncertainty emitting from my skin.

Coach thought long and hard before he rolled his chair back to the utility cabinet. He hesitated again, "BJ, against my better judgement, I'll allow you to join. Obviously, indoor season has already begun."

He yanked open the cabinet.

"You still wear the same size?"

I nodded.

Coach scrounged through the leftover track gear of practice shorts, tops, and pullovers.

"You can attend practices for the next couple of weeks and I'll assess your progress. But I won't let you participate in any meets until I feel you're ready."

He handed me the gently used apparel.

I nodded again, feeling relieved that I wasn't just getting tossed to the wolves right away.

CHAPTER 5

OLD ACQUAINTANCES

/

Since I rejoined the team, I could no longer pick Monica up from day care or take her to her kid's class. That job was a toss-up between Mr. James and Auntie Emma, whoever was available.

One day when I got home from practice, I found Monica sitting at the kitchen table in her Gi watching *Inspector Gadget* on our nineteen-inch color TV, snacking on a giant bag of peanut M&Ms—*my* peanut M&Ms.

"Where'd you get that?" I asked.

"Umm..."

"Stay out of my room, Monica," I said, snatching the bag from her.

I went to my bedroom to change out of my practice gear. While getting undressed, I heard several voices coming from my bedroom vent. I squatted down getting closer to the vent which was by the floor. The vent led to only one place, the basement. I rushed back into the kitchen.

"Spud, where's your dad?"

"Downstairs."

"Is someone with him?"

"Yes," Monica said, chewing the last few M&Ms she had in her hand.

I waited a few seconds for her to tell me who was in the basement but then I remembered *she's only six*.

"Who's downstairs with him, Monica?"

"Some homies from back in the day."

That's all I needed to hear.

I found it odd that Mr. James would suddenly have company over, so I crept toward the basement stairs to investigate. He hasn't had anyone visit since the funeral, at least, not to my knowledge.

I eased the basement door open and crept down the first few steps, so I could ear-hustle in on their conversation.

"I don't get what you're doing, Keko," said a vaguely familiar voice.

"Just trying to be a better man," Mr. James responded.

"Better than who, us? So you better than us now? That what you sayin'?"

"Take it how you want it, L.O."

/

LIGHTS-OUT

L.O., that's why the voice sounded familiar.

"L.O." was short for "Lights-Out," the nickname my father gave his onetime best friend for the consistency in which he knocked people out when he fought someone.

Lights-Out had to be high up in the gang hierarchy, possibly a regent, or even a governor, like Keko. They used to "run" together when my dad lived on the West Side and had been tight ever since.

"C'mon, preacher-man, show me," taunted L.O.

I didn't know what was going on but the way L.O. and my dad were going at it, I knew I had to get down there quick.

I scrambled down the stairs and was met with a cloud of smoke that hugged me like a T-shirt three sizes too small.

Mr. James was sitting behind the long homemade bar he built shortly after purchasing the house. Lights-Out was standing in the middle of the floor and two other Gangster Disciples were sitting on a nearby sofa.

As soon as Lights-Out saw me, he went and sat down at the bar.

"Hey BJ, you remember the homie Lights-Out?"

"What up, Keko Jr.?" L.O. greeted me with a smile.

I walked over to the bar, looking into the ashtray. "I know y'all ain't smoking weed up in here?"

"BJ, calm down. This is just tobacco and rolling paper, cigarettes. You know I don't smoke weed no more."

Lights-Out laughed, "We know who hasn't smoked before if he thought this was bud."

His flunkies on the sofa laughed as well.

Before I knew it, I had gotten right in L.O.'s face. My pops had given this bum his nickname for knocking people out. I was ready to test that theory. Something inside of me seethed with hatred for everything Lights-Out and his boys stood for. His mascots followed him around giggling at his every attempt to be funny. It made me feel sad for how weak they were. That they wouldn't stand up to him. But not me.

With no hesitation, I snatched the cigarette from L.O.'s lips and squished it to smithereens in the ashtray.

"Man, I don't care what type of smoke it is. I don't want it up in my house, especially when my little sister's home."

That remark finally wiped the smirk off that jerk's face.

His two soldiers stood to their feet.

One of them rushed over taking a swing. I slipped the punch stepped to the side and gave him a quick jab-cross combo then finished him off with a hook for his trouble.

He dropped to the floor.

"Eh! Eh, cut it out! BJ?" Mr. James yelped.

The other punk threw a wild haymaker. I leaned back then popped him with a counter right-hand cross.

Mr. James rushed from behind the bar and grabbed me, "Calm down, son."

The two guys hopped up, looking at Lights-Out for direction.

Unexpectedly, the smile resurfaced on L.O.'s face, he stood, clapping with vigor, "There it is. There he is! Whoo! You got a little Keko up in you after all. I was beginning to wonder. Maybe he is yours."

I felt conflicted. I wasn't sorry for cleaning those two goons' clocks. Yet it deeply disturbed me that L.O. would compare me to Keko. I had let my anger get the best of me. I wanted to be nothing like him. I yanked away from Keko's grip.

Lights-Out wafted his hand telling his hoods to "stand down."

"Yeah, that's my boy," Mr. James answered. "Look here, um, maybe y'all should go."

"Yeah, yeah, maybe you're right," L.O. agreed.

Lights-Out waved his hand again. The soldiers glared at me as they obeyed their master. Mr. James ushered them upstairs, and I followed them the whole way.

Mr. James walked his guests onto the front porch. I stayed inside. I wanted to deal with Mr. James once and for all. I quickly got Monica situated in her room with a few coloring books, then I returned to the living room to wait for Mr. James to come back inside.

I looked out the window. Mr. James and L.O. seemed to still be beefing about something. To my surprise, they eventually did end up giving each other dap, and a hug, and L.O. headed down the stairs. That's when I got an idea.

I sprinted through the house and went out the back door. I scrambled down the back steps and through the gangway. When I reached the front of the house, I peeked around the corner to see if Mr. James had gone back inside, he had. Then, I sprinted again, chasing down L.O.'s car.

"Hey. Hey!" I yelled out, catching up to the car. They pulled over to the curb and Lights-Out rolled down his passenger side window. I leaned inside to speak with him.

"What up Keko Jr.?" L.O. said calmly.

"Do me a favor. Don't call me that."

"Oh, you don't like being called Keko Jr.?" interrupted the goon in the back seat.

"I wonder why," commented the driver.

Both foot soldiers laughed, which I found strange. *What were they laughing about?*

"Hey, shut up!" L.O. barked. "What's on your mind, shorty?"

"I wanna know what's up?" I asked. "Looked like you and Mr. Jam...Keko were beefing. Ain't y'all supposed to be boys?"

"Don't you argue with your boys? It ain't nuttin'. Yo pops making some dangerous moves. I came to warn him to be careful, that's all."

"Dangerous moves like what?"

Lights-Out smiled, "Stay in school, shorty." He waved his driver to take off.

I watched them drive farther down the street. *What was going on*? I wondered. *What were these dangerous moves Lights-Out was speaking of?*

Mr. James had a past—a past that was rudely pushing its way into my present, which according to Lights-Out, will lead to danger. Who would that danger impact, Mr. James alone or me, Auntie Em, and Monica too?

CHAPTER 6

VANESSA COLBY

/

Vanessa Colby was the girl of my dreams—caramel-complexioned, silky jet-black hair down to her shoulders with the smell of Luster's Pink hair lotion, really sweet yet kind of sassy at the same time. And absolutely gorgeous! Vanessa, sometimes I called her "Van" or "Vee" for short, had one dimple that was perfectly placed in her left cheek that accentuated her pearly white smile that could stop traffic both ways. I'd seen her shoot down many brothers that tried to talk to her. That's if the brothers even had the courage to try to get her number. She was just that fine.

Many would say that it's "luck" that I ended up with a girl like her. I would say "longevity" had more to do with it than luck. Though our relationship was relatively new, just a few months, we'd been friends since I was in the seventh grade and she was in sixth, back in the day when we went to All Saints together. Mom knew Vanessa as that cute little girl who lived on the next block, but we didn't start dating until a few months after Mom passed away.

Vanessa transferred to Mendel from Willibrord, another Catholic school on the South Side. We usually walked home together considering that she lived only a block away from me on 113th Place. Friday track practices were usually pretty short. Coach didn't want to wear us out the day before our meet, so after practice, I went to spend a little time with my sweetie.

The sunshine glistened off the melting snow as I walked down Vanessa's block. To my surprise, there she was, outside, shoveling what little snow there was in front of her house. I stopped and just watched her.

/

FIRST DATE

I can still remember our first date, mainly because of the big trouble I was in afterwards. I didn't exactly have Mr. James' permission to use his car for the date. But I was no fool. I knew a chance to go out with one of the most beautiful, popular girls in the hood doesn't come around often. The crackly phone line made her sultry voice more intoxicating than it usually was. Each word she uttered was as if Angela Winbush was serenading my soul. Vanessa told me how much she was looking forward to our date with a level of giddiness I hadn't heard from Vanessa before. So taking my father's car keys without permission was worth the risk.

I pulled up in front of Vanessa's house and blew the horn. Instantly, the guilt of "borrowing" my father's car surfaced. I looked deeply into the rearview mirror knowing I had buckled under the pressure soon as I heard how happy Vanessa was over the phone.

Vanessa came out of the house looking as fine as ever. She had on a blue jean skirt, blue jean top to match, with white sneakers. Vanessa hopped in the car smelling all good and delicious, smiling brightly at me. I said to myself, *Self, if you're gonna get in trouble anyway, you might as well have some fun.*

First, we went to a restaurant named Shoney's to get a bite to eat. After Mom died, Auntie Emma took it upon herself to teach me the finer points of dating. "Us, girls get really crabby when we're hungry, so feed her within the first hour of a date."

I picked Shoney's because it had a great variety of pizza, wings, fries, and shrimp, practically anything you wanted. Kevin told me to take her to Red Lobster or someplace fancy like that. Cutting the fellas hair in the neighborhood provided me some money, but I didn't have that kind of money. It was best Vanessa found out early that I wasn't Big Money Grip. I was pleasantly surprised she was down with Shoney's all the way.

I was also shocked to find out Vanessa wasn't shy when it came to getting her grub on. *Ole girl could eat!* Not in a slobby kind of way, but real, like Mom or Auntie Emma—a meat and potatoes kind of gal.

After Shoney's, she asked, "What's next?" as we were walking back to the car.

I wanted to say, *Nothing, I'm taking you back before my old man gets off work.* But I didn't. "I don't know. What do you want to do?" I asked instead.

"Ooh, I know," she yelped. "I heard there was a great arcade out here somewhere."

"Yeah, Friar Tuck's."

"Can we go there?" she asked batting her soft brown eyes.

It was ten fifteen exactly. I knew that the second shift ended at about eleven thirty. So I guesstimated Mr. James would make it home around midnight or just after. I tried to convince myself that I could get away with it if I made it back before midnight.

"Let's go," I said.

I found out about Friar Tucks about a year and half ago. My boys and I were always on the lookout for secret hang out spots away from the city. We liked getting out of the drama of the hood. It was rare to find a place where we could occasionally let our guard down but when we did, it was usually in the suburbs. In Calumet City, I didn't have to worry about some fool trying to hit on Vanessa while I'm standing right next to her.

A huge smile plastered Vanessa's face as we entered Friar Tuck's Game Room. Right as you enter, there's a small pond full of what I always thought were giant goldfish, but Vanessa told me they were actually called koi.

Who knew? At the bottom of the pond was loose change people threw in to make a wish.

"This place is dope," Vanessa said.

I nodded in agreement. "C'mon, let's get some tokens."

As we got our tokens and headed off into video-land, I suggested we walk around first so she could see all of the games they had to offer before we settled on a spot.

She liked that idea and walked on ahead of me to browse at her leisure.

"Ooh, they got *Centipede*," she squealed. "Look, *Q*bert* too. Oh man, we gotta play *Donkey Kong*."

At first, I was worried about not making it home before Mr. James. But the more time I spent with Vanessa, it made me forget all about the punishment I would have had waiting for me. Besides, Monica and Auntie Emma would have noticed that I took the car anyway, so the odds of keeping what I did a secret from Mr. James were slim to none.

Vanessa and I held hands, running from game to game like two little kids loose for the summer. Whenever we ran out of tokens, we'd zoom to the front of the game room, insert several dollars and out came tokes galore.

Vanessa was having a great time and I couldn't front, so was I. Never had I met a girl who liked video games as much as she did, let alone who was any good at them. Vanessa smoked me in *Centipede*, *Galaga*, and *Ms. Pac-Man*. But I couldn't go out like no sucker, so I challenged her to come to the back of the arcade to play a game that I was great at, *Pole Position*. She didn't even flinch, "Let's do this," she fired back. Her confidence shook me at first. But I was determined to leave with at least one win under my belt. I won by a lap and a half.

I immediately hopped up from the *Pole Position*'s boxcar seat and told her we had to go. But the competitor inside her demanded a rematch. I kept walking to the door like I didn't hear her. Vanessa grabbed me by the arm. I thought to myself, *This girl's gonna make me have a rematch.*

"Ooh, BJ, look at this one."

Vanessa dragged me into one of the little side nooks of the game room where there was an upright cabinet version of *Track & Field*. I didn't even know they had this game at Friar Tuck's.

"We got the same one at school. C'mon, put in a token," she urged.

"Vanessa, I don't think you want none of this."

"Boy, quit being silly and put the tokens in."

I reached in my pocket and pulled out the last two tokens, shaking my head as I slid them into the slot. Vanessa had no clue she'd just signed her death certificate. She was right, inside Mendel's student lounge we had the exact version of this game. But since she was new to Mendel, what she didn't know was this game had been at the school for years and any free time me and the fellas had, we were up in the student lounge playing *Track & Field*.

Vanessa didn't stand a chance. I beat her in hurdles, in the sprints, in the javelin throw, in the long jump. It was getting so bad I began feeling sorry for the poor girl. Yet the whooping I was giving her didn't dampen her mood one bit. After each defeat she just laughed and vowed to beat me on the next event. *What a gal!*

/

STEALING FIRST BASE

We pulled up in front of Vanessa's house at about 1:20 a.m. I had never enjoyed anyone's company like I enjoyed Vanessa's that night. We laughed the whole ride home. I ain't Eddie Murphy or Richard Pryor but I had her cracking up. That was something else Auntie Emma told me, "We love guys who can make us laugh." And it was true, so true.

"I had a wonderful time tonight, BJ."

I couldn't agree more. The entire night was like a dream that I didn't want to end. But of course, I couldn't let her know that.

"Yeah, it was cool," I nodded.

"It was nice of your father to let us use the car."

I nodded sheepishly again.

"Oh, what's up with this quiet stuff all of a sudden," Vanessa said. "It's too late to play 'Mr. Cool' I've already seen fun BJ. Where is he? Where is he?"

Vanessa began tickling me, which again, I liked, but I just played it smooth. I kept pushing her hands away.

"C'mon girl, stop playing. Cool out."

We got closer and closer as we tussled inside the front seat. Then that moment happened. That moment most of the guys in my hood would die for. That magical moment that would solidify our relationship and make us the most envied couple in the *Wild-Wild*.

I leaned in slowly for the perfect kiss, from the perfect girl, on that perfect night. My poor heart was skipping like Laura Ingalls through the field on the opening credits of *Little House on the Prairie*. Vanessa eased toward me pouting her smooth lips. *Yes. Yes, yes.* I couldn't believe it. I was about to kiss Vanessa Colby. My lips were only inches away when Vanessa shoved her polished index finger to my mouth, *shushing* me like a schoolteacher.

"BJ, I know you didn't think it was gonna be that easy, did ya? Ha!"

She played me! I swore I heard Marv Albert in the background, "Olajuwon with the rejection!"

I came so close to kissing Vanessa; I could practically taste the strawberry lip balm.

All I could do was laugh with her.

"All right, you got me, Vee."

Without saying a word, Vanessa got out of the car and went up the stairs to her house. She turned and waved goodbye, smiling that irresistible smile of hers.

"Byyyye, BJ."

I waved back, "Later, girl."

She disappeared inside.

I sat there shaking my head for a second or two before starting the car and driving back home. I thought of strawberries the entire ride.

/

VICTOR

"Yo slim? What's your name? You got a woman?" Vanessa chirped all sassy-like bringing me back to reality; winter coat unzipped, *smurfing* her skull cap.

"Yeah, I got a woman," I quipped, walking toward her. "But I'm thinking bout dropping her. So what you talkin' bout?"

Without warning, Vanessa flipped snow from her shovel into my face. I yelped and skipped around shaking the snow from my track practice hoodie. Vanessa ran over to help, but she laughed more than helped.

"Stop being such a girl," she chortled. "You're fine."

Just as we got all the snow out of my hoodie, we noticed a black mustang creeping down the block toward us. My eyes were glued to the vehicle. In our hood, drive-by-shootings were as common as traffic lights changing from red to green. As the car crept closer, I instantly recognized two of the three people inside.

The front passenger was the biggest jerk I'd ever met, Vanessa's big brother, Victor. He was only a year older than Vanessa. And for reasons known only to Victor, he hated my guts. The feeling was mutual. I didn't care much for that *mark* either. We used the term "mark" as another name for a "lame" or a "chump." Nearly all the guys that went to St. Paul Academy were marks in my book, but Vanessa's brother was unique. Victor was the neighborhood intimidator, the jokester, the arrogant jerk who terrorized everybody, but no one would ever cross him. Not that there weren't reasons for the average joe to be afraid of him. Victor routinely traveled with an entourage of yes-men, ready to protect him if anyone dared to stand up to his torturous bullying. Exhibit A, the meathead in the back seat, Bruce, Victor's right-hand, flunky bodyguard.

I didn't know the driver, but it didn't take long for Vanessa to fill me in that the mystery guy was she and Victor's infamous cousin, David. He was a Gangster Disciple, ruthless, uncaring, and rumored to be a stone-cold killer. This was confirmed by Vanessa's reaction.

"Beej, you gotta go," Vanessa said gently ushering me along. But I continued to watch as the car slowly pulled over to the curb.

"BJ!? Stop it!" Vanessa yelped.

"Stop what?"

"Don't be getting into staring contests with them. My cousin David is crazy. He's dangerous. Victor's all 'bark' but David 'bites.'"

"OK, all right, I'll go," I said.

The group exited the car. David appeared harmless enough, goatee, fresh fade, jeans, Air Jordans, pretty clean cut, which was typical of most gangbangers. Not every thug was tatted up, with dirty jeans looking all disheveled.

Vanessa gave me a peck on the cheek, and I slowly began to jog away. As I got a little farther away, my hood-senses urged me to watch my back.

Sure enough, Vanessa was struggling to hold Victor from chasing after me.

"Eh dog!" Victor yipped. "I better not catch you back around here. I told you, my sister would never date a buster from Mendel."

This caught the attention of Vanessa's cousin. He muttered something to Victor, but I couldn't hear it from my distance.

Vanessa looked to have everything under control pushing her brother up the stairs. So I nonchalantly waved off Victor's weak threat and kept jogging down the block.

Before I knew it, I heard footsteps coming in my direction. I turned, and Victor circled around to get in front of me.

I quickly looked to see if I could expect any other visitors.

David was holding Vanessa as she flailed around. Bruce stood a few feet away watching.

"Eh, wave me off to my face, dog?" Victor stated, then muffed me in the face.

I was shocked. I had known Victor just as long as I'd known Vanessa and even though we've had minor verbal spats before, they had never turned physical. The only thing I could think of was Victor wanted to show off in front of his thug cousin.

"Vic, what are you doing? Stop," Vanessa pleaded.

Everything was happening all so fast. David and Bruce switched places. Bruce now held Vanessa while David trotted toward me and Victor. My thoughts bounced back and forth like a ping-pong ball. *Were they gonna try to jump me?*

"Get 'em, Cuz. Handle yo business," David cheered him on.

Nope, David just came to be Victor's hype-man. I looked over at Vanessa. She shook her head no with a worried look on her face. She didn't want to see her boyfriend and brother in an all-out brawl just several feet from her house.

"Don't be looking at her," Victor shouted, giving me another shove to the face, this time, a lot harder.

I had to decide quickly what to do. Apparently, Victor wasn't going to stop as long as David was there egging him on. I had to stop him myself. I looked over at Vanessa again, apologizing with my eyes. She mouthed, "it's OK," shaking her head yes. Permission granted.

Victor stepped in for the kill. He took a huge swing attempting to knock my block off. I ducked just enough so that his hand glided over top of my head. He swung so hard that his own momentum threw him off balance. But I was in perfect position for what I needed to do.

Bop, bop, bop, I tagged Victor with three stiff shots, taking him totally by surprise. He must have thought he was dealing with Martin Luther King's kid or something. I wasn't violent, but I wasn't going let him keep pushing me in the face either.

Victor wobbled a bit with a stunned look on his face.

David must have thought that I was going to pounce all over his dazed cousin, so he got between us and held up his hand to hold me back. Although, I was done with Victor, my mind was still in attack mode. I slapped David's hand down which grabbed his full attention.

David squared off against me. I hadn't noticed before, but he was a couple inches taller than I was. But that didn't matter.

"Boy, you sure you wanna make this mistake?" he asked through gritted teeth. "It'll be a big one."

Before I could respond Vanessa and Bruce had rushed over.

Bruce grabbed Victor before he could topple over, and Vanessa tugged me away from David.

"Lemme go, lemme go! This ain't over, dog!" Victor huffed while Bruce pulled him toward the house. David walked away joining them.

"You OK?" Vanessa asked compassionately.

"Yeah, I'm straight."

"I'm so sorry, BJ. I don't know why he keeps antagonizing you."

"It's cool, Van."

Vanessa gave me the most reassuring hug a guy could have after beating down her brother. I looked over her shoulder as we embraced watching Victor and Bruce enter the house. But just then, David turned and glared back down at me from the porch. Instantly, a shudder went down my spine. Not that I was nervous or scared of David. But the look on his face screamed I had just started something that he intended to finish one day.

CHAPTER 7

FIRST TRACK MEET

/

My probationary season of practice was officially over, and Coach allowed me to participate in the last few remaining indoor meets to get ready for outdoor season. There were about twenty-one of us on the team during the indoor season which didn't worry me. More students usually joined during the outdoor season because other sports like football and basketball will have ended.

I was familiar with everyone on the team, but we only had a handful of certified studs. There was Derrick Ayers a senior, Quan Mitchell, also a senior, who was one of the captains along with Joe Marshall, a junior and most of the time, quiet. Daniel Winters, "Shadow," was a sophomore and the only White student at Mendel. Shadow and Joe were both transfers who followed Coach Abrams to Mendel after he led his old school to a track state championship a few years ago on the West Side. There was also Esau Hawk, a junior who was half Black and half Native American with long black hair. And lastly, another one of my closest friends next to

Kev and Box was Antwan Benson. We called him Squirt. Though he was a senior, he still got teased a lot because not only was he short, five foot two, if that, but also he talked with a lisp. Over the years, to take the attention from his speech impediment, Squirt became an all-around class clown. And you could always find Squirt somewhere trying to holla at girls. That didn't mean he got any play. Though, rejection has never been a deterrent for Squirt.

Our little ragamuffin group filed onto the bus on our way to the Homewood-Flossmoor meet. On the bus ride over, Coach Abrams drummed two specific concepts into our heads: effort and attitude. About effort, he stressed the importance of expending maximum effort every single time we stepped onto the track or field. Concerning attitude, Coach Abrams said, "Remember, you are not just representing yourselves today. The name on your uniform reads 'Mendel.' Do I make myself clear?"

"Yes sir," we all responded like little robots.

"Oh, also as a reminder for those just joining us," Coach said, looking directly at me. "We do not drop batons...ever!"

The comment didn't bother me; that's just how Coach was, direct. Besides, baton passes had never been a problem for me. I was more concerned about getting into track-shape.

We got off the bus and went into the track and field house. The place was already buzzing as the other schools were inside warming up and claiming their sections in the stands.

Mendel didn't have an actual track at the school, indoor or outdoor. The closest thing we had was the gravel road across the street that circled the basketball court at Palmer Park and none of us ran on that. I remember as a kid watching track on television during the Olympics—the stadiums were always so grand. In person, not so much. We all found a spot on the bleachers to put our belongings.

The atmosphere inside the arena was more than electric. I was so nervous, it felt like bats were dive-bombing into a vat of blood inside my stomach. It always amazed me how track meets ran smoothly, like well-oiled machinery. There were countless working parts from the competitors to umpires and referees, to block and hurdle setters to the announcer. The other thing that amazed me was the number of fans that showed up to watch people run around an oval.

The one and only event that I was running finally rolled around, the mile relay.

Squirt, Hawk, Joe, and I were stretching out on the track infield when Coach Abrams approached. We all acknowledged him with head nods.

"Gentlemen, I'm making some changes to the lineup. Hawk, you'll lead off," he said, handing Hawk the shiny blue baton.

He continued, "BJ's going to run anchor."

"What?" Squirt interjected. "I'm supposed to be anchor."

"Antwan, I need to assess everyone's strengths for the upcoming indoor championship, that OK with you?"

Coach asked sarcastically. "Focus on the leg you have. I'm putting you second."

With that, Coach walked away leaving us to continue stretching. Coach didn't understand. Squirt wasn't trying to be disrespectful. He was just a competitor. He'd challenge a person to see who could spit the farthest if he felt he had a chance of winning.

/

MILE RELAY

We joined the other mile-relay teams who were gathering at the starting line. Squirt and Hawk began to strip off their sweats.

The starter gathered the first legs onto the track, instructing them to their appropriate lanes. The entire arena became quiet.

All of a sudden, my stomach bubbled, and my mouth became as dry as a cotton gin as I began to remember what my body already instinctively knew. I flashed back to the very last track meet a year ago. The meet where I decided I didn't want to do this.

Mom had badgered me my freshman and sophomore years to join the track team. Well, I guess that's not fair. She strongly hinted at it. I never knew why she wanted me to run. When I did join my junior year, I found out I was good at it. I improved so much throughout the year, I was getting mostly first and second place finishes.

Yet my heart wasn't in it. Keko wasn't around, so Mom struggled financially to keep Monica and me in private school and pay all the other bills. I felt my time would be more useful bringing in money from my side-hustle, cutting hair, than running in circles around a track.

That final meet, I was tied for third coming into the final stretch of a 400-meter race. I gave it everything I had. I pushed and pushed, giving my absolute best, straining across the line just to get edged out at the tape, fourth place. I had had it, mentally and physically. When Mom passed away, it was a no brainer for me to quit to help Auntie Emma keep things afloat.

The stampede of runners yanked me from my daydream. I didn't even hear the announcer yell "runners to your mark."

The crowd rose in unison to their feet followed by a frantic roar that banged on my eardrums. I thought I would throw up any second.

"Man, you hear that crowd?" Squirt asked rhetorically.

I lamented, *How did I get myself back into this situation?* Squirt said something else to me, but I couldn't hear him, I was busy counting Hawk's laps. On an indoor track, four completed laps around equaled 400 meters. So, all four of us would have to run four laps apiece to complete the full 1600 meters, one mile.

Slowly my anxiety began to settle when I saw how well Hawk was doing. Coming into Hawk's fourth lap, he was battling for third place. This made me feel even more comfortable. Squirt could potentially move us into second place and there was no way anyone was going to fade Joe. So, all I had to do was not mess it up.

Just then, *ding-ding-ding-ding*, the final lap bell rang. It always sounded like a dinner bell to me.

"Squirt, get ready," warned Joe.

I took a deep breath to center myself. There was no turning back, I had to press through the jitters of last year and focus on the now.

"A'ight Squirt, you can move us into second place, baby," I encouraged him.

Squirt glanced over at me looking like "death warmed over," as Auntie Emma would say. I could have sworn I heard his teeth chattering. The referee came over and ordered Evanston's second leg onto the track. Then, he waved over Squirt to get in the second place position and Leo after that.

I looked again, and the ref was right, Hawk had moved into second. My guy was doing it.

Hawk came in and handed off the baton to Squirt.

Squirt took off like a bat out of hell.

"Slow down," Joe yelled immediately. Joe was sitting on the floor yanking his sweatpants off. Joe looked up at me, "He's starting out way too fast."

I nodded in agreement. Within the first lap he caught up to Evanston and was battling back and forth for first place. He even stayed in first for a few strides. When Squirt came by, I yelled out more encouragement to him.

The Evanston cat was right on Squirt's heels, just pacing him, waiting for my boy to run out of gas. Coming into the third lap not only did the Evanston guy catch and pass Squirt, but so did Leo, Brother Rice, St. Rita, and all the other schools.

Squirt had slowed down so much that fourth lap that he was in threat of being lapped by Evanston, who was still in first place. The referee called over the third-leg runners placing them in their respective positions. One by one, they each snatched the batons from their teammates stampeding right by Joe and there was nothing he could do but watch.

Joe bounced in place impatiently waving Squirt in. When Squirt got there—dead last, he inched the baton into Joe's hand.

Squirt stumbled off the track over to me and collapsed into my arms. I had never seen anyone breathe so hard that didn't have asthma.

"Squirt, you a'ight dog?" I asked.

But instead of answering he began making these wheezing sounds that reminded me of Monica trying to breathe through a busted balloon at her last birthday party. At that point, I thought it best to just lay him on the infield. I mean, Squirt was my boy and all, but I had to keep my concentration on the task at hand.

I heard another glorious uproar. I turned around and saw why Joe is the Thoroughbred of the team. Remarkably, he had overtaken the fifth-place runner and showed no signs of slowing down. What a seesaw battle. Even Evanston lost their huge grip on first place to Brother Rice who came out of nowhere.

Coming into the third lap, Joe seemed to be getting stronger. He was slowly, steadily moving up and up and up, fourth place, a little farther, third place, a little farther.

"Yeah, Joe, yeah," I screamed at the top of my lungs. I was so into the race I had almost forgotten that I was up next.

That's when I felt a strong tug at my leg. Squirt looked up at me deliriously licking his crusty lips. But I couldn't worry about Squirt right then, I had to pay attention to the race. The bell for the last lap rang and Joe had a lock on third place and wasn't stopping there. He had fought back from last potentially into second—unbelievable. The referee told us remaining runners to get ready. Squirt yanked at my leg again.

"What?" I yelped.

Squirt squeezed out two little words that didn't mean much to me at that moment. Truthfully, I had forgotten the validity of those words and how they impacted this race in particular. I didn't know those simple words would eventually come back to haunt me like a ghost.

"Man leave me alone," I snapped again.

It was time to put up or shut up. My mind was going a mile a minute. The crowd was going bonkers as Joe made his final move of heroism pushing us back into second place.

"Brother Rice, Leo. No, no, Mendel then Leo," the referee yelled out and waved us over.

I took a few deep breaths and calmly waved that *stud muffin* over.

Joe tumbled in, utterly exhausted from making up for Squirt's deficit.

Joe passed off the baton and I set my sights on Brother Rice.

I took off with caution, keeping in mind that I didn't want what just happened to Squirt to happen to me.

I couldn't believe how quickly the first lap went. Funny, I wasn't even tired and better yet, I held the second-place position.

During the second lap the pace was just as blistering. It was frustrating that I wasn't making up much ground on the first-place runner, so I decided to kick it up another notch.

Anyone that made an aggressive move was promptly rewarded by the crowd. Their cheers echoed inside my head, energizing me, pushing me to dig deeper. Now I was gaining on the one guy ahead of me.

The crowd was completely out of control and for the first time ever, *I loved it!* I soaked up every cheer. But of course, what I didn't know at the time was that several other competitors were making their move also, on me. Coming into the third lap, I hadn't closed any more distance on Brother Rice. I began to concede in my mind, *Well, second place isn't that bad.*

As I settled into my pace, I noticed how hard I was breathing. I tried to pump myself up, *Come on, BJ. A lap and a half to go.* Just as I thought this, the runner from Leo zoomed passed me as if I were standing still. I felt someone else on my backside, so I took a quick glance to see where the other runners were.

St. Rita and Evanston were right on my heels and so was the rest of the crowd. Desperately, I kicked it into overdrive, holding off the St. Rita runner as best I could. But he also passed me. The crowd exploded again, *Those Judases*.

I heard the final lap bell ring. Brother Rice had just passed the finish line going into his last lap and Squirt's prophetic words now began ringing in my ears. I tried not to listen. I blocked Squirt's negativity out of my mind and kept going.

As I passed the finish line entering my final lap, the strength from my entire body seemed to ooze onto the track. At practice, we often joked about the "invisible monkey" who hops on your back during the last stretch of a tough race. That day I felt no cute little monkey, I would have welcomed several monkeys, in fact. No, what I got were *gorillas*, a family of invisible overgrown gorillas and my body was the tree limb too flimsy to hold their weight.

My hamstrings tightened. My quads burned. My lower back stiffened. My shoulders hunched, and my left side cramped so badly I thought I was in labor. *Hold up, did my water just break?*

The crowd was still going bananas. Every school team was on their feet clapping and cheering their teammates on, Mendel included. Coming toward the finish line, I saw Joe, Squirt, and Hawk frantically waving me in. I knew if I went all out, I could probably, maybe, hold onto fourth place.

But every time I tried, like the killer in a bad horror movie, Squirt's two little words would repeat themselves, whispering, "It hurts." Every muscle in my body succumbed to Squirt's airy, sweet-sounding words. Soon, it was a battle of attrition, and I lost.

Mind over matter. Coming off the last turn and into the straight away, Evanston finally whizzed by me, and our fourth-place aspirations went up in smoke. I shuffled across the finish line clutching my cramped side in fifth place, which is next to last as indoor tracks only have six lanes. The guy in last place at least had the common sense to fake a torn hammy. *Hmph, maybe I'll do that next time.* Who was I kidding? There wasn't going to be a *next time*. My heart wasn't in this. The referees and umpires scrambled to give everyone their times. I clomped over to where my sweats were.

Squirt handed me my belongings.

"That race hurt, don't it?" Squirt asked me way too chipper.

If I wasn't so tired, I would've snatched a hole out of his esophagus. I just glared at him and snatched my clothes from him instead. I looked around to see if anyone else was watching then limped away.

"What's wrong with you?" my personal jinx Squirt asked me.

/

COMING HOME

"Ooh, BJ's home! Did you win, BJ?"

Mr. James, Auntie Emma, and Monica were all in the living room playing UNO when I got home. I didn't mean to be rude. I truly didn't. But I wasn't about to play one-thousand questions with Monica about some stupid track meet. So instead, I chose to ignore *her* for once.

I headed to my room. I could feel the soft comfort of bedspring and mattress welcoming me. I entered my room and swung the door closed behind me. I threw my bag to the floor hearing the expected *thud*. That's when I noticed the expected *wham* of the closed door was missing.

I turned to see Mr. James standing in the doorway.

"Your sister asked you a question."

"No, I didn't win," I admitted sulking. I flopped onto my bed finding it not as comfortable with Mr. James interrogating me from the doorway.

"So you ignore her cuz you mad?"

"Well, she won't have to worry about that happening again. Thinking bout quitting."

"Whoa, whoa, whoa. Hold up. You just don't quit something because it's hard."

"Why not? Isn't that what you did? It was too hard for you to be a law-abiding citizen, so you just gave into your emotions cuz someone made you mad. That was the easy way out. In the meantime, you left your family responsibilities for my mother to handle."

"Easy way, huh? Is that what you think?"

I ripped out of bed and got right in his face.

"That's what I know," I growled. "I was right there, remember?"

"You don't know nothing," he shot back.

Once again, Auntie Emma came to the rescue, foiling my plans of finding out the reason Mr. James snapped the day he was incarcerated. She stepped into the doorway.

"Hey, knock it off you two. Keko?"

Mr. James looked at his sister then back to me. He shook his head then left.

I plopped back down on my bed. Auntie Em sat next to me.

"Wow," she chuckled. "You must've really been awful."

I wanted so badly to be upset but I couldn't with Auntie Em cracking jokes. We looked at each other and burst into laughter.

"I really was," I admitted.

"Oh baby, don't worry about that. Kathy would have been proud of you no matter what."

Auntie Emma kissed me on the forehead and left. I spread out on the bed staring up at the ceiling. I finally remembered; it wasn't about me. I couldn't let one meet bury Mom's dreams. I couldn't quit on her again.

CHAPTER 8

TWO EDUCATIONS

/

Every inner-city kid knows growing up, we get two educations. One, from the streets. The other from the classroom. Father Louis Cooper, Mendel's principal marched into our sixth-period US history class like it was his second home. We called him "Father Lou" for short, which he didn't seem to mind. He was low and compact like a bulldog, loyal, but at times vicious. His demeanor alone demanded respect. The instant we saw him, gentle cheers and clapping rang out over the class. Our history class didn't give him that kind of respect just because he was the principal. No, we gave him props because it was unanimous around the entire school that Father Lou was more than a walking history book; he was a living time capsule, full of historical treats and goodies packed in a five-foot five-inch pudgy White man's body. Father Lou could take the most ordinarily drab history class and teleport us through time, space, decade, and century all within the span of fifty minutes.

What we loved most as a class full of Black and Brown students was that when Father Lou substituted, he didn't teach from the school's ancient textbooks that were thicker than Monica's Children's Picture Bible. We knew we weren't going to learn that same old, tired George Washington, Thomas Jefferson US history stuff either. No, our principal enjoyed educating us about Black and Latino heritage, and not just in February and September either.

He was a firm believer that American history should also reflect the actual students of the class. *Hmm, what an original concept.* But not only that, Father Lou also loved to teach us different historical facts about the city we lived in. I did not know that one of the first known serial killers in America was a White man named Dr. Henry Howard Holmes from Chicago's South Side. H.H. Holmes, as he was known by, owned a hotel, which brandished the name "Murder Castle" because of the homicides he committed there. Another fact, Holmes' hotel was located on Sixty-Third and Wallace in the Englewood neighborhood. Father Lou told us that Holmes took a number of his victims from the 1893 Chicago World's Fair, which was just a few blocks from Murder Castle.

We learned from Father Lou about the Great Chicago Fire that happened back in 1871. The inferno lasted three whole days, killing more than 300 people. It burned up about thirty-four blocks, spanning over three miles long.

Father Lou put us up on the race riots that happened in the fifties and sixties. He schooled us on how the Chicago Housing Authority began in 1937 and about the history of several high-rise housing projects and how they began. Father Lou was dedicated to educating us on useful, relevant stuff.

The historical events he taught were almost unimaginable. We were amazed with how much Father Lou knew about Chicago and world history in general. He confessed that he knew a lot about Chicago's history just by living through it. Everything else he said he learned from his father. Turned out that Father Lou grew up in Roseland and so did his dad. Unlike a lot of his neighbors, Father Lou stated he saw no reason to leave Roseland just because the area was filling up with people that didn't look like him. Then he made a comment that had all of us scratching our heads, but I was the only one brave enough to raise my hand.

"Mr. James, question?"

"Father Lou, did you just make that up?"

"You all never heard the phrase 'White Flight' before?"

We all shook our heads no. I knew I hadn't. It was shocking to us to know it was an actual phrase, let alone, to hear a White person say it. And just like that we had our topic for the day.

"All right, White Flight is a phrase used to describe how large groups of White people would relocate from an area when other ethnicities settled in the same area."

Box blurted out from the back of the room, "In hood vernacular, the White folks dipped once the Blacks and Lats came to town."

Everyone laughed.

Even Father Lou got a chuckle out of Box's comment.

"Yes, that's one way to put it Mr. Hughs. But that's not the whole story. See, White residents didn't pack up and leave just because they saw a few Blacks and Latinos in their neighborhoods. Some tried to quote, unquote, defend their neighborhoods from integration. They were ready to fight to keep the neighborhoods White."

"Is that when the race riots started?" Vanessa asked.

"Not really. There were some threats of violence to try to intimidate the new families. But resistance was mainly done by legal tactics."

"What kind of legal tactics?" Box asked.

"All right, remember what Jim Crow is, right? So imagine Jim Crow laws implemented in the late sixties, early seventies but not just for public places, for private sectors too. What would that have looked like back then...Antwan?"

"Why you asking me?" Squirt replied.

"Because you're part of this class discussion. And I'm sure you don't want detention for not participating."

"I don't know, Father Lou."

"Would someone care to elaborate for the mentally incompetent this morning?"

"Hey, I take offense to that," Squirt quipped.

"As you should," retorted Father Lou.

"Basically, it would be legal discrimination, right?" I chimed in.

"Go on," said Father Lou.

"Well, for instance, I'm guessing there would be laws prohibiting Black families to live in certain areas. Instead of segregation being limited to public restaurants or department stores, the laws would have had stipulations on things like home ownership or maybe even small Black-owned or minority businesses."

"Yes, but, not only racial restrictions or stipulations, like you said, Mr. James. There was mortgage discrimination and hidden fees to offset a decrease in profitability, because after all, these area's property value will inevitably plummet because of all the Black and Latino families who live there now."

"Wow, is that what happened here in Roseland?" Kevin asked.

"Not just Roseland, a lot of neighborhoods in Chicago," Father Lou replied.

It was amazing to me that people would go to such great lengths all because of racism disguised as *separate but equal.* But Father Lou was on a roll that day.

"Let me give you a real-life example," Father Lou continued. "It's called 'blockbusting' and it went hand-in-hand with White Flight. Back when the diversity changes began happening here in Roseland, several of my neighbors were fearful that the neighborhoods would be over-run by people who didn't look like them. One day I saw a Black woman in her mid-to-late twenties playing with a soccer ball on the front lawn of the house next door with her son, who looked to be around six or seven years old."

Father Lou stated a few hours later someone rang his doorbell. It was a real estate agent. The agent asked Father Lou if he happened to see the young lady and her son playing out front. Then he went on and on about how he knew that several more Black families were moving into the neighborhood and he completely understood if

Father Lou no longer wanted to live there. That's when the agent shoved his business card in Father Lou's hand and told him to contact him when he was ready to move, then he went on to the next house.

About two days later, Father Lou saw the same woman and her son at a McDonald's. So Father Lou, being who he was, went over and introduced himself.

"Did you get her number, Father Lou?" Squirt blurted out.

A few people laughed but most of us were irritated because we wanted to know what happened next.

"No, I didn't get her number," Father Lou said, rather annoyed. "Instead, I got her apology. She explained that she wasn't my new neighbor and that some guy paid her one-hundred dollars to kick the soccer ball around the yard with her son. Turned out to be that same real estate agent. She said he had about four or five soccer balls in his trunk and that my neighborhood was the third one they visited that day."

"Why'd he have her do that?" Squirt asked.

"To reinforce the scam, what you think?" Kevin answered.

"Precisely," Father Lou continued. "First the agent spreads the rumor about different ethnicities moving into the all-White neighborhood. Then he plants a phony neighbor to prove the rumors are true. Next, he goes door to door, calling everyone's attention to the young woman playing ball with her child. He's sure to point out that there's no dad around, to help perpetuate stereotypes. He gives out his business cards just in case people want to move. Then. . .you tell me, what happens next?"

"He gets the sale," Vanessa answered.

"Ahh, not quite yet, Ms. Colby," Father Lou adds. "He's not satisfied with just one deal. The agent hands out a few more one-hundred-dollar bills, plants a few more phony neighbors, Latino ones this time, but not on the same block, a few blocks over. He goes door to door again. This time adding more stereotypes, perhaps, these new neighbors don't even speak English. Now, the dirty work is done. The agent is out of soccer balls, out of money, but it doesn't matter. It was a great investment. By the time he gets back to his office, the phone is already ringing off the hook with people who want to move and fast."

"That's how 'The Man' gets down, huh?" exclaimed Squirt.

"But here's the kicker," Father Lou continued.

"That's not enough," I interjected.

"This agent not only helps sell the house of the White folks who want to move, but also follows through with selling the vacant house to a Black family. After all, no White families will move there anyway. Oh and, the vacant house where the staged family was playing soccer, the real estate agent actually had bought that house for the purpose of planting the phony family in the yard."

"So his investment pays for itself," Kevin surmised.

"And needless to say, six months to a year later. . ." Father Lou waited for the answer.

"He runs the same scam all over again in a different community," Box added.

"And that's blockbusting," Father Lou concluded.

"Deg, it's kinda smart," Kevin stated.

It seemed the entire class turned and glared at Kevin.

"It's dirty, but smart," he reasoned.

"Well, it's illegal for real estate agents to do that now," Father Lou explained. "But my personal opinion, I think racism and discrimination just change forms; the essence remains the same."

The school bell rang and that was that. Father Lou's history lesson explained a lot to me. I had often wondered how Roseland flipped from being a predominately White area to mostly all Black. Yet I never would have thought it happened in such an underhanded manner. The reason we all respected Father Lou was because he was real enough to tell us the truth no matter how it made his own people look. More than once, Father Lou has stood in an assembly of his all-minority students with tears in his eyes and apologized about the racism in Chicago and even America. That type of open honesty and acknowledgement would make the average White person squirm, our principal, Father Louis Cooper, owned it. There was no way any of us expected him to take the blame for what many of his ancestors did back in the day. But we all loved him for his courage in acknowledging there was an atrocity and injustice done to Blacks and other minorities by Whites, even if not by him personally. There was no mistaking it, our principal loved us. And we loved him back.

CHAPTER 9

GANG GATHERING

/

Monday practices were never any fun. On Mondays we found that Coach would work us the hardest because, for one, our next meet was at its farthest point away, and two, the meet was fresh on his mind and that first practice back was meant to punish us, if we had a crappy meet.

Walking to and from school was never an issue until I started running track. Mercifully, that Monday I made it onto my block. The pain from practice would soon be over once I collapsed on my bed and propped up my barking mutts. As I got closer to my house, I saw several guys that looked to be leaving my place. The silhouette of one of them looked strangely familiar, but I was too far away to recognize who he was. Whoever they were, they divvied up hopping in three cars and sped off.

Just as I got to the steps of my house, four more guys exited the front door. But these guys, I definitely recognized as infamous gangbangers from the hood. They were maybe several years older than me but certainly not old enough to be friends with Mr. James.

"What up shorty?" said the biggest of the four.

"What up man," I said back.

They trotted down the steps and quickly hopped into a car then left. *What was going on?*

I hurried inside to find Mr. James in the kitchen, his head buried in the freezer.

"Yo, why you got thugs up in my mama's house?"

Mr. James emerged from the freezer, a package of catfish fillets in one hand, chicken wings in the other.

"I felt like having some friends over," he said way too matter of fact for my taste. "It really doesn't concern you, BJ."

"You got killers up in here like Ice-Cold, Bugger, and Raymore? And it doesn't concern me?"

"Boy, who have. . .name me one person you know they've killed?"

"I don't know, but I heard—"

"That's what I thought, hood rumors, BJ."

"Yeah, well, I know what's not a rumor."

Keko glared at me with bad intentions.

"Let it go, BJ," he warned, then held up the respective packages. "Now, you want chicken or fish?"

But I couldn't let it go. Not any longer. This family has been skirting around the obvious for way too long and I had just about enough of it. Keko was in jail for nearly ten years of my life, and I needed to know exactly why.

"I'm not letting anything go," I growled. "I don't remember him doing anything to you to make you snap like that."

"You were a kid—"

"I know I was a kid. A kid you were supposed to protect—"

"I was protecting you."

"No, you scarred me for life. How do you think I
felt seeing my father being dragged off by police? I had
nightmares for years."

"BJ, you. . .you just don't understand."

"Well explain it to me. I'm not nine years old anymore. I'm a man. What did that guy do to you to make
you snap like that?"

My father stood there in silence. At that point I knew
I wouldn't get anything out of him. So I switched tactics.

"Fine, you don't want to talk about the past; let's talk
about the present. What are these 'dangerous moves'
you're doing?"

"What are you talking about now?" Keko questioned.

"I chased down Lights-Out after they left the other
day. He said you doing something so dangerous he came
to warn you to stop. What you into? Is there gonna be a
repeat performance or will it be something different to
land you in jail?"

He placed the frozen foods on the counter.

"BJ, again," he began softly. "It does not concern you."

"Man, I swear, if Monica gets hurt because of something you're wrapped up in—"

"BJ, I'm sick and tired of having to prove myself to
you," he exploded. "Yes, I did a lot of horrible things in
the past. But I've done my time. The good Lord has forgiven me and that's not who I am anymore."

"The Lord has forgiven you? Now that's funny. That's a good one."

"Brandon, go upstairs and get Monica for dinner. Now please! Now!"

I scoffed aloud before storming out of the back door, slamming it shut behind me. If he wasn't going to give me answers, I knew who I could get them from.

/

MORE LIES, LIES, LIES

Auntie Emma and Monica were at the dining room table playing checkers with the local news on the TV in the next room blaring way too loud. Auntie Em knew everything about her baby brother, and it was time for her to come clean.

I rushed into the room and before I could say anything Monica was giving me information I didn't care to know.

"Hey, BJ! They almost caught the Bumpy-Thumpy-Burglar today."

"Bump and Thump Thief," Auntie Emma corrected.

"Mr. James wants you," I announced, promptly lifting Monica out of the chair to the floor so she would know I meant *now*.

But Monica, being Monica, stayed put, staring at me. "BJ, why do you call Daddy, 'Mr. James'?"

"It's a sign of respect," I said lying through my teeth.

"BJ!" Auntie Em scolded.

"Monica-downstairs-now-bye."

Monica gave a snort and huffed away. Seconds later we heard a *ka-boom* as she slammed the back door. Auntie Emma jumped, startled.

"You all won't be satisfied till y'all tear this house down."

I sat in Monica's chair and resumed her game. Monica and my auntie were horrible at checkers. I went for the kill.

"King me."

"What's the matter with you?" Auntie Emma asked, crowning my player.

"What's the deal with these meetings Mr. James is having downstairs?"

"What? Um, baby, I don't know. Did you ask him?" Auntie Emma stammered, now lying through *her* teeth. She played another move. I triple jumped the remainder of her pieces.

"I did. He keeps lying saying he's not banging anymore."

"BJ, Keko's in that lifestyle about as much as I am."

"Well, I just know, old habits die hard."

"Spit it out, what are you trying to say?"

"I asked him about why he went to jail too. Why he beat that guy half to death."

"Did he tell you?" she asked me hesitantly.

"Nope. Just said he was protecting me."

"Oh," Auntie Emma replied.

I waited for her to offer up something, anything more to the story. But she didn't.

I finally said, "Auntie, you know something. Tell me what it is."

"BJ, I don't know. You were there with him. I wasn't."

"Auntie, sorry, I don't believe you."

"BJ, sorry, I-don't-care."

Aunt Emma stood, then swiped the checkerboard clean with her hand before storming out of the room.

CHAPTER 10

THE GREAT DISCOVERY

/

I stood in awe inside the men's restroom admiring Squirt's fresh new *kicks*. This wasn't my original plan entering the restroom. As soon as the bell rang, I sprang up from my Geology Genius class, *yup that's what it's called*, and zipped through the hallway. Vanessa tried to stop me to chat, but I was on a mission. I only had a few minutes before the next bell and I had to urinate so badly I was seconds away from starting my own clothing line, "River Pants," for men.

I zigzagged my way through the between-class traffic that was cluttering the hall. I bust into the restroom where I found Squirt, polishing off his new Air Jordans.

"How'd you get the new Jordans? You ain't got no job."

"What, I got mad loot." Squirt answered pulling out a wad of money bigger than his fist.

"OK dude, what you into now?"

"Who are you, my mother?"

"Nah, your father. You didn't know? Your mother should have told you, son."

"Man, shut up."

We both laughed until another contraction hit my abdomen. I rushed over to the urinal to handle my business.

"C'mon, dog, what's up?" I asked again.

"A'ight dude, you gotta promise not to tell nobody."

"Man, I ain't gonna tell nobody," I said flushing the urinal and going over to wash my hands. While I was doing that, Squirt rushed over to the door and peeked outside. The coast was clear. He came back over to the sink.

"I'm the stick-up-kid," he whispered.

"What?" I asked drying my hands.

"You know, that guy that's been on the news. . .for robbing the old ladies? It's their Social Security money."

"Yo, stupid, don't you think they need that money?"

"*Shush*, keep your voice down. I know, but that's the brilliant part. They just get reimbursed anyway. I wait for them to cash their check at the Currency Exchange, follow them and steal the loot. It's simple. Quick."

I couldn't believe my ears. One of my best friends was robbing little old ladies for their Social Security checks. What was next, snatching candy from kids on Halloween? I just shook my head. There was no way I could hide my disappointment.

"I don't know what you looking at me like that for. It's hard out here, man."

"Get a job."

"I do. I have a couple of them," Squirt laughed.

"What, you selling too?"

"Maybe. A little something."

Just as I was about to storm out of the restroom, it dawned on me. This was my boy. I knew him. I grew up with him. And this. . .*this* wasn't Squirt at all. Someone's gotta be manipulating him, pulling the strings. He's either being bullied into this or owes someone money or something. Being short with a big mouth wasn't a good combination for the hood.

He continued, "BJ, I'm just doing what I gotta do to survive out here. Remember, keep your mouth shut," he commanded before storming out the restroom door.

Not only was Mr. James trippin', but now I also had to find out what was going on with Squirt.

/

HEART TO HEART

With some very hard work and added pointers from Coach Abrams, I was able to rebound from Squirt's jinx, placing second and third in my last few relays. One day after practice I cornered Coach Abrams inside his office to talk with him about more than just track strategies. I shared with him in detail how much I'd struggled since Mom's death, and I wanted to get his advice about Mr. James keeping in touch with active gang members.

"Change is hard, BJ. Sometimes it takes a while. Be patient. You can't penalize your father for what he used to be. Look at the man he is today."

It wasn't what I wanted to hear.

"I guess."

I stood up and began browsing around Coach's office. I went to his bookshelf. He had a lot of different books, but it was the pictures that caught my attention. There were several framed pictures of an attractive woman and a teenaged girl, who looked around my age. I didn't remember him having pictures up in his office last year.

"Coach, this your family?"

I picked up one of the framed pictures. Coach promptly took the picture from me and placed it back on its shelf.

"Word is you used to live down south, like waaay down south. That true?"

"I did for about twelve years or so," Coach answered.

"Where'd you go?"

"Mississippi. . .to a small town named Louin."

"What was that like?"

"It wasn't too bad. Hot. Lot of snakes though."

"Snakes!?" I interrupted. "Poisonous?"

"Yeah, some were. You get used to it."

"What would make you leave Chicago to go to a place that has poisonous snakes, then move back after so long?"

Coach Abrams became eerily quiet. I called his name, but he just stared off into space as if he was in another place altogether. *Had I crossed a boundary?* I thought. Maybe Coach's reason for leaving Chicago was something I ought not push.

"Coach, you OK?"

"What?" he gasped, snapping out of his daze. "Yeah, I'm fine."

Coach grabbed his car keys, bag, and stood up.

We entered the hall but before exiting, Coach offered me a ride home. I politely declined and we both went our separate ways. I figured I could use the walk home to ponder Coach's weird reaction to my questions about his relocation from and back to Chicago.

/

CHESS NOT CHECKERS

I unlocked the front door and went to my room to change. I heard voices coming from my bedroom vent. Was Mr. James entertaining gangbanger friends again? I laid on the floor putting my ear to the vent.

I overheard Mr. James speaking like he was addressing a group of people. Yet by his tone, he wasn't speaking to dastardly foot soldiers. This was different.

"It's not your mama's job to teach you how to become a man. That's your father's job. Many of us men have failed you in that area, including me. I'm sorry every day I wasn't there for my son."

Wow! My mouth dropped. I was shocked, not only by what he said about me, but that it was evident Mr. James was mentoring kids. I heard it with my own ears, yet I was still having a terrible time believing it. Was Mr. James some type of rehabilitated, ghetto-fied scholar kicking knowledge to the underprivileged youth of Roseland? *No way! Un-uh!* I needed ocular proof.

I popped off my bedroom floor and gingerly crept through the living room. I carefully made my way to the top of the staircase that led to the basement. I opened the door easing my way down several of the creaky steps and slowly peeked around the corner.

There they were, right before my very eyes, fat, tall, short, and small; a group of maybe twelve to fourteen boys, ages ranging probably from eight to fifteen years old. Most of the boys were Black but I did spot a few Latino boys sprinkled around. They were spread about the basement sitting in pairs each with chessboards in front of them. Mr. James walked amongst the boys, watching while they played.

"Today we're gonna learn about love," he announced getting the response of scattered giggles.

"Love?" rang out a squeaky voice. "I thought you was teaching us how to be a man?"

I was eager to see how Mr. James would handle the preadolescent heckler.

"Well," he began, "the priority of a real man is to love God and his family. He provides for his family, protects them, supports them, all of this is done from the foundation of love."

"But how do rooks and pawns show love?" one of the older boys with a high-top fade asked.

"Well, love is sacrificial," Keko answered assuredly.

Another dark-skinned thirteen-year-old interjected, "Ooh, I get it. The pieces sacrifice themselves for one another, right Keko?"

"Not only that but chess teaches us to think two, sometimes three steps ahead, right? So how would this look on the street?"

Right as the older boy was answering, I examined each group more closely. It appeared to me that each group had an older boy teamed up with a younger one. Instantly, I realized that this structure was set up with a mentor focus. Whenever there was side chatter or inappropriate joking and laughing, I noticed the older boys would gently rebuke the youngsters. *Brilliant.*

"Say, if I shoot somebody," the teen continued, "or steal on them in the face or rob them, that person may take it out on my little brother 'stead-o-me. So I should think about stuff like that first to help me decide what I should do."

I was utterly mesmerized. A permanent smile engrained itself on my face. Just then, I noticed something else, Keko was looking right at me while I sat on the steps. *Busted!* He gave me a smirk and a slight head nod. I nodded back in return.

"Great example. Everybody see that?" Mr. James asked, returning his attention back to the boys. "The love for his younger brother helps him make the right decision."

You would have thought Mr. James had a master's degree in secondary education the way that he broke subjects down so that the kids would relate. I knew he was good with Monica, but I didn't know just how far his skills expanded.

Keko continued, "All right, let's wrap it up early today. I'd like y'all to meet somebody very special to me."

In unison, all the little faces swung around looking in my direction. If I weren't so dark skinned, I'm sure I would have turned beet red.

"Come meet the fellas, BJ." Mr. James waved me over.

I edged down the steps walking slowly toward the group.

"This is my son BJ. He's a senior at Mendel. He graduates this year," Mr. James bragged.

With no prompting, one by one, from the older to the younger ones, the guys came over and shook my hand firmly, looking me in the eyes, introducing themselves by their first names. Who knew respect was contagious? *Was I still on the South Side?*

"Yo, what up fellas?" I said to them as they approached.

"OK, guys, let's wrap it up," Mr. James encouraged.

The young men circled around Mr. James like he was a head basketball coach ready to assign the starting lineup.

"When you truly love others more than yourselves," Mr. James began, "you make better decisions because most decisions we make in life will always affect more than just yourself. Life isn't about just getting what we want all the time. True love makes sacrifices."

As I looked around at all the bright faces, I couldn't help but notice how they hung to Keko's every word. They believed him. They trusted in him.

"All right pick up these chessboards and get outta here," he continued. "Don't forget to do your homework. Stay out of trouble. Let's clap it up, guys, c'mon."

The group began clapping and slowly walking away. An older fella playfully grabbed a younger one in a headlock. Others dapped one another up. Another successful group. But suddenly, a tiny voice squealed out from a frail Latino boy about nine, "No, wait, Keko, the memory verse."

"Oh, you're absolutely right, Leslie. How could I forget that? Fellas, hold up." Everyone stopped what they were doing.

"C'mon, everybody say it together," Mr. James instructed.

All the boys in semi-unison recited, "It is better to be godly and have little than to be evil and possess much. Psalm, chapter 37, verse 16."

The fellas clapped it up again then went back to the business of cleaning up the chessboards. Mr. James scooped Leslie up in his arms and gave him a huge hug.

/

MEN'S GROUP

I was officially flabbergasted at what I just witnessed. I parked myself at the living room window to watch the parade of tween-agers leaving my home.

The two older boys who were answering all the questions downstairs were last to leave the front porch. That's when something unexpected happened. As they got ready to leave, they both pulled baseball caps from their bags and broke them hard to the right. I couldn't believe it, barely thirteen and little Gangster Disciples. They trotted down the steps without a care in the world.

The overpowering scent of seasoned ground beef drew me away from the window. Mr. James cleverly instituted Taco Tuesday when he found out that tacos were Monica's favorite meal. Auntie Emma thought it was a sweet gesture. To me, it was just another ploy to sink his hooks deeper into Monica's little heart. I mean what type of person would bribe a kid with tacos to get her to like him.

Mr. James didn't only cook on Taco Tuesday but every day. I didn't eat much of his cooking though. I usually waited until Auntie Emma came around then I'd pass by her with my stomach growling. Sometimes I had to fake it with my throat, but she was never the wiser. "BJ, baby, you hungry? Want me to fix you something to eat?" *Heh, it worked every time.*

I don't know where Mr. James learned to cook but it looked like every meal was a culinary experiment. The kitchen was always in total disarray, and Mr. James looked exhausted as if he was the lone chef preparing meals for the entire Bears team roster.

I made my way to the kitchen. Smoke billowed from a skillet on top of the stove. Mr. James seemed to be in the middle of a disaster. He bounced back and forth from the countertop to the fridge to the stove. He had on a white apron that read, "Can't stand the heat? Move to *Minnesnow-ta.*"

"Tacos cool with you, BJ?" he asked over his shoulder, halfway looking at me.

I didn't answer. I just sat down at the kitchen table and stared at him. I was still trying to understand how he began "the hood-boy-scouts" in our basement. Little boys from the South Side—from Roseland, *my* neighborhood—learning morals, values, and of all things, Bible verses, from *my* dad? What was Mr. James up to? My silence finally got his attention. He turned to look at me.

"Who are you, really?" I asked sincerely.

"What?"

"Are you this big, bad gangbanger? Or a guy who teaches kids Bible verses and about the consequences of their actions through chess? I mean, who are you?"

Mr. James laughed as he turned the fire to simmer then joined me at the table with a cup of coffee.

"Do you even want me to answer, BJ? Seems like you made your mind up about me a long time ago."

"How long have you been trying to get kids out of gangs?"

"It didn't start out that way. I just wanted to teach them how to be men. To have integrity, respect for themselves and others. But the ones that showed up just happened to bang. But I told them they couldn't do both."

"What do you mean?" I asked.

"You can't both gangbang and be a man. They're polar opposites. They had to choose: be a man or a thug. So kids started coming, asking me how to get out the gang life."

"So the guys I saw the other day?"

"I started the men's group about a month after this kid one. Some aren't too happy about that though."

It suddenly dawned on me, "Hmph, Lights-Out."

Mr. James nodded taking a swig from his cup.

"My groups affect their bottom line."

"Bottom line?" I asked.

"Gangs are about making money, BJ. Don't let anybody fool you. It ain't about love for ya boys or them looking out for one another. That loyalty lasts about as long as the person's ability to make them money. You see, the less members mean less membership dues, less people out selling drugs, guns, sex trafficking—whatever their hustle might be. My hope is the ones that come will detach themselves from the streets permanently. I just have to keep them coming."

Though I was unsure how things would play out, one thing was certain, it took vision and courage to do what Mr. James was attempting. It was admirable. Mr. James eventually opened up about all the different types of men's groups he held right under my nose inside my mother's house.

The group of shorties I saw that day was, what he called, his MIT group, "Men in Training." These were kids ages eight to fourteen. He explained that the next group was the Prime Picks aged fifteen to about twenty-one. He called them Prime Picks because that was the age group most heavily recruited by gangs. Most people knew about being "jumped in" to a gang. Yet before that could happen, there needs to be a recruitment phase.

Mr. James explained that just like the US Army, gangs were looking for "a few good men" as well. They would go to elementary and high schools or even house parties to ask guys and gals to join. They would entice people with the potential to make lots of money, protection, or just having fun. And most of all having a "family" that will always have each other's back. If all else failed, he said that guys would recruit biological family members, like younger brothers, cousins, or nephews. And there was usually some talent or skill or connection that appealed to the recruiter, whether the person could fight well, had access to guns, was a fast runner—any trait that would make the set stronger was appealing. No one wants a liability, I guess, even in gangs.

The last group, the one I saw with all the killers leaving the house, was called the No Nonsense group. This was the *real* men's group. It had the most active gangbangers in them, all with at least seven years or more of banging under their belt. That group was for adults, twenty-two and up and it was the most secretive, therefore, in my book, the most dangerous for Mr. James to be involved with.

Mr. James explained that the men in this group had to totally buy into the fact that there was life outside the set. For a new member to even join this group, he had to be walked in by an already existing member. This was the group that had the greatest potential to sell out Mr. James to L.O. And now I understood the "dangerous moves" that Lights-Out was trying to warn my dad about. L.O. informed my dad that the set's higher-ups got wind of what he was doing and out of respect, I guess for past services rendered, were giving him a chance to stop willingly before they made him stop, permanently.

CHAPTER 11

MY CONFIDANT

/

Mr. James and I stayed up that night talking for hours. It was the first time we had really connected since he had gotten back.

Could God really change a man that much? I wondered silently the next day while watching Vanessa thumb through clothes hanging up on the frayed laundry lines in the attic.

This question continually rang in my head after Mr. James told me that he felt God used my mom to get him out of the gang life. She told him she didn't want her son born into gang life and he said he totally agreed with her. Mr. James compared being in a gang to being in prison. He said, "God wanted our child to be born free."

I hadn't spent much time considering what God wanted. Maybe because I've never felt as if He ever cared much about what I wanted.

"I can't believe it," Vanessa exclaimed while shoving another hanger with seventies gear aside. "Squirt's robbing little old ladies."

Her rhetorical question jolted me awake from daydreaming about Dad.

"Yeah, me neither."

"Well, maybe you can talk some sense into him," Vanessa suggested.

I shrugged, *maybe*.

See, Vanessa didn't understand. Squirt's head is what cement and granite would produce if they had a baby. When I talked with him in the men's room, he seemed fairly certain this was the lifestyle he wanted. Which meant I could've talked to him until I was as blue as Papa Smurf; he wasn't going to stop.

I propped up a couple of new folding chairs that I had gotten from the basement and placed them by the black footlocker. I finally threw out that broken chair.

Vanessa held up a sequin shirt in front of her. "What do you think?" She laughed, then shook her head, "No."

I joined her shaking my head, "Negative."

We both laughed.

She placed the shirt back on the laundry line and came over to have a seat. She leaned over and began sifting through Mom's "treasure chest." Searching through the random items she found a photo of my mother.

"Aww, your mom was so pretty."

I smiled as I walked back over with the journals. Vanessa took a journal from me then handed me the picture.

"Find out anything about your mom that you didn't know before?" she asked thumbing through the pages.

"Few things," I said, sitting down. "Think some pages might be missing though."

"Uh-oh, you know what that means?"

"No, what?"

"Your mama hiding some skeletons."

We both laughed again.

"Yeah, right. My mom was an angel."

Vanessa looked at the date on the journal, "Wait a minute, you started all the way from the beginning?"

"Don't most people?"

Vanessa put the journal aside and dove into the crusty shopping bag bringing out all the diaries. And she wasn't gentle about it either. I wanted to slap her wrist like one of our nuns from school.

"You gotta start from the most recent and work your way back. This way you start with all the good stuff first."

"Vee, there you go, messing up my system."

"You shouldn't have invited me over then," she retorted giving me that shimmering smile.

I was putty in that girl's hands, and she knew it. Vanessa began reading.

December 11, 1984

Dear God,

> *I tried to get BJ to go to church with me again today. It was like trying to change the diaper on an angry baby. He still hasn't noticed I hid the Bible I gave him just to see if he'd miss it. He hasn't.*

Vanessa stopped, "BJ!?"

"I know. I knew she took it," I quickly lied to save face.

"So you know where it is?"

"Yeah. Of course. We always played jokes like that on each other."

Thankfully, Vanessa never asked me where it was. She continued reading.

> *I finally told BJ about my cancer but couldn't bring myself to tell him just how sick I really am. Lord, our biggest test is yet to come. BJ doesn't know I've been talking to Keko about four months now. I've tried to teach BJ to forgive. But he has so much anger inside toward Keko. Lord, will I ever have my family together again?*

Vanessa stopped again, "Maybe this isn't a good idea."

"Nah, you straight. I would just end up telling you about it anyway."

Vanessa closed the journal and looked at me softly. *Putty.*

Vanessa had a different plan. She told me she'd rather *hear* about my mother, than *read* about her. Vanessa asked me questions about Mom's personality. What was she like when she was happy. . .sad. . .upset? Van asked about my mother's laugh—not "what made her laugh" but to *describe* my mother's laugh. She asked what I missed most about the woman who gave me life.

Vanessa asked hypothetical open-ended questions that had me rambling on and on as she listened and smiled. It was then I realized that I hadn't truly reminisced about my mom until I shared her with Vanessa that night. Yet I didn't do all the talking, Vanessa communicated with me by holding my hand, batting her eyes, comforting me with her smile and sexy giggle.

I had never confided in anyone so completely other than my mother. We talked for so long that we never did get back to the journals that night. I promised Vanessa that we would read from them again another time.

/

COLLEGE DREAM DEFERRED

I waited nervously in Mrs. Morales' empty classroom during lunch break. I knew the conversation we had at the end of last semester wasn't over. She cornered me in the hallway and told me she wanted an update on the plan I had for my future. I sat, eating my fingernails and dreading the conversation to come. She was certainly taking her sweet little time to come back with a few sheets of computerized paper.

Mrs. Morales ordered me to her classroom while she took the liberty of printing out my school transcript. She wanted to see if I would qualify for an academic scholarship, "just in case."

Finally, the door ripped open and Mrs. Morales rushed in.

"Sorry I'm late, Brandon."

"You get the transcript?" I asked a little too eagerly.

Mrs. Morales held up the forms in her hand, "What do you think this is, Brandon, my mail?" she quipped.

"So. . .what do you think?" I asked.

Mrs. Morales took a seat and handed me the stack of papers, the transcript of all my years at Mendel to date. I scanned the pages frantically seeing Bs. . .a lot of Bs, some Cs but less As. . .way less As than I remember getting during my tenure at Mendel.

"Your grades are good. Very good. But for an academic scholarship, I'm afraid, they must be excellent. Brandon, I'm sorry."

I stopped browsing the transcripts for what wasn't there. My grades weren't good enough to get me a free ride into college. And with the bomb Coach dropped on me about the scarcity of track scholarships this late in the season, who was I kidding, college was a fantasy.

I got up slowly, leaving the papers on the desk.

"Thanks, Mrs. Morales."

"Brandon, wait."

I stopped at the door, dejected. She got up and walked toward me. Not even Mrs. Morales' sexy sauntering could pull me out of the depression that was deepening by the second. *What had I gotten myself into?* Maybe Mrs. Morales was right. Maybe I will be shot in the head. Another teen statistic from the South Side that people will shake their heads at while watching the evening news. *Mm-Mm-Mmm, poor BJ, what a tragedy. On to the sports highlights.* Why hadn't I spent more time planning my future? I never once thought my mother wouldn't be here to help me sort through these life decisions.

"You joined the track team, right?"

"Yeah, but I might as well not have. Coach Abrams, himself, told me that colleges and universities have already sent out their award letters. So there's nothing I can do."

"There's always a chance, Brandon. Have faith," Mrs. Morales encouraged me. "Just be so good that you stand out. Attract the recruiter's attention. It's not rocket science, it's running. Just run faster than the other kids."

"It's not that easy, Mrs. Morales."

"Yes, it is."

"No, it's not!"

"Well, I guess I'll be seeing you on the nine o'clock news then." Mrs. Morales shoved the transcript in my chest. "Go. Go!"

"What's wrong with you?"

"What's wrong with *you*! Why do I care more about your life than you do? Brandon, if there were a gun pointed at you right now, what would you do?"

"What?"

"What would you do?" Mrs. Morales pointed her index finger at me like it was a gun.

"Run! I'd run."

"How would you run!?" she screamed, waving her "hand-gun" all around like a mad woman.

"Fast, I'd run fast!"

She pointed the "gun" between my eyes. "You'd run for your life, wouldn't you?"

I opened my mouth to answer but couldn't. My heart had leapt into my throat. As Mrs. Morales held me up at "gunpoint," her index fingernail digging into my forehead, her arm quivering and before I knew it, tears rolled down her rouge cheek.

"Yes, Mrs. Morales. I would run for my life."

"Then run for your *life*," she said weeping softly, lowering her hand only to bring it to her face to wipe the tears.

/

KATHY'S SECRET PAST

I couldn't get to sleep that night. I tossed and turned like a fat guy in a defective waterbed. The explosion of thunder shaking the house wasn't helping either. I sat on the edge of the bed seething over the annoying sound of rain crackling like bubble wrap against the window's pane. Only in the Midwest can we get a thunderstorm in the middle of winter.

I hated when it rained during the wintertime. The whole city became an ice rink filled with idiots who would continue to drive 65 mph on the Dan Ryan. I squinted to see the time on the clock. It was one-thirty, in the morning. Because of the constant thunder and rain dancing, I knew it would be impossible to get any real sleep. Not that I would have anyway. The images of Mrs. Morales pointing her finger at me like a gun and crying, haunted me. Crabby and wide awake, I was not about to just lay there looking around at the four walls.

I wrestled into some sweats, a hoodie, grabbed a skull cap, gloves, and my winter coat. The only thing I didn't grab were my winter boots. I crept out the back door into the pitch of night. Lightning lit the back porch as I tiptoed up the stairs to my hideout.

I never realized how scary the attic was at night. Complete darkness mixed with sporadic lightning was the perfect recipe for the eyes to play tricks. I wasn't afraid of the bogeyman. But a basehead, high off smack hiding in the attic would scare the hell out of me. I grew tired of bumping into things in the darkness while trying to maneuver in the attic, so I waited patiently and only moved when the lightning struck. Which, that night, happened about every thirty seconds. I shuffled a couple of inches here, a few feet there until I made my way to the lamp. I clicked it on and set up my makeshift library once again. I chose not to stick with Vanessa's method and flipped to where I had left off when I was reading solo. I had just found out about Mom being bullied and wanted to see if she wrote anything about how that panned out.

April 5, 1967

Dear Diary,

> *What am I gonna do? They beat that girl to a bloody pulp, and I know everybody's gonna think I had something to do with it. I should've never gone back up to that school after getting suspended. I told Crystal not to*

get her cousin involved. Emily's crazy and so are Trina and Brenda. Now we're both expelled from Corliss and Crystal's friends don't care. They don't even go to school. Diary, this was the worst day of my life. Nobody asked Crystal to jump Allie for me. That freshman, Justin warned me not to hang with Crystal because all her friends bang. Crystal never told me her cousin was in a gang. But Justin wouldn't lie. He gets straight As and goes to church. As much as I hated Allie, I never wanted this to happen. But I'm glad Crystal stuck up for me. No one's ever stuck up for me like that before.

April 13, 1967

Dear Diary,

Who knew cutting class would be such a rush, ahhhh!!! I can't believe we outran those cops. That was soooo much fun! I can't keep this up much longer, though. It took Mother a lot of begging to get Harlan to take me. I told her I didn't want to go to no Harlan. And I haven't gone a full day since I got accepted. I'm glad Justin was wrong about Crystal's friends though. They're not too bad. They just wanna have fun. Crystal's cousin Emily is so crazy!!! I can see us being friends. I can't believe she's almost five years older than us. I can't believe she stole those steaks from Hillman's today. I can't believe she knows how to cook steaks. They were good. What will we do tomorrow? Emily says she got some big surprise for me and Crystal. I can't wait!!!

April 15, 1967

Dear Diary,

I <u>CANNOT</u> believe Crystal and I got jumped in last night. I know if Mother hears about this, she'll disown me without a second thought. Miriam Hunt's daughter in a gang? "Scandalous!" But I don't care anymore. She's not perfect either. She never gives me the benefit of the doubt. All she does is ride me. I'm better off without her. I don't really know what it means to be "GD." Emily says it means I never have to be afraid again because they always got my back, just like with Allie. I guess that means I'm untouchable? They all love me. This is my family now.

What? *My mother gangbanged.* I was speechless. Who was this woman? Of course, I knew about my dad's gang ties. And I knew the "Emily" in the journals was talking about Auntie Emma. But not once had it ever crossed my mind that my own mother gangbanged too. I felt so betrayed. I felt the same way I did when I found out how sick Mom was, after the fact. I thought finding these journals would be a good thing. Instead, it's been nothing but unpleasant surprises and family secrets. From reading just a few brief journal entries, I found out, my mom never wanted me, she was a high school dropout, and was in a gang too. Guess I never knew my mother at all.

CHAPTER 12

TRACK PRACTICE

/

oach's routine for track practice during the week was pretty simple. Monday and Wednesday practices were for the harder, more physically taxing workouts. Tuesday was full of drills, baton passes, and weight lifting. Because our track meets were on Saturdays, Thursdays and Fridays were for light lifting, drill work, and recuperation.

Thank goodness it was Thursday which meant it was going to be a relatively laid-back day. I couldn't sleep a wink after reading about my mother. Since we didn't have a track at the school, the team had to jog up and down the hallway of the main school building for twenty or thirty minutes to do our mileage workouts. Most of the guys decided to stay inside to run their mileage. I felt that was a great opportunity for me to jog outside and be alone for a while.

After stretching, Squirt asked if I was ready to jog the hallways. I told him that I was probably going outside to run, thinking there was no way he'd want to brave the winter elements.

"Cool, lemme grab my sweat top."

Deg, there goes my peace and quiet. Just then Coach Abrams approached me, "Did I hear you and Squirt were going to run mileage outside?"

"Yeeeeah," I responded curiously.

"Good, Shadow's going outside too. You all stick together."

With that, Coach left me alone to wonder how the heck I just got volun-told to babysit Squirt and the White boy?

Once we stepped outside the wind whistled and howled as if to say, "Are y'all fools crazy?" I had on a hat, gloves, and double the sweats and was still cold. Shadow and Squirt walked on ahead of me blabbing away seemingly unaffected by "the Hawk" that whipped past our ears. Squirt had the idea of jogging down King Drive to Ninety-Fifth Street. I didn't care. I just wanted to start moving before my corpuscles began to freeze.

We exited the school grounds heading down King Drive. One of the serene aspects of running that I liked was that you can let your mind wander the whole time. Mama used to talk about hearing her heartbeat when she ran. She said that on a good run her heartbeat and footsteps would make music together. I never reached that level of peace when I ran. And I wasn't going to find that great joy with Shadow and Squirt yapping away. They laughed and joked like old friends reunited after twenty long years. We were barely past 110th and I was already sick of their cackling.

I decided to slow down to let the bosom pals enjoy one another's company. When they got a good distance away from me, I attempted to see if I could get in this running zone that Mom used to talk about. I cleared my mind and allowed myself to just be in the moment. It wasn't surprising that my thoughts took me straight to Mom's journal entries. I hypothesized about why she and my grandmother's relationship was so rotten. I never had the pleasure of meeting my grandmother, though reading about her, I doubt it would have been pleasurable. I also thought about what made Mom decide to change. According to Keko, Mom was the reason he left the gang life, so obviously she grew tired of that lifestyle. *What happened?*

A loud buzz of chatter brought me back to the reality of the South Side. I knew that Shadow and Squirt couldn't possibly be making that much noise. I took quick inventory of my surroundings. Shadow and Squirt were now about a half a block ahead of me. And I was coming up to 103rd and King Drive. There was usually a good-sized crowd of people that came up the hill from Corliss, one of the neighboring public high schools, to catch the King Drive bus.

I scanned the crowd to spot any potential threats. I felt a bit safer because the crowd was on the other side of the street when I passed. After assessing that there was no danger, I set my sights on catching up to Shadow and Squirt. But to my surprise they had turned around and were already coming back. They must've changed their minds about jogging all the way to Ninety-Fifth Street.

Without thinking, I turned around as well and began to head back to Mendel. Unfortunately, I didn't think how this would look to the criminal element who might have been in the crowd across the street. Like tiger sharks drawn to O-Positive blood, several guys, who seemed to be minding their own business seconds ago, slowly trotted across the street angling toward me.

In my neighborhood, one of the worst things a person can do when confronted by a brood of hoodlums is turn the opposite direction. It's always better to put on a brave face, avoid eye contact, and pass by hoping no one bothered you. But turning to head in the other direction was to alert the guard dog to sniff the air for fear and then attack.

When I noticed my new admirers coming toward me, I stopped jogging and began to walk. I took another quick glance down the street and was relieved to see that Shadow and Squirt were getting closer.

The dude that appeared to be the ringleader stepped to me.

"What you running for, homie?"

"I ain't running from nothing, just jogging," I said firmly.

"He look scared, don't he?" said another goon. A few of them start laughing. The leader chimed in again.

"Oh, wait, I see your little track uniform. You go to Mendel, huh? Look, I bet he happy girls go there now."

A few of them chuckled giving each other five. But that was fine with me. The more they clowned around the closer my own boys got. Although, at that point, I hadn't a clue if Shadow would sell us out if we had to scrap. I was about to find out soon enough.

The leader stepped closer to me asking what I had for him. I called smart guy's attention to the fact that I had no pockets on my track sweats, so I couldn't possibly have any money. But the "gooch" wouldn't take my word for it.

He stepped a bit closer like he wanted to search me. I prepared myself for the worst, knowing that if they did get the best of me, I wouldn't get stomped for too long. Shadow and Squirt were closing fast.

I angled to the side to keep them from seeing my surprise visitors. Two of the guys tried to get behind me. I circled quickly to keep them in plain view.

The leader tried to grab me. I slapped his hand away and backed up.

"I know you got something for me, homie," the leader said again.

"Nah, he ain't got nuttin' for you, dog," Squirt said, busting into the thug's circle getting side by side with me.

Suddenly, Shadow ran up behind the biggest of the thugs and body checked him like he was Wayne Gretzky.

The thug went flying several feet before crashing to the ground. Shadow totally caught him off guard.

Oh snap, once again it's on, I thought. There was no way of avoiding a fight this time. The three of us squared off against the five of them. I told the leader that no one was getting punked today.

He said, "We'll see about that."

The leader turned toward the bus stop and whistled. What happened next was like something straight out of a bad movie. Every single person that was standing at the bus stop looked over at us. Then the leader yelled two of the most frightening words a person can hear on the South Side of Chicago, "Move out!"

The entire crowd from the bus stop—jocks, nerds, even the girls—began sprinting across the street to get us.

I turned to see Squirt humping down the sidewalk. Shadow and I looked at each other and took off right behind him.

Complete chaos erupted. The mob clogged up traffic in both directions. They were yelling and screaming as they chased us, "Get 'em" and "Catch those Mendel marks."

Car tires were screeching, and horns were honking.

After a little while, Shadow and I caught up to Squirt.

"What we gonna do?" Squirt asked.

"Yo, just keep running!" I shouted back.

About a full block into our sprint, I turned around and saw the crowd stopping one by one.

"Yo, why they stopping," I asked.

"Look, look," Shadow said pointing to the street.

Two squad cars happened to be cruising down King Drive coming straight at us. I had never been so excited to hear police sirens in my life. The cop cars screeched to a halt.

The crowd dispersed in several directions as the four officers hopped out their cars, barking orders and tackling anybody they could get their hands on.

"What about them?" I heard one of the officers yelp.

"Leave 'em. It's just the track team," his partner replied.

We all looked at each other and started busting up laughing as we continued running down the block.

Utterly exhausted, Shadow, Squirt, and I made it back to Mendel's campus unscathed. We told the rest of the team what happened and a few of the fellas began putting on sweats and hats getting ready to go back to 103rd. Although Mendel was a Catholic school, it was still on the South Side of Chicago. There were no choir boys being bussed in from the suburbs. Mendel was composed of inner-city boys and girls, meaning, we had our own share of gangbanging hoods. Sure, they were *educated thugs*, but thugs, nonetheless.

Coach Abrams put a quick end to that revenge nonsense. There was something positive that came from "The Chase," as it became known as: from that day forth most of the guys began jogging outside together, bringing us closer as a team.

/

DAVID

Vanessa and I had made plans to hang out. She wanted to come over to read more of Mom's journal, but I didn't want her to discover Mom's sordid past, so I convinced her to watch a movie instead.

Before she arrived, I decided to go to the store to pick up some snacks. Her favorite? Strawberry ice cream. Mine? I can't watch movies without Jiffy Pop popcorn. On my way out, Monica and Auntie Emma were coming in from kid's class. Monica asked if she could tag along because she wanted to get a box of cereal. I said, "sure," then wet Gi and all we walked to the neighborhood market.

I had my popcorn; I had Van's strawberry ice cream, but Monica was awestruck, drooling in the middle of the aisle while anguishing how to narrow down her selection.

"Spud, c'mon; just pick one."

"But I want Trix."

Just then, I heard one of the last voices I ever wanted to hear that day.

"Now, let's see what type of man you are," said David, Vanessa's killer cousin. "Fruity Pebbles or Lucky Charms."

David chuckled at his own lame attempt to be funny. I acknowledged him with a quick head nod and returned my attention to helping Monica pick out a brand of cereal, which I'm sure was much more interesting.

"What, can't take a joke?" David chuckled again, playfully punching me in the arm.

Monica giggled, "Who's your friend, BJ?"

"Friend?" Why was this dude even talking to me? We weren't friends nor were we ever going to be. David bent over placing his hands on his knees.

"Hey little one. What's your name?"

"Monica," she said, giggling even more.

David reached over gently taking the tip of Monica's orange belt of her Gi top.

"Whoa, you know kung fu?"

"Monica," I said, removing David's hand from her Gi belt, "why don't you check the end of the aisle for the Trix."

I waited until I knew Monica was out of earshot and I cut to the chase.

"Man, what you want?"

"Whoa, whoa, why the aggressive tone? I'm just trying to be nice man."

"I'm being nice too. What do *you* want?"

David inhaled deeply. *Like I was the one annoying him.*

"OK, check this out, BJ. Um, I had a long talk with Vanessa, and she really likes you. So I'm warning you, treat her right."

"Yep."

I figured David's finger wagging was over, so I started down the aisle toward Monica. David grabbed me by the arm. I snatched away from him.

David got right in my face, "I'm trying real hard to be nice for Van's sake."

I looked down the aisle quickly to make sure Monica wasn't watching.

David continued, "But you got one more time to disrespect me, shorty. For real."

"Dog, who are you? Gangster-thug wannabe. Dude, I ain't scared of none of y'all."

That's when I noticed Monica finally had her box of Trix and was skipping back toward us. David saw Monica as well and turned his back to her.

"Youngster," David whispered sternly, "you ain't gotta be scared of them; be scared of me. She may know kung fu, but I know 'gun fu.'"

David lifted his shirt just enough to reveal the butt of his gun buried deep in his waistband.

"Look," Monica announced.

David lowered his shirt sneakily and turned facing Monica, "Wow, you found the Trix, huh?"

"You like Trix too?"

David glared at me, "Nah, I never did liked *Tricks* much."

"Monica, lets go," I put my arm around her, and we left David standing there.

David continued to glare at me while me and Monica stood in line to pay for our stuff. He finally went outside, and I expected him to be there waiting. I was thankful that he was gone, but just like Mrs. Morales, I was sure we would talk again.

/

MOVIE NIGHT

Vanessa and I sat cozy-comfy on the sofa with our snacks. I frowned playfully as she sprinkled a few kernels of my popcorn in her strawberry ice cream, *straight-nasty*. Vee rented *Back to the Future*, with Michael J. Fox. As entertaining as the movie was, I couldn't stop my mind from contemplating what just happened at the corner market. It made me think about my own family ties.

If someone peeked through the window on Christmas day, my father, an ex-Gangster Disciple governor, and my auntie, an ex-Gangster Nation queen would have looked like any normal, loving family. No one would ever think that that sweet little unassuming woman formerly drove getaway cars, chauffeured drive-by shootings, and won fist fights against grown men. And to see Mr. James play with Monica, no one would think that just twenty or so years ago, he literally ran gangs on the West and South Side. That he was third in command in one of the most historic gangs in Chicago with just as much clout as the prince, himself.

As Vanessa was laughing at Marty McFly, I was considering just how much I'd been cheated out of in my life. It didn't take me long to conclude that almost all the issues in my life were gang related, though I had never banged a day in my life.

I didn't have a solid relationship with my father because he banged and was carted off to jail for half my existence. My dear auntie had constant nightmares and could not even bring up the past without nearly having a breakdown because of the things her gang had her do. My grandmother, whom I never met, practically forced my mom into gang life all because she didn't love Mom the way she should have.

The more I thought about it, the angrier I became. I wished I had a huge AK-47 with endless bullets and a car with an endless gas tank. I'd get Kevin to drive us from New York to L.A. to do a drive-by on every single gang member.

Tears burned my eyes. I removed my arm from Vanessa's shoulder to fake a couple of sneezes, so I could wipe my face. I knew my drive-by dream was delusional. There was nothing I could do to bring Mom back or change my family's past. And I knew there was nothing I could do about the gangs in Chicago, even though their very existence, it seemed, was ruining my life. The weight of it all made me exhausted.

Suddenly, keys rattled at the front door and in clomped Mr. James.

"Hey Beej. And well, well, well, hellloo there Ms. Vanessa!" he said excitedly once he saw her. *What up with that, was she his kid or me?* I thought.

"Hi Mr. James! How you doing this evening?" Vanessa responded with equal enthusiasm.

"I'm doing good, Ms. Vanessa. Uh, you all sitting a little bit too close, ain't cha?"

"Yes sir," Vanessa answered through a playful sigh as she moved almost to the other side of the couch.

"Don't worry, she can't get pregnant just sitting next to me."

Vanessa swiftly punched me in the arm.

Keko stared at me briefly, shaking his head.

"Thank you, Vanessa, at least somebody is respectful around here," Mr. James said walking away.

"Got your crabby pants on tonight," scolded Vanessa.

"I'm tired of people like him demanding respect."

"BJ, honey, what are you talking about?"

I didn't know if I should tell her. Of course, I knew that I could trust her, but just how much dirty laundry can be dumped on a person before they crawled out from under the heap feeling just as filthy. I'd been pouring out my heart to Vanessa about my mom, could she take hearing about my father too?

Vanessa took the remote and muted the television. She looked at me with full attention. I didn't know where to start. I know she liked my father and what I was about to tell her might change her view of him.

"C'mon," she urged. "You can tell me."

"You know my dad used to bang, right?" I began after a deep breath.

Vanessa nodded.

"And you know he was in jail for a long time?"

"I'd heard rumors about it. But I don't know what he did."

"Well, I was with him when he got arrested. It was for first-degree assault."

"What happened?"

"We were at the corner store. Matter of fact the same store Monica and I went to this evening. I was nine years old. It was summer. One of those kinds of sunny days where you had to wait for your eyes to adjust to the brightness when you came outside."

I admitted to Vanessa I didn't remember much about the guy, other than he was a little taller than Keko and kinda chubby but average built at the same time. As Keko and I were leaving the store this guy was coming in. The sun was extra bright as it beamed off the glass door so I couldn't see his face really.

"He held the door for me," I explained to Vanessa. "But apparently when Keko walked through, they must have bumped shoulders or something, cuz I heard the guy say, 'my bad.' When I turned around, all I saw was Keko grab this guy and fling him to the ground. I remember thinking to myself, 'Dad, what are you doing?' But I was in shock. The guy scrambled back to his feet, but Keko scooped him up, like a WWF wrestler and wham! Slammed him so hard on the sidewalk, I thought for sure he was dead. The man didn't move a muscle, he just moaned like a wounded animal. Then Keko stood over that poor dude and just wailed on him."

"No warning or nothing," Vanessa asked. "He just started beating the guy?"

"Yeah…" I replied.

"Brandon, that doesn't make sense," Vanessa argued. "Either the guy or Mr. James had to have said something. You just don't beat up a person for accidentally bumping you as he's holding the door for you."

"Vanessa, I know what I saw. I begged Keko to stop. I tried pulling him off myself, but he just flung me aside. It took about five people to finally pull him off. The police came, cuffed him, and carted his butt off to jail. Because my mom didn't allow me to visit him in jail, the next time I saw my dad was in the hospital the day she died."

"BJ, I'm sorry all of that happened. And I'm not disputing what you saw. I just think there has to be more to—"

"There's not. That's how people like him operate. They snap at the slightest sign of someone dissing them."

"People like who?"

"Like him…thugs…wannabe, tough guys always wanting their respect, respect, respect, just like your cousin.

I ran into him earlier today. It was the same thing, 'you dissing me?'"

"What? You ran into David? Tell me exactly what happened." Vanessa demanded.

"Nothing. He 'warned me,' I had one more time to disrespect him, or else...Oooh."

Vanessa stared down at her lap for what seemed like a full minute as if searching for the right words. She sighed heavily then looked me deep in the eyes.

"BJ, honey," she began very calmly. "I'ma tell you this one more time because evidently you thought I was playing the first time. Stay. . .away. . .from. . .David."

"He walked up on me in the store."

"I don't care, Brandon!"

"What was I supposed to do?"

"Go! Leave! God, why is that so hard for guys to walk away?"

"Cuz I refuse to live in 'Black-Slavery' in my own neighborhood."

"Black Sla—what is that?"

"Oh, 'run for your lives the thugs are shooting up the place again. Lock your doors and windows. Live in fear in your own community'. . .like some prisoners. Man, I'm sick of it."

Vanessa exploded up almost knocking over the popcorn. She grabbed her jacket from the recliner and stormed to the front door.

"BJ, you won't have to worry about being a prisoner when you're dead," Vanessa heaved the door open and left, slamming it behind her.

I didn't get it. *Why was she all bent out of shape? She lived here too. Shouldn't we all be tired of the gangland martial law in Chicago? Whatever, man.* I slid the popcorn over and unmuted the television just in time to see Marty stiff it to Biff. *Yeah Marty. . .man, bullies suck.*

/

SQUIRT'S PROPOSITION

It was so ridiculous all I could do was laugh.

"C'mon, Beej," Squirt pleaded.

"Are you sick in the head?"

"Father Lou is coming to search my locker any minute. Look, I'll never ask you for another favor as long as I live."

"Dude, there is no way I'm holding drugs for you. Are you stupid? Are you actually *high* right now?"

Unbelievable the audacity of Squirt. He was so confident that I would hold his drugs that he came to the restroom with the white paper package, wrapped in duct tape, practically forcing it into my hands.

I was still chuckling a bit as I walked into the hallway, that's when I saw Vanessa with a hoard of homegirls mixing in with the between-class chaos. I dropped my bag near my locker and went over to kiss some serious butt. We hadn't spoken in several days since the fight we had about her killer-cousin.

Good thing for me Vanessa's mean streaks last about as long as a mayfly's lifespan, even with her nosey friend Kim egging her on to dump me anytime I mess up.

Right in the middle of pouring my heart out to Van, down the stairs came Father Lou and Dean Greene, our infamous dean of students. We dubbed him, "Mean Dean Greene." He was a man that was respected but mostly feared, partly because, he had the strength of Sampson. I'd seen him break up fights by slinging two-hundred-pound-plus athletic studs across the hall. I made the mistake of shaking his hand once, *once*. His grip felt like a car door slammed shut on my fingers.

The cluttered hallway parted like there was a drunken blind man with a pitbull for a Seeing Eye dog. It could have been the huge bolt cutters that Dean Greene was carrying. We watched as they stormed down the hall toward Squirt's locker.

Squirt had just come out of the restroom and was standing over by my locker. He slowly escorted his guests farther down the hall to his own locker. At least Squirt was there to open the combination for them as opposed to having the lock cut off. I felt sorry for Squirt. But not sorry enough to take the fall for him. Vanessa, Kim, and I gathered up our respective belongings and walked by Squirt as Father Lou was searching his book bag and Dean Greene was tossing the locker.

If only this was a small infraction, Squirt would get a slap on the wrist and hit with a JUG, our version of the public school's detention. JUGS stood for, "Juveniles Under Guidance and Supervision." We called it, "Jokers Under Grueling Surveillance."

The concept of detention seems straight forward but nothing was ever simple at Mendel. The JUG system was set up on a "three strikes, you're out" rule. If a student received three JUGS within a school year, he or she was automatically suspended. And in order to return to school, that student had to serve a fourth JUG with none other than the "Dean of Mean," himself for six hours on a Saturday.

Dean Greene assigned only the meanest teachers to supervise JUGS. And what's more, he allowed the teachers to come up with their own methods of torture for students that received JUGS. That and the overtime pay, made it all worthwhile for the teachers to stay after school for the two-and-a-half hours to watch the misbehaving deviants.

Mr. Chandler thought of writing lines with the opposite hand.

Brother Brooks made his students work on one college level advanced calculus problem. If the student got the question right, they could leave, even if it was in the first five or ten minutes of detention. Everyone always tried, but no one ever got the math problem correct.

These were tip of the iceberg when it came to creatively cruel forms of JUGS. There were other methods by various teachers like writing a one-syllable, three-thousand-word composition on "Why Teachers Hate JUGS More Than Students," helping teachers grade papers, even arm-wrestling competitions. That was an idea drummed up by Mr. Echols, the wrestling coach.

However, Sister Cawley was as mean as they came. She seemed amused whenever she got a rise out of a student. I say that because a tiny smirk would appear on that wrinkly mug of hers whenever someone challenged her—student, teacher, it didn't matter. Sister Cawley successfully antagonized many of us with her accusatory tone. If she said, "Good morning" to me, my first inclination would be to yelp, "I didn't do it!" She thought up the doozy of standing. . .*for the whole two-and-a-half hours.* If a student sat or even leaned against a desk or wall, he or she got another JUG.

But Squirt would not have it that easy, I'm afraid. Mendel had a strict no drugs policy, so as soon as they find his stash he would be expelled for sure. Which made it more baffling when the three of us walked past and I saw Squirt chuckle at me as if he didn't have a care in the world.

CHAPTER 13

INDOOR CATHOLIC LEAGUE CHAMPIONSHIP

/

Mendel and St. Paul Academy had been bitter rivals ever since I could remember. Our rivalries were synonymous with the Bears and Green Bay Packers, Dallas Cowboys and The Philadelphia Eagles, Duke and North Carolina. Our schools were so closely matched over the years that we'd seesaw back and forth for bragging rights in every sport: baseball, football, hoop, and especially track. It was well-known that St. Paul would stack their basketball team with track members, so they could run their opponents to death.

Our bus pulled up in front of our archenemies' establishment. St. Paul had one of the largest high schools in the Chicagoland area. You could fit three Mendels inside of St. Paul. But we weren't intimidated by the size of their school.

Coach's genius was well documented. Coach had masterminded perfect symmetry of relay runners, sprinters, distance runners, and jumpers. By the time we got to the indoor championship, Coach knew the combinations of teammates and individuals to give us the best chance at winning every race and every field event we competed in.

Mrs. Morales' gun-point motivation pushed me to work my butt off over the weeks leading to the indoor championship. I was determined to win over any recruiters who might happen to be there to see Joe or Shadow or some other underclassmen from a different school. Mrs. Morales was right, I had to do whatever it took to earn a scholarship.

Shadow and I were in two relays together that day and there was no way we wouldn't dominate with the legs coach put together. In the 4x200-meter relay the pecking order was me, Shadow, Quan, and Joe. In the mile relay: Joe, Hawk, me, then Shadow.

Out the gate, Joe won the 55-meter dash, no shocker there. He didn't have much time before the 4x200 relay, so he just decided to stretch on the side to stay loose as Shadow, Quan, and I warmed up with a light jog.

While going around the track we came across Victor and his relay team warming up for the same race. We knew we were in their house, but we weren't going to back down one iota. The two relay teams jogged cordially side by side, eyeing one another for weaknesses. The tension was so thick you could choke on it.

After eyeballing me several times, Victor broke the ice, "Van tells me you still haven't gotten recruited?"

Victor immediately turned to his boys and chuckled.

"What's so funny?" I demanded.

"They must not want you, dog," he replied. "But I do, I haven't forgot we got unfinished business. But first, lemme school you in this relay."

"What's with all the jaw-jacking?" demanded Shadow.

"Man, who's this chump?" Vic retorted.

"Oh, that's Shadow."

"You'll remember me if we ever race," Shadow explained calmly.

"And why is that?" Vic asked.

"Cuz, all you'll see is my *shadow*," he said with a straight face.

Quan and I couldn't help but laugh which infuriated Victor. He lunged at Shadow but his teammates dragged him away. *Yeah buddy.* This was going to be fun. I was so excited that my body was tingling all over. Quan and Shadow were amped up too. I could see it in their eyes, relaxed yet laser focused. We made our way back over to grab Joe then we all reported for the race.

"Yo, start us off BJ," Shadow said, giving me a pound and the baton. I nodded my head in acknowledgment then went over to lane four and set my blocks. I saw that Victor was in lane two, perfect. I was oozing with confidence as this was a short race, I could go all out and not have to worry about dying at the end.

I set my blocks and got in a few practice starts. The official walked by checking everyone's positioning. I looked back at Victor and caught him scowling at me. *Hmph, the feeling was mutual.* The official began calling the cadence. I thought to myself, *It's time to shut this clown up once and for all.*

A hush fell over the stadium as we got on our marks. The official waited until we were all steady then, "Set!"

Bang! The gun sounded. Everyone exploded out of their blocks. . .except me. I didn't move. I waited. I waited just like how Mom use to wait before coming back to smoke me. I imagine everyone else thought I had a horrible start. But I waited purposely in the blocks until Victor zoomed by me; *he* was my start gun.

When I saw Victor pass by me, I leapt out of the blocks with my prey dead ahead in my sights. I didn't care about any other school in that race. I wanted Victor. I didn't make up ground as quickly as I thought I would, but that didn't deter me. I knew I was better than him and soon everyone in the arena would know it too.

Going into the second lap, my legs kicked me into a gear that even I didn't know I had. I sucked up Victor and the other sprinters like a Hoover vacuum cleaner in a room full of dust mites. Victor was in first place. I passed person after person, keeping my eyes glued to the back of Victor's big head.

By the time we approached the passing zone for the second leg, Victor and I were neck and neck. But I wasn't interested in a tie. I wanted him demoralized. And a guy getting a late start out of the blocks coming in first to the baton exchange would do just that.

I pushed myself to find that fifth gear. But Victor wasn't going down without a fight. We both strained toward our respective teammates. Shadow was waving like crazy. I knew that if I could just get the baton to Shadow first that he would die before letting the lead go. I belted out a ferocious yell that somehow acted like a rocket booster, propelling me ahead of Victor by two to three steps.

"Yahhh stick." "Stick," Victor and I yelled at just about the same time.

Shadow's hand flung back, grabbing the baton and off he went. Moments after, St. Paul's second leg got the baton from Victor, but it was a moot point by that time. Shadow had at least four to six strides in before their second leg even secured the baton.

I strutted over to the infield clapping arrogantly the entire way. Shadow not only held the lead he extended it which made it a cakewalk for Quan and not to mention Joe. But classic Joe, he only had one speed, *blazing*. It didn't matter how far ahead we were in the race; he was going to go all out. By this time, Victor was nowhere to be found. I guess he didn't want to see me gloat. *Gloat?* I was jumping up and down like Monica on Taco Tuesday.

Quan joined Shadow and me as we high-fived and laughed jubilantly. Joe zoomed by us heading toward the finish line well ahead of any other school. About twenty meters or so from crossing the tape, he let out an agonizing shout, grabbing his right hamstring and drops to the track.

Our celebration halted. All I could think was *get up*. But I didn't say it aloud. I didn't want to seem insensitive just in case it was a serious injury. Thankfully he did get up. Joe's competitive nature wouldn't allow him to sit there. He hobbled to his feet and limped his way to the finish line still edging out the pack of wild dogs behind him.

Once Joe crossed the line, securing first place, he buckled again. Coach and several teammates ran over to his aid. I just stood there in awe. I didn't want to believe it. *Superman was hurt.*

/

ANCHOR

As the day dragged on, we began to feel the pressure as a team. I would have never thought that one injury would plague us like it did. There were four teams who were battling it out for first place: St. Paul Academy, Mt. Carmel, St. Rita, and us.

A blonde female medic had wrapped Joe's hamstring up with ice sidelining him indefinitely over an hour ago. Once again coach had to do some nifty maneuvering to figure this one out. It was time for the mile relay.

Coach came over to the bleachers with Red and Hawk. Shadow and I were next to Joe for moral support.

"All right," Coach began. "This is how we're going to do the 4x4. Shadow, you'll lead us off. Second leg, Red. Third, Hawk. And, BJ will take Joe's place as our anchor. Questions?"

Coach glared at each of us individually. When he landed on me, I must have had a look on my face like I swallowed a gnat.

"Question, BJ?" Coach demanded rather than asked.

I was only a few meets in since quitting the team. I didn't run a lick all summer, Thanksgiving, or Christmas break. Sure, I worked hard on my individual events, but I was still nowhere near my full form. And this was for the Catholic League Championship, bragging rights for the entire school.

"Yeah," I began nervously. "Coach, maybe Shadow should—"

"Maybe Shadow should what?" Coach interrupted.

Coach's vocal tone warned me that it was best for my health if I didn't complete my sentence. So I kept my mouth shut. After all, Coach placed me in this position. He must've felt that I was ready.

"All right then," he continued, "let's go to work."

The last event of the day was moments from starting. St. Paul was in first and we were tied for second place with St. Rita, Carmel was third. To win Catholic league, we had to come in first place in the mile relay and hope it would be enough to win by points.

As the race began, I was in a total fog. I heard the bang of the gun and heard the cheers but had no clue what was going on around me. My face felt hot. My stomach, bubbly. I jumped up and down a few times trying to settle myself. It didn't help.

My eyes darted to the passing runners trying to locate the one dressed like me. *Who was I after?* I tried to remember the new order Coach gave us moments ago.

Hawk and this light-skinned, wavy-haired pretty boy for St. Paul literally fought each other tooth and nail for the lead. A nudge here, a subtle elbow there. Hawk would lead for four or five strides then St. Paul would take over and lead for a few steps. Back and forth they went, neither one of them seemed to tire or lose much ground to the other. As they went at it, they continued to separate themselves from the pack. That's when it hit me, Shadow, Red, and Hawk. I was up next, anchor.

Coming into the last fifty meters or so, pretty boy began to pull forward a little bit. But this time, Hawk couldn't catch him. I saw the desperation on Hawk's face. I knew he had given his all and couldn't do anymore. It was my turn.

Bruce and I took the track, lining up one and two with our respective teammates. Bruce looked over at me shaking his head with a wry smirk on his face. He snickered.

"First Vic, now you? What's funny?" I demanded.

"I was just thinking," Bruce said smugly. "Isn't it ironic how Mendel is always the first team to come in second place?"

Bruce laughed again arrogantly.

Those kinds of comments were the reason Mendel and St. Paul were always at odds. It was those types of smart-aleck jabs that fueled the bad intentions with every sacked quarterback, every wild pitch thrown right at a St. Paul batter's head, every blocked shot or slam dunk down the throat of a St. Paul opponent. If there was ever a competition to see who could hold their breath the longest, every Mendel student I knew would risk blacking out before giving St. Paul the satisfaction of winning.

Bruce snatched the baton from his teammate and took off. I glared at him murderously. If looks could kill, gravediggers would have just finished shoveling. His smirk had etched a permanent groove into my brain. His comment repeated in my ears like the annoying hook of an awful song.

Hawk staggered into my daydream, jabbing the baton into my side. "Go, go," he gasped. I gripped the baton so hard I felt my fingers making ridges in the aluminum. A starving lion had just spotted a three-legged gazelle loose in the prairie. My spikes dug up little divots of clay from the track. My tongued wagged with blood lust.

There was no way Bruce was escaping. Against all reason, logic, and strategy, I sprinted as hard as I could. I had run this race plenty times. I knew very well what would happen if I went out too hard. It happened to Hawk. Squirt said it a few meets back, and I knew it; it'll hurt. But I didn't care. I had to catch Bruce and I had to catch him *now*. I had to let him know he was in for the race of his life so maybe, at the end, he'd be the one to crack.

The crowd roared so loudly that I couldn't hear myself think. The closer I got to Bruce, the more noise they made, stomping on the bleachers. It felt like an earthquake. The stale air inside the track and field arena rushed by my face. My mouth dried, my eyes watered but I did not slow down. I was determined to catch Bruce. And if I was able to catch him, I knew I could beat him.

The bell tolled signifying the last lap. Unexpectedly, Bruce turned around to spot me. *Got him.* This time I smirked while panic covered the mangy gazelle's face. Lunchtime.

I inched my way over to the second lane to make my move. Bruce cleverly, slinked over himself, blocking my path. He was determined not to let me pass him.

The finish line was in sight. I knew I didn't have much time. And then it happened. Magilla and his whole family came back to say "hello." My legs began to buckle. Fatigue attacked me like an armed robber. I tried to focus on my form by pumping my arms, but I couldn't feel them. I tried to concentrate on my breathing but discovered I was suddenly asthmatic.

My mind was going a mile a minute. I was running out of options. I had always thought of myself as a mentally strong person, but the time I needed mental strength the most, my mind was mush. As much as I wanted to beat Bruce and St. Paul Academy, at that point, all I wanted to do was lay down on my bed.

Negative thoughts began to assault me, forcing me to shut down my engine, and call it quits. That's when I heard a distinct voice calling out to me. It was a very familiar voice, but more than that, deep within, I knew that it was a voice I had to listen to.

My eyes searched the bleachers for the owner of the voice. I looked at the interior of the track, toward the stadium's field area and that's when I saw him. Coach Abrams on the side of the track yelling at the top of his lungs, "Refuse to lose. Refuse to lose."

It was the first time I'd ever seen Coach cheer for any of his athletes, and he was cheering for me. When I saw how animated Coach was on the sideline, that competitive flame began to stoke. I'm not a person who ups and quits. That's not who I am. I had accepted the challenge from Lights-Out's flunkies in the basement. I had accepted Victor's challenge on his own front lawn. And I happily accepted David's challenge inside the corner market. It was time to accept the challenge at hand.

Coach's words were like jumper cables to a weakened battery. Each time he repeated his phrase "refuse to lose" my mind and body revved up more and more until I was able to charge myself. *Yes, I do refuse to lose. Let's go, BJ, let's go. Let's go!*

Rejuvenated, I made my move again but this time with a little twist.

I started toward the second lane once more, then quickly shifted back to lane one when Bruce tried to cut me off. Bruce looked to his right; I stole the lead on his left. Bruce stumbled and almost fell when he finally figured out what just happened.

Once I took the lead, I forgot all about Bruce and focused on the finish line tape.

"Aghhh!"

I let out a ferocious growl as I crossed the tape first.

Bruce tripped across the line after me, flopping to the ground.

What a great idea, I thought. I collapsed on the track beside him sucking oxygen through my cotton mouth and newly diagnosed asthmatic lungs. *Hurts, it hurts!*

Suddenly, a wave of blue track uniforms buried me alive while I laid on the track, smiling through the hurt.

/

AND THE WINNER IS

Mendel, St. Paul, and St. Rita were the only teams left in the arena, all mingling amongst their respective teammates.

"Man, what's taking so long?" Squirt asked me and Quan.

"Oh, here they come now," Quan replied, pointing.

Several of the track officials marched over to where we were all sitting. The three officials stood at the base of the stands looking up at us. I glanced at Coach Abrams; he was calm as could be.

"All right," the tubby head official began. "Third place for the Indoor Catholic League Championship goes to. . .St. Rita. Rita, come get your trophy."

Polite claps echoed from all of us as Rita's coach bumbled down the stands to receive the third-place trophy.

Quan and I traded looks accompanied with deep sighs.

"Congratulations Rita," the official continued. "Second place goes to. . .Mendel. And first—"

The St. Paul team erupted with cheers and clapping, as soon as Mendel was announced, drowning out their own names. The St. Paul coaches rushed down the stands to grab their huge first-place trophy. The rest of the team quickly joined them, clamoring over their win.

As the St. Paul team began to funnel out of the arena, Bruce tapped Victor on the shoulder and pointed up at us.

"And first team to second place is. . ." Bruce holds for dramatic effect, "Mendel!"

Victor, Bruce, and several other St. Paul guys burst out laughing.

"Look, Cindy Brady's with them," Victor said, tapping Bruce on the arm. He points up at Squirt.

"Better luck next time, Cindy," Bruce quipped.

"Squirt, can you say, 'Sally sells seashells by the sea-shore'?" Victor added.

The St. Paul team continued to laugh as they exited the arena. We were peeved, but what could we do? Squirt was especially pissed off. Vic and his crew constantly made fun of Squirt because of his lisp. I could tell by the look on his face he wanted to say something but didn't.

Coach Abrams bellowed for us to get on the bus. Everyone grabbed their belongings and their disappointment and headed for the parking lot.

It was completely silent apart from the hum of the bus engine. No one said a word. Not even Squirt, who always had something to say. I didn't know whether it was the defeat that had him down or the embarrassing ridicule from Bruce and Victor.

Shadow plopped down next to me.

"Yo, dog, awesome anchor leg." He held out his hand and gave me some dap.

"Thanks. Shadow. It was all for nothing though."

"Is that what you think?"

I kind of looked at him incredulously, wondering, *Didn't you see St. Paul celebrating?* Just when I was about to forewarn Shadow that I wasn't in the mood for a moral victory speech, Coach Abrams came aboard the bus. He put our second-place trophy on the seat in front of him then walked down the aisle a couple rows.

With all certainty and confidence, Coach began, "Get your heads up! St. Paul only won by three points with one of our best sprinters sidelined and another one who's barely in shape. I know you're hurting but I want you to remember this feeling. Use it to motivate you. To fuel you."

I don't know what it was, but Coach Abrams words still had control of me. I wondered if anyone else felt the same surge of energy.

I looked at Shadow, he was locked in. I looked around at Quan, Hawk, and several others, everyone was hanging to Coach's words as if they were air.

"We will never lose to St. Paul Academy again! Is that clear?" Coach bellowed.

Scattered claps erupted throughout the bus. He ended with a rhetorical question, but deep down inside, we *knew* it was a command—a "you-understood command."

"From now on we win all major meets. Is that clear?"

More claps echoed forth. This time, I joined in with several other guys, "Yes sir!"

"And we are going to win outdoor Catholic league! Do I make myself clear?"

"Yes sir!" the whole team responded, cheering, clapping, stomping their feet. The bus was rocking as if we'd just won the meet. I realized quickly that I was dead wrong. I did need a speech, not a moral victory speech but a speech that reminded me that one defeat doesn't make us losers. One setback does not have to be the end of the story. I felt the jerk of the bus taking off while high-fiving several teammates. Coach Abrams handed the trophy to Derrick, and we passed it around as if it was indeed the first-place trophy. After all, in our minds, with Joe sidelined with his hamstring injury, it was St. Paul Academy who had the moral victory.

CHAPTER 14

LIFE-CHANGING MOMENT

/

Perspective. It's ironic how two people can experience the same event and have totally different life-changing outcomes. When *life* happens, we either adapt or fail to adapt, then suffer. Life always seemed to thrust *change* upon me, change I never asked for nor wanted. My mother stricken with a rare form of cancer, change. My ex-con father released from jail the same day Mom died, change. Our team bus pulled into the back of the school's parking lot after losing indoor Catholic league. . .*change*.

"I'm telling you," Quan continues, "we're gonna dominate soon as Joe gets back."

Shadow and I grabbed our bags and followed Quan to the front of the bus.

"Who needs Joe, we got BJ to run anchor leg now, dog," Shadow joked.

"Yeah, right," I added sarcastically.

The three of us laughed as we got off the bus. Immediately, I spotted two adults who were not having as much fun as Shadow, Quan, and me.

Mrs. Morales had pulled Coach off the bus and was speaking with him privately. Once they laid eyes on me, they both stopped talking and walked toward me as if floating in some type of movie-magic slow motion.

"Brandon, you have to come with me right now," she said.

Before I could object, Mrs. Morales whisked me away to her car.

I remember the engine revving as Mrs. Morales ran red lights and honked impatiently at those who weren't breaking traffic laws. The smart aleck in me laughed while pondering, *Is it moral or amoral to drive recklessly with your teenaged student?* But my serious side was horrified by what I would soon discover once we arrived at our destination, which didn't take very long.

Before I knew it, Mrs. Morales was whisking me off again through the revolving doors of Roseland Community Hospital, while her hazard lights blinked furiously at the security guard who mumbled something about parking illegally and a tow truck.

To her credit, Mrs. Morales was only doing what she felt was right. During the erratic drive to Roseland, she never told me what was going on. I suppose she didn't want to worry me. How could she know that my imagination was way worse than any tragedy she could have dropped on me? So I played along, not asking many questions, knowing that it takes all of three minutes to drive from Mendel to the hospital.

We stormed upon the hospital emergency department room. My heart fluttered when I saw Auntie Emma, standing there, silently stroking Monica's hair as she laid asleep in the hospital bed. Processing the scene, I quickly assessed, *OK, no tubes or hoses plugged into my little sister. No IVs dripping unknown liquids into her puny body. There's a beeping monitor that's pretty normal inside an ER. OK, OK, she's good, I'm good.* I exhaled a sigh of relief only to have my next breath knocked from my body with unbelievable dominance.

Mr. James had me by the scruff of my track uniform hoodie plowing me into the wall. The peaceful serenity in ER room one hundred was replaced with indistinct screaming and chaos as Mrs. Morales, Auntie Emma, and Nurse Sharon Kimble, who dashed in from the hallway, uselessly attempted to pry Mr. James' fingers from my throat.

/

CHANGE IS GONNA COME

Disappointment, anger, rage, all these emotions had surfaced at one time or another toward Squirt during our tenure as friends. Yet none more than at the moment when I discovered he was the reason my little sister was hospitalized.

I had threatened Monica countless times to stay out of my room. Oh, how I wished she had feared these warnings.

I could feel the heat of Mr. James' eyes peering at me from the other side of the sofa we shared while waiting in the family and visitors lounge. Not even a year ago, Nurse Sharon tried to coax me into this very room after my mother had passed away. I'm sure these walls have heard its share of good news before, just not with my family.

Mr. James slowly scooted past the invisible barrier between us on the couch. Whatever he had to say, I just wasn't in the mood for it. Monica was alive, that was the most important thing to me. I'd deal with Squirt myself at school. Maybe I'd break his hand or arm, possibly his nose.

"Son, hasn't my life been enough of a warning?"

"What?" I scowled back.

"The friends we keep influence the person we become."

It was on the tip of my tongue to ask him what kind of friends he had to land himself in jail, but I figured I was already in enough trouble. How was I to know Squirt would hide his drugs in my bag after we left the restroom? I hated the fact that Mr. James, the ex-con turned Mother Teresa, was always preaching at me. This clearly was not my fault.

"Man, my boys and I are nothing like you."

"Really? Squirt's selling crack and robbing people. You sure?"

"So you have the right to judge him now? Is that it?"

"I'm not judg—"

"You've been mentoring kids all of two minutes and you think that wipes away a lifetime of doing dirt? Get real."

I got up and went over to the window. I figured the passing traffic outside would be more interesting than whatever Mr. James was preaching at me.

"All I'm saying is watch the company you keep. We'll just pray Monica will be all right. And we'll pray for Squirt too."

"Yeah, cuz that always works."

"Ohh, now I see," Mr. James reasoned. "Why pray? It doesn't work anyway, right? Your mom certainly believed in it."

"She was wrong," I snapped angrily. "You know what I think? God doesn't care about us."

"Really?"

"Really. All prayer is is a hope and a wish that never comes true. You know how many times I prayed for Mama not to die? How many times I prayed, as a kid, for you to come home to rescue us out of the hood? What's the use of a God who doesn't answer when you need Him?"

"Brandon, I didn't purposely abandon you all, I—"

"Yes, you did! You chose to beat that man half to death. I pleaded with you to stop but you wouldn't. So in my mind, you chose to leave us. You chose to go to jail. What did you think was going to happen? You beat him down in front of the whole neighborhood. And we suffered because of your out-of-control actions. Takes a real man to beat someone down who obviously couldn't defend himself against you. That was you! Not us, you!"

Keko walked over to me. I turned my back to look at the traffic again.

"You're right son. I've done horrible things and my family had to suffer for it. And I'm sorry. But BJ, you can't blame God for what I did. You can't blame Him for what happened to Kathy."

"Why not?"

"So God is just here to do whatever we want, but if he doesn't, who needs Him, right?"

I ignored his condescending, rhetorical question and kept looking outside. All I wanted was peace. Some peace to be grateful that my baby sister was still on this earth and not taken away from me after ingesting some useless drug...like my mother was taken from me by some useless disease.

Just then, Nurse Sharon barged in.

"Mr. James, BJ, you can take her home now."

"Great. Thanks for everything," Mr. James replied.

"Sure, sure," Nurse Sharon said as she exited.

Mr. James hurried behind her but then stopped at the door. I could see his reflection in the window as he looked back at me, "Know what your problem is, BJ?"

"Oh, I have the problem," I scoffed. "This'll be good."

"You go to God to get something from Him, and not *for* Him. You want Santa Claus, not Jesus."

I whipped around to respond but he was already gone. I waited for a few moments and followed him out.

/

CONFRONTING SUBMISSION

I sat across from him in his office not knowing if he was joking or not. He had recently, yet often, been a positive sounding board in my life. I shifted uncomfortably in my chair.

"What are you saying, Coach?" I asked.

"I think you're blinded by your resentment toward your father," Coach replied. "You can only see him through the lens of what he used to be."

"Cuz, I think he's a big, fat hypocrite."

"How, when his working with these kids is an outpouring of the change he's experienced? Is it true what he said?"

"About me wanting Santa Claus instead of God," I scoffed. "C'mon, Coach. I went to church all the time with my mom. Well, maybe not all the time, butI go to school here, remember? We have Mass every week."

"We're talking about submission, BJ. Submitting to God will always result in change, purpose. Your father has changed. He's in his purpose. The question is why are you so afraid of change?"

"I'm not."

"Sure you are. You're petrified of a life without your mom."

"That's ridiculous."

"Every decision you've made is to please her."

"Coach, that is so not true."

"Oh no?" Coach Abrams accused, leaning forward in his chair. "Tell me, why'd you join the track team the first time?"

"Because, I. . .um—"

"Your mom begged you to join, and you caved in. Then once she died, you quit, right, because you never wanted to do it in the first place. So why'd you join this second time? And it had nothing to do with a conversation you had with Mrs. Morales."

There was nothing I could say. Coach was right. I was actively living in limbo, still unsure of what I really wanted out of life.

Coach in his wisdom must have known something. He whiffed out an empathic sigh then spun around in his office chair. He grabbed a framed picture from the bookshelf behind him. Coach examined the portrait before handing it to me.

"It's time you know why I left Chicago."

I looked at the picture and it was the same one of the middle-aged, attractive woman and the teenaged girl that I looked at before when in his office.

Coach took another deep sigh then he thoughtfully began to divulge the deep dark secret from his past.

"One summer day after grocery shopping, I stopped to chat with a neighbor of mine while my wife and daughter finished bringing the groceries into the house. My friend and I had only been talking a few minutes when we heard a huge crash and screaming from inside the house."

Coach explained he and his neighbor darted across the street. The inside of the house was completely trashed. Picture frames, vases, and lamps were smashed to smithereens on the living room floor. The furniture was disheveled from its original positions, the groceries his wife and daughter had brought in were strewn about the place.

As Coach and his neighbor navigated through the mess, they saw Constance sprawled out behind the couch on the living room floor, barely conscious and bleeding from her nose, mouth, and forehead. Coach ordered his neighbor to call 911.

"I knelt down to help my wife," Coach explained. "But she gasped for me to go help our daughter, Melanie, instead."

Suddenly, their daughter yelped. Coach's neighbor took off for the kitchen, Coach right on his tail. They entered the kitchen finding two men ransacking the cupboards, another kneeling down over Melanie with a knife in hand.

The knifeman was the first to look up. He spotted Coach and the neighbor and jumped to his feet. He bolted out the back door, while Coach's daughter lay on the floor bleeding profusely from her neck.

"BJ," he said stoically, almost not even sounding like his regular self. "When I saw him with that knife to my little girl's throat. . ." Coach swallowed roughly, then looked right at me, "I froze."

Coach cleared his throat softly then continued, "My neighbor chased off the other two but ended up tripping on a kitchen chair. They escaped out the back door. By the time the ambulance arrived Constance and Mel...they um...they both died while waiting on the ambulance."

There weren't words to describe the agony on Coach's face as he recounted that tragic day.

Coach wiped his soggy face. "So," Coach cleared the phlegm from his throat, "that's why I left Chicago. For years I felt an enormous amount of guilt after freezing up in the kitchen that day. I know I could have caught at least one of them. But when I saw my baby girl covered in. . .I, I couldn't move."

"Did they ever catch the guys who did it?" I asked.

"No. Authorities said it was likely junkies looking for money or drugs. After that, I just couldn't stay here any longer. I hated the community. I hated the people. I hated myself. I couldn't bring myself to live in the same city where my two girls were taken from me."

"Man, Coach, I'm really sorry that happened."

Coach nodded in acknowledgement as he put the picture back on the shelf behind him. When he turned back around to face me, I guess he could sense I had one more question.

"What is it, BJ?"

"Why'd you come back?"

He sighed before answering, "Deep down, I always felt if someone would have made a difference in those young men's lives, my wife and daughter would still be here. Ultimately, I came back to live out my purpose, to have an impact. BJ, you have to find your *own* purpose in life, not your mother's."

"How did you find yours?"

Coach didn't answer me right away. Instead, he opened his bottom desk drawer and pulled out a Bible. He plopped it down in front of me. My heart cried for Coach, but I was so irritated that he and Mr. James felt religion was the answer for every life's problem. That just wasn't my experience.

God's never answered my prayers and from what I've seen on the South Side, God must not care. How could

He? What did Coach feel was inside the Bible that would relate to me here and now? Was God even aware of where we were, the South Side of Chicago? We got drug infested streets, crooked cops, teen pregnancy, rapes, muggings, and murder. Who knew this better than Coach Alexander Abrams?

"What could I possibly learn from that?" I asked sarcastically.

Without flinching Coach looked me in my eyes and answered, "Forgiveness."

/

THE MARVELOUS LIGHT

On my walk home from school, I couldn't stop thinking about the conversation I had with Coach. I didn't know why it bothered me so much, but it did.

When I got home, I quickly went to my room and shut the door. I tried my best to concentrate on my homework but couldn't. Every time I tried to think of the answer to my trigonometry, my mind would shift to thinking about the meaning of life. The topic loomed in my face and would not go away.

Why am I here? Why is the world so messed up? If God is real, why doesn't He do something? I didn't care to know the answers to these kinds of questions before, so why was it bothering me so much now? Mom had sent me to Catholic schools my whole life, though we weren't Catholic. I was raised by Protestant religious zealots. I even had a "religious-ish" aunt who I thought gangbanging was part of her DNA, change because of God. But never has life-altering enigmatic musings haunted my very soul the way this invisible entity called "God" was doing so obviously now.

For, I knew *He* was pursuing me, and I'd rather have a long, sloppy kiss with asphyxia than be caught by Him. He grated against me like drywall, stubbornly refusing to answer the most important question, *why*.

Why did you take my mother from me, God? And why was my mom so desperate to have Him in my life? Then the thought hit me. In anger, it hit me. In raging, terrible anger, I jerked myself from my chair and tore a path from my bedroom to the attic. I decided if I couldn't run from God, I'd run to Him and have it out.

"Where is it?" I muttered to myself flinging open the blue footlocker. Nothing. I went to the red, then the green one, digging, searching for what Mom hid from me over a year ago. We'd cleaned this house from top to bottom and everything she once owned was crammed into these five footlockers. Finally, I saw it, inside the very footlocker I lugged up to the attic many months ago, exactly where she must've placed it.

I scooped up the black leather Bible. It still had that new smell. The spine creaked when I opened it. I ripped through the gentle pages anxious to see if there was something inside the antiquated text for me. Extreme guilt poured over me as I opened Mama's gift for the first time. I whimpered softly when I allowed my mind to think of my ingratitude. The one gift most precious to her was the one I paid the least attention to. The only time I had ever read the Bible was to follow along during Mass at school.

Slowly, my indignation subsided and all I was left with was the pain. The crispy-thin pages swept over my shaky fingers. I didn't know where to start so I took a breath and just dove in. The pages stopped at the book of John, so I flipped furiously until I came to the beginning of John and started to read. And I read and read until I fell asleep.

When I awoke, I found myself sprawled out on the attic floor. I looked at the Bible only inches from my head and remembered that I had just about finished the entire book of John before crashing. Still a bit groggy, I grabbed my Bible and headed downstairs.

I entered through the kitchen back door just as Keko came in the kitchen. He looked to be coming from Monica's bedroom that was connected to the same small hallway.

"You still up? It's school tomorrow."

"Yeah, I know. How's she doing?" I asked through a gravelly voice.

"She's fine. Sleeping. Don't beat yourself up, son. She's OK."

"Yeah, she said she forgives me and that I owe her some real candy now."

Mr. James and I both laughed and had a seat at the kitchen table. I placed the Bible on the table. Mr. James slid it over to himself and thumbed through the fine pages. I looked at him. Really looked at him. He handled the pages so tenderly, almost respectfully. Mr. James appeared to be a man at total peace and totally in love with a book. I thought of what Coach Abrams said about Mr. James being a changed man and pondered, *Could it be true?*

"Can I ask you something?" I began humbly.

Keko didn't respond verbally, he just looked up at me. I took that as my cue to continue.

"What made you wanna change?"

"Wanna change?" he chuckled. "Shoot, I didn't have a choice. Once I truly let God in, BJ, change just sorta happens. Why do you ask?"

I hesitated. I wasn't sure if I wanted to open my heart to the man who's caused my family so much pain. I took a deep breath. Then another.

"Coach. . .Coach seems to think that I'm afraid of change."

This time it was Mr. James' turn to pause. He considered what I said then began turning the Bible pages with purpose. I examined him again, face focused, concentrating, eyes fluttering back and forth searching for something. My interest piqued more when I saw that he was searching through the only book of the Bible I've ever read, John.

Mr. James skimmed section by section, then page by page, still searching, until he finally stopped. His index finger skimmed the page. I couldn't see exactly where he landed because that glazed ham, he calls a hand blocked my view.

"Here," Mr. James began reading, "My command is this: Love each other as I have loved you."

He stopped reading then looked up at me.

Did I just miss something? I thought. Mr. James' face brightened into a smile as if he had successfully explained two plus two equals four to Monica.

"Sooo, I don't get it."

"Authentic change, BJ. Is it that the disciples didn't love before? Or does Jesus want them to love differently? Think about it."

I truly did want to understand but I was coming up with crickets. Nothing came to mind. Finally, I had to shrug, "I don't know."

"What did Jesus do, BJ?"

"Lots of stuff. Miracles and wonders."

"BJ, *love*. I just read it. Love each other as 'I have loved you.' So how did He love us? What is Jesus most known for?"

"Dying. . .and rising again, I guess?"

"Among other things, but, here, read for yourself. John 15, verse 13."

Keko pushed the Bible over to me and pointed exactly where he wanted me to read.

"Greater love has no one than this, that he lay down his life for his friends."

"Get it?" he asked excitedly again.

I shook my head *no*.

"Love is sacrificial, BJ," Keko continued. "And it's hard to do. True acceptance of God eventually *requires* us to change, to love 'as Jesus has loved us,' sacrificially, unselfishly. BJ, you have the chance to have all your sins forgiven and to forgive others. I know I hurt you. But your unforgiveness toward me has nothing to do with me. That's between you and God. Don't be afraid of becoming who God wants you to be, son."

My heart was on fire at the same time roaring waves were capsizing my stomach, churning it over and over. True change, like what happened to my dad, could only come from a close encounter with *the* Father. I had never wanted to change because I felt there was nothing wrong with me. He was right. I never came to God *for* God because I never needed Him. I was fine. An intelligent, independent, good person all on my own, but that was a lie.

I could never love others like Jesus commanded without *knowing* Jesus, without Him enabling me to. I couldn't give a love I didn't have.

Suddenly, Mr. James slid his chair close to mine and hugged me. This caught me completely off guard. *What was he doing?*

Gently, lovingly, he began wiping my face. I hadn't even realized I was crying until he did that. But once I knew, the tears gushed down my face as if my tear ducts had broken. I was an emotional wreck and didn't know why. *What did all this mean?*

Through sniffles and sobs, I asked, "What am I supposed to do?"

Keko turned to another verse and pointed again, giving me the answer.

Through blurred vision, I read, "Whoever has the Son, has life; whoever does not have the Son of God, does not have life."

Easing the Bible from me, he said, "BJ. . .choose 'Life.'"

My throat felt swollen and sore. All I could do was nod *yes* to his suggestion. Then my earthly father hugged me again after wiping his own tears.

CHAPTER 15

OUTDOOR TRACK SEASON

/

asketball season had just ended, so a few good men rejoined the track team for the outdoor season. There was Kevin and Box who both threw shot put and discus and a few other sprinters and distance guys. Heck, even Eddie-Ed joined. Although, I think, it was more so he could continue to harass Box for a battle.

I rushed into the men's locker room to change for practice. I stopped dead in my tracks. It was my first time seeing Squirt since Monica ended up in the hospital. Several other guys were in the locker room changing as well. I didn't know what to do. After the incident happened, I envisioned myself walking up to Squirt and popping him square in the nose.

I eased my way toward him. Squirt was joking and laughing with Kevin and Box at the lockers. As I got closer, I saw that he had a black eye. *Hmph, somebody beat me to it?*

"Eh man," I interrupted.

"What up, Beej?" Squirt said then turned around to continue his regaling story.

"What happened to you?" I interrupted again.

"Nuttin'. I'm straight."

I turned to Kevin and Box, "Man, what happened to him?"

"He wouldn't tell us either," Box answered.

"Let it go, man, he said he straight," Kevin chimed in.

"He's standing up here with a black eye, and y'all joking around like everything's cool."

"What you want us to do, force him to tell us?" Kevin snipped. "If he don't wanna tell us, he don't wanna tell us." Kevin shut his locker and walked out the locker room.

"Squirt, we're boys, man, you can tell us," I said again.

"Ugh, what man? I fell, BJ. I fell."

"Yeah, on somebody's fist," Box chirped.

"Box, lemme holla at him for a second."

Box closed his locker, shaking his head as he left. I knew I wouldn't get Squirt to admit he's being bullied by someone, but now that we were alone, I wanted to confront him about the drugs.

"BJ, dude, I'm not in the mood for a lecture. We gotta get to practice."

Squirt tried to walk off. I grabbed him.

"Why'd you put that stuff in my bag?"

"What?" Squirt asked, apparently not catching on that I had switched subjects.

"Last week?"

"Ohh," Squirt remembers, "Yeah, that was pretty slick, huh? See, I told you you wouldn't get caught. A-yo, keep hold of that for me till I need it." Squirt tried to walk out again.

"Squirt! Monica found it inside my bag."

"What?" He turned around.

"Yeah, she thought it was candy and ate some. She almost died cuz of you."

"Aww man, BJ, I'm sorry. How's she doing now? Is she OK?"

Just then Coach Abrams came into the locker room.

"You two need special invitations?" Coach shouted.

Squirt hurried out of the locker room.

"BJ, you're not even dressed yet?"

"Sorry, Coach. I'm coming."

I scrambled to open my locker to get my belongings. Coach stepped closer, "Listen, BJ, while we have a moment, I wanted to talk with you."

"What's up, Coach?" I said, still gathering my gear.

"Mrs. Morales told me you two looked over your school transcript."

"Yeah, it's a no go," I said still busily gathering my things.

Coach put his hand on top of mine to stop me. I looked up giving him my full attention.

"BJ, maybe you can join the service or get a job somewhere."

"No, I already told you what I have to do."

"Get a track scholarship and go to college," Coach said in a sing-song manner like he'd heard it all before. "I told you, it's impossible."

"Coach, recruits get hurt. I'm sure some recruits change their minds at the last moment and go with a different school. I can do this. I know I can. The only question is, are you gonna help me?"

We both stood in silence for a moment, neither budging. Then Coach asked me, "For the third time. BJ, why have you joined the track team?"

"Because most of the memories I have of my mother are of us, running. That was the happiest time in my life. Racing my mother as a kid, seeing the joy she had on her face. But not only her joy, mine as well. I guess I'm trying to find that joy again."

Coach peered at me. "Get dressed. I'll see you outside."

/

TEAM IS THE GOAL

I marched onto the practice football field behind the monastery to find several of the guys untangling long plastic cords that looked like giant rubber bands.

Coach was in the middle of reminding the team of the goals we had set after losing indoor Catholic league: to win all major meets, in addition to winning the Outdoor Catholic League Championship. He stated that these new drills would help us attain those goals.

"Several of you grab a harness and put it on," Coach instructed.

Joe helped pass out harnesses since he was still injured.

"We only have a few," Coach explained, "so the rest of you just wait till the other groups are done. This is something they're doing over in Germany to make their sprinters faster."

After a few of us had strapped the harnesses onto our backs, Coach paired us up. I was paired with Derrick. Quan was paired with Shadow. And Hawk with Red. Coach then explained that the drill was basically a game of tag. The first three guys walked ahead stretching the bungee cords until it became taut. The second group of guys was to stay put until Coach told them to run. Then, all six runners sprinted at the same time going the same direction. The second set of runners attempted to catch the first set. The first set tried to avoid getting caught.

"Coach, what is this drill supposed to do?" I asked.

"You'll find out, BJ," Coach said. "Derrick, Quan, and Hawk, you're the first runners, get going. I'll tell you when to stop."

Derrick, Quan, and Hawk began walking down the worn, patchy field. None of us could figure out logistically how the cords were supposed to make us faster sprinters. As the fellas got farther away the huge bungee cords started to stretch, which in turn, began to pull us second runners forward a bit. Coach told Joe and a few others who weren't harnessed to hold us in place, so we wouldn't be pulled by the force of the bands.

"I got a bad feeling about this," Shadow whispered to me.

"C'mon, Coach, there's gotta be something you can tell us about this drill?" I begged.

"I'll give you a hint. Run as fast as you can, or you'll be sorry," he said while attempting to hold back laughter.

I looked over at Shadow and Red; they looked back at me.

"That it?" Red asked quizzically.

"It's called resistance training. You're building and training your muscles to push through the tension of the cords."

Coach yelled out for our partners to stop walking.

The cords were bouncing in the wind as Hawk and the rest of the fellas tried to hold still. Each of us in the second group dug our heels into the brownish grass trying not to be yanked away.

"All right, when I say go, go!" Coach yelled, then turned to us, "That means you guys too, all right?"

We nodded in agreement.

"One, two, three. . .Go!"

Our spotters let us go and the bands shot us forward as if we were smooth stones fired from a perfectly made slingshot.

I jostled down the field like a twin-engine plane experiencing severe turbulence. We were less than ten strides in when Red wiped out to my left. But not only did he wipe out, he was being dragged mercilessly by Hawk, who had no clue Red had fallen.

Shadow looked over at me. The panic in his eyes said, *Help! Stop this crazy thing!*

"Go. Keep running," I shouted over to him.

We both tried to kick it into overdrive, but the bungee cords were way too strong. *Wham!* Shadow slammed into the ground next.

I knew it would be only a matter of seconds before I was biting the dust too. Suddenly, I remembered that

Coach told us run as fast as we could. Apparently, he meant we should run with the cord, but I was already at top speed. I felt my feet searching for the ground. I couldn't keep up with the pull of the cord. I gave one more valiant effort to sprint faster, then *whop*! I hit the grass.

Watching Shadow and Red fall didn't prepare me at all for just how awful it would be. I spun and spun like a kid rolling downhill. The only difference, I wasn't having any of the fun that came with it.

Coach finally yelled stop. I was so thankful the guys heard him. When I got up, I had grass and dirt on my face, in my hair, and all over my practice gear.

"All right, bring it back," Coach yelled to us.

We turned around to find that Coach had the next six runners strapped up and ready to go. On the way back, Quan and the others were still in the dark about our experience.

"What the heck happened to y'all?" Hawk asked.

"What do you think? We fell," Shadow answered rather annoyed.

"All of y'all?"

"Yeah," I snipped. "Look, watch what happens."

Just then the next set of sprinters shot past us as we walked back to the starting line. It was déjà vu all over again. All three of the runners in the second group fell and were being dragged several feet like amateur cowboys at a rodeo to Coach's slight amusement, I might add.

"Stop!" he yelled out again. "Come back."

Since there were only enough harnesses for half of us, we graciously got a break when we had to take off the harnesses for the fourth and last group. However, the break was short lived. Before we knew it, we were clinking and clanking ourselves back into the harness straps.

"First group, BJ, Shadow, and Red, reverse the order, you're the first runners now. Hawk and the others chase. C'mon, let's go. To the line. BJ, you guys start walking."

Shadow, Red, and I were eager to let the other guys be the stones. We walked and walked until the bungee cords were stretched out again. Right away we felt how being the front runner was totally different than the back runner, yet it wasn't any better. It was all we could do to keep from being yanked backwards by the strength of the cords. We didn't have spotters to help hold us this time. It was like climbing a mountain although we were on level ground.

Coach yelled, "Go" again and we took off. At least, we tried to take off. The three of us vigorously pumped our arms and knees. We ran in place for almost half a minute before we actually moved. Derrick might as well had been a semitruck strapped behind me. Eventually, we inched a few feet, then a few more, until we were finally able to get some speed behind us. Very shortly after laboring to sprint full speed, we heard "Stop!"

We turned around, not in the least surprised to see our teammates picking themselves up from the earth.

Once our group was done, the other group was already running, and the next were all harnessed up and ready to go, with the last group on deck reluctant to take the harnesses we were eagerly handing over.

This was about the time that some of us began to grumble. It was tedious work sprinting, falling, getting up, climbing in and out of those stupid harnesses, just to do it over again. Coach's new drill was getting old quick. I didn't care if sprinters in Germany were using this crap. They could keep it for all I cared. This drill was the pits!

"Wait a minute," Coach said as he noticed the team's apathy. I knew this wasn't going to be good. He had that look in his eyes like he could rip the head off a grizzly. But to my surprise, he didn't make his way over to Quan or Joe, who were the captains, he marched straight toward me.

Pulling me aside slightly, he scolded, "I will not put myself out there again if you're not willing to work. I looked like a fool last time, so I need to know, how serious are you?"

I hesitated. "Wait, does that mean you'll—"

"If you truly want a track scholarship, you're going to have to earn it, every day in practice. You have to want it like you've never wanted anything before."

"Coach, I'm trying. But this drill—"

"Were you expecting this to be easy? There's never any progress without pain, BJ. No pain, no gain."

Coach returned his attention back to the whole team.

"Win all major meets! Win outdoor Catholic league! That's what we agreed to on the bus, right? Will mediocre work accomplish these goals? Or hard work, giving our best every single day, every single practice, every single meet! That's the only way to get this done! Now, BJ, Shadow, Red to the line!"

"C'mon fellas, let's do this," I said.

We stepped to the line and were promptly dragged again. That's when Coach decided to douse more gasoline on the fire.

"C'mon. Get up. You better figure this out," Coach yelled from the starting line. "We'll be out here all night until we do. No pain, no gain. Let's go. Next group."

After hearing that, I decided to have a chitchat session with the fellas as we walked back to the start line.

"A'ight y'all, we gotta figure this out. The point of this drill can't be to teach us how to fall. Any ideas?"

"Man, I've been trying to think of some," Shadow said.

"We gotta come up with something," Quan added. "I ain't trying to be out here all night. And you know he crazy enough to do it."

Then it occurred to me, I asked, "What would happen if the second group just resisted?"

"What do you mean?" asked Shadow.

"Look, we know the cords are faster than us. That's why we're losing it, following Coach's dumb advice to run with the cords. But what if we leaned back as we ran, resisting the tug, letting the cords do all the work? That should slow it down some."

"Bet, bet that might work," Shadow agreed.

"And the first group wait a few seconds before going," Quan added. "Even when Coach yells 'go,' don't go, just wait a few seconds."

We all agreed to give it a shot. Amazingly we each made it a little farther before falling. So we knew we were on to something. With each attempt, we began to get the hang of it. We made it through two rounds without any falls. We quickly spread the word to the other groups on how to manage the drill.

Coach belted out that we were only halfway through because all the times we fell didn't count. A collective moan echoed about the field. But I wasn't having it. We were too close to completing this sadistic drill and I didn't want our bad attitudes to earn us extras, so I had to do something to keep us motivated.

I thought back to what helped me when I wanted to give up on that anchor leg of the mile relay. Coach jumped up and down like a madman cheering me on. So I began cheering and clapping for the groups that were running through the drill. Then the idea hit me to ad-lib a chant right there in the middle of practice.

When the other group approached the start line, I yelled at them, "C'mon fellas, no pain, no gain. Let's go!" They looked at me like I had two heads. But I kept screaming, "No pain, no gain. No pain, no gain. No pain, no gain." Then, out of nowhere, this hand clap cadence popped into my head. I thought to myself, *What the heck? I might as well try it*.

I began to clap, ad-libbing a beat to go with the "No pain, no gain" chant I created.

"Go," Coach screamed.

I clapped and screamed even louder,

> *Clap-Clap. Clap-Clap-Clap-Clap!*
> *Clap-Clap. Clap-Clap-Clap-Clap!*

No pain, no gain! No pain, no gain!
No pain, no gain! No pain, no gain!

I clapped and sang that stupid song the whole time the other group ran. But the guys were so tired that not one person joined me.

Coach called my group to the line. "Go."

We took off being yanked and pulled by the bungee cords, I tried my best to just concentrate on my form, and that's when I heard it.

Clap-Clap. Clap-Clap-Clap-Clap!
Clap-Clap. Clap-Clap-Clap-Clap!
No pain, no gain! No pain, no gain!
No pain, no gain! No pain, no gain!

I looked to my right and saw Kev and Mark and the rest of the group that I just cheered carrying on with my silly impromptu chant. Although, I was beginning to think it wasn't that silly after all.

/

THE STREAK

We had the blueprint. The next day at practice felt like a pep rally all over again. We continued the no pain, no gain chant, clapping and yelling encouragement for our teammates, this time in front of the school building.

Since we didn't have an actual track, the whole Mendel campus became our practice facility.

Me, Shadow, Quan, Hawk, and Derrick galloped down the semicircle driveway like Vikings chasing off marauders. Coach was holding a stopwatch at the finish line, two hundred meters away, while Joe stood next to him with a clip board balancing on his one crutch.

We all jockeyed for position as Coach screamed out the time, "Sixteen! Seventeen! Eighteen!" Shadow came in first. I was right on his heels for a close second, just edging out Quan. Hawk and Derrick were close behind.

Week after week I felt myself improving. But not only me, the whole team was peaking. The inner-squad competition elevated the team's performance to new heights, which paid dividends immediately. We won our next meet, then the one after that, and the one after that.

One day after practice Coach had all of us congregate inside the first-floor hallway of the main building. He and Shadow came onto the floor lugging two huge white cardboard boxes. He called Quan over to help him tear one open.

Inside were royal blue letterman's jackets for each of us, with our names stitched in cursive on the left-hand side of the chest area. "Mendel Track" was printed across the back in huge lettering. We were stoked. Everybody was dapping each other up, checking out one another's jackets. As I examined my own, I saw the word "co-captain" underneath my name. I was shocked. Shadow came over almost tackling me, showing me his jacket and name. He was made a co-captain as well.

There was no better feeling than walking into track and field arenas with our new Mendel track jackets, knowing all eyes were on us. It felt good to be a part of something greater than ourselves. And that one practice with the harnesses and bungee cords brought it all together for us. We had momentum that couldn't be stopped.

Kevin really got into the act after the ad-lib "No pain, no gain" slogan. He took the lead on creating our motivational chants we would belt out in practice and especially at the meets. Man, he had some dope concepts too. Everything he came up with was great, but sometimes he would just hit it out of the park. Like the one he made up for us to sing every time we walked into the track and field complex to claim our spot on the bleachers. It went:

> *I go to Mendel; Monarchs never quit!*
> *I go to Mendel; Monarchs represent!*

And we'd just repeat that over and over until we took our spots in the stands. The brilliance behind the school chants was it seemed to destroy the other teams' psyche. We were in their heads from the time we stepped on the track until we went back to the bus. We felt that if the other athletes were thinking about us, calling us arrogant, prideful, or whatever, they probably weren't too focused on their races.

We loved the "No pain, no gain" chant during sprints because it had a quick, up-tempo cadence. But Kevin created chants for relays as well, specifically the 4x100 and

4x200. We named it "Reach Back" because that's what Coach Abrams would always yell at us when he wanted us to dig deeper, to give everything we had. It was a little different than the other chants Kevin came up with because half the team had to say an underlying echo of "Reach back, reach back, reach back." While the rest of us yelled:

Lift your knees! Pump your arms!
Perfect form! Reach back!
Lift your knees! Pump your arms!
Perfect form! Reach back!

Kevin promised to work on a slogan for the mile relay just for me because Coach made it one of my main events. Since that was the last event of the day, he wanted that chant to be memorable, by "memorable" he meant "hyped."

But the chants weren't just to distract the opposition; they were really for us, to get us pumped up. And it worked. Week after week we went into other school's houses highly motivated and confident. The entire team was in a zone.

When Joe's hamstring healed, he continued his reign of first-place terror in the 100-meter and 400-meter races. Me, Shadow, and Quan ruled in the 200-meter. Even Coach was in a coaching zone. He finally had all the relays set just how he wanted them, and I was on three of them, the 4x100, 4x200, and the 4x400.

With our new attitudes and new inspirational team slogans to go with it, we were doing just what we set out to do—dominate! We creamed the competition for five straight meets on the way to accomplishing our goal of winning out the season. And the best part about it, recruiters were coming out of the woodwork to check us out.

I knew this year was a lock for scholarships and that the recruiters were technically there scouting for the following school year. But I was glad to be back on full display. Like Mrs. Morales said, "Stand out, grab recruiters' attention anyway." And with Coach Abrams working his contacts, who knew, a slot just might open.

CHAPTER 16

PREACHER MAN

/

I entered the front door, exhausted from another grueling practice, and feeling strangely like I had entered the wrong house for a moment. Angry, loud voices assaulted my ears. I was terrified to take another step. I heard lumbering shoes trekking upstairs, drowning out the commotion coming from the basement.

Mr. James squeezed out of the basement door and quickly shut it behind him.

"I thought I heard you come in," he said, almost out of breath.

"What is going on down there?"

Mr. James opened his mouth, then hesitated. He took me by the arm then walked me into the dining room.

"Terry and Little Jay were on their way here. They got blasted by some Vice Lords. Jay's dead."

Terry and Little Jay were part of the No Nonsense men's group. This was the group with all the active gang members that Lights-Out warned my dad to stop.

"Oh wow...is, is Terry OK?"

"Yeah, yeah, he's fine. It's just a flesh wound to the shoulder."

At that time another ruckus uproar came from the basement.

"Look, I gotta get back down there. You can't be here right now, son. Go on upstairs to Emily's and don't come back down till I tell you. Understand?"

I nodded my head yes but had no intentions of going upstairs to Auntie Emma's. As soon as he went back downstairs closing the door behind him, I crept to my bedroom, closed the door, laid on my belly with my ear glued to the vent so I could ear-hustle.

I quickly discovered what the arguing was about. Half of the group wanted to retaliate. The other half were against it, including Mr. James.

He asked them, "Are y'all doing this for Little Jay or yourselves? Cuz, Jay won't know y'all got revenge."

A familiar voice shot back, "I'll know."

"So it *is* about you?" Mr. James accused. "If that's the case, why wait, shoot me. Go upstairs, kill my sister, my son, my little girl. Matter fact, go outside and just start capping people at random. Kids and elderly people."

The whole room went quiet. I pressed my ear harder to the iron vent until the sharp pain against my gristle coerced me to back up some. That's when I realized, I wasn't missing anything, they were just. . .quiet. It was killing me that I couldn't see what was going on. I wanted to see the men's faces, look into their eyes to see if any of what Mr. James was saying was penetrating their minds, their hearts.

"Keko, two of our boys was shot," began the familiar voice again. "Jay got smoked right in front of Terry's face. We just supposed to let that ride? Hell nah! Somebody's gotta pay for that, dog."

"It's nonsense to believe Jay will rest in peace just because we smoke the fools who shot him. Jay's got way bigger problems right now."

"What? What are you talking about?" the familiar voice asked.

Another voice, this time an unfamiliar one answered for Mr. James, "God, man."

"God!? Mannn, y'all trippin,'" scoffed the familiar voice.

Mr. James interjected, "No, you trippin', cuz Jay's on his knees, right now, answering to God for every low-down, shady thing he's ever done. His fate is way worse now than it could ever be bangin on the South Side. Y'all better wake up!"

"Hey, hey, hey, *preacher man*, kill that noise," said the familiar voice. "Terry was the one who got shot. Let him decide. Yo, Tee, what cha wanna do man? I got yo back. Let's ride out on these marks."

It was silent again for a few moments before a rugged, baritone voice bellowed out, "Then what? I'm saying, dog, what we been doing all this time at these meetings? Reshaping our thinking. Learning to think two and three steps ahead. If we retaliate in the heat of the moment and get smoked, who's gonna look after my daughters? Who's gonna take care of your son?"

"They mamas! What you thought?"

An enormous outburst of voices cried out, arguing again, this time more intense. I couldn't tell who from who anymore. And it was evident, I didn't know many of the people in the basement anyway. However, I was able to distinguish there were about five to six different voices including Mr. James.

Suddenly, my dad's voice began to stand out above the rest, "See, see, that's the problem. We got mamas raising unruly boys who when they turn fifteen, sixteen, seventeen run all over them. We're asking our women to do mission impossible. The best moms in the world can never know what it's like being a young Black male growing up on the South Side. But we do. It ain't fair to expect them to teach our sons to be men because we ain't in the homes, we sitting in jail, or on the run, nodding off somewhere addicted to smack, or dead in some graveyard."

"So that's it, huh? I'm outvoted? We just gonna let people shoot us up and do nothing about, huh?" asked the familiar voice.

Commotion erupted again. Lively chatter and talking but nothing I could distinguish that had to do with the shootings. That's when I heard someone running up the stairs from the basement and Mr. James calling out the name of a person I would have never guessed was in my basement. The name was attached to the familiar voice that I couldn't place.

/

PROTECT YOUR QUEEN

I waited. Impatiently. I had to time it just right. *Bump it, I'm going.* I started to yank the door open but thought better of it. I waited some more then gently clasped the knob and caressed the door opened. I didn't hear anything except the blathering coming from downstairs. I knew then the coast was clear.

I tiptoed like a ninja out of my room, through the dining room, into the living room easing softly, to the sheer curtains at the front window. I took my time, careful not to be noticed. I saw them. Their bodies silhouetted through the light lime-green curtain fabric as they stood on the front porch talking. I lowered myself, sitting on my bum with my back against the windowsill listening to Mr. James and David's conversation.

I thought back to several weeks ago when I first saw the mob of people leaving my house as I walked home. It's clear to me now, it was David's body and gait I had recognized and couldn't put my finger on.

"We can both stop pretending," Mr. James said calmly. "I know you're spying on me for L.O."

David chuckled before asking, "What gave me away?"

"Well, I was skeptical when Ice-Cold first introduced you. You never really seemed to buy into what we were doing. But you gave yourself away today when you called me 'preacher man.' No one calls me that but L.O."

"You're too smart for your own good," David retorted.

"So. . .what has he told you about me?"

"That you're a traitor. A big phony. Sneaking around teaching shorties to play chess. 'Love's a sacrifice. Think three steps ahead. The rooks and pawns, kids.'" David laughed. "You couldn't even protect your own queen. Yeah, I know all about it. What was her name? Kathy? You let that disgraceful abomination happen. Pitiful."

What had I stumbled upon? It was like they were speaking code. And it seemed David knew something about my mother's death. I couldn't hide behind the curtains any longer. I needed to see their faces. To sneak a better view, I rolled over onto my knees, staying crouched and peeling back the corner of the curtain just in time to see Mr. James walk over and get right in David's face.

"So you think I'm a traitor, huh?"

"Oh, for sure."

"So why don't you smoke me then? I'm here. You're here. That's what y'all do right? Kill Black people."

Shockingly, David didn't respond. He just glared at Keko getting angrier by the second.

"Ahh, that's right," Keko murmured, condescendingly. "You're just a foot solider. I was third in command. I've put in more years of work for the set than you've been alive. You can't even pass gas in my direction without L.O.'s permission."

David whipped out his gun. Mr. James placed his forehead against the gun's barrel. He looked squarely at David and continued speaking casually as if fondly greeting our elderly neighbor, Ms. Kling.

"Little homie, how many more times do you have to pull that trigger for them before you become a man? One more? Two more? Or is it possible pulling that trigger won't make you a man at all, but a slave."

David was so incensed his hand began to shake. But he wasn't shaking nearly as much as I was. My mother died practically in front of me and now my dad was about to get his head blown off right before my eyes. David's finger nervously hovered on the trigger. I wanted to scream out but feared it would startle David instead of stopping him.

Thankfully, boisterous voices and numerous galloping footsteps began to climb the basement stairs. David quickly removed the gun from Keko's head and jetted down the steps before the remaining guys from the men's group came to the porch.

I sprang up and ran back to my room as fast as I could. I didn't want to risk someone seeing me and reporting back to Keko that I was eavesdropping at the window. I laid on my bed staring at the ceiling trying my best to wrap my mind around what I just witnessed on my mother's porch. *Would David have truly killed my father if the guys hadn't interrupted? How would I have felt about that knowing that I likely could have stopped it?* To lose both parents in the same year would be unfathomable.

Just then there was a slight wrap at my bedroom door. I was about to answer, but then it dawned on me that I was supposed to be upstairs at Auntie Emma's. There was only one thing to do. As the door creaked open, I quickly shut my eyes, turned toward the wall and pretended to be asleep. Childish, yes, but it was better than him knowing that I was awake and potentially heard everything through my bedroom vent.

He lingered for a while. I could *feel* his concerned breathing. The door gently closed. But I didn't open my eyes. I took comfort in a needed nap and the fact that I still had one parent left.

/

THE KING IS HERE

The entire team lounged about the wrestling room in factions of four and five, except Squirt. We had no clue where he was, yet that didn't stop him from being the topic of conversation as me, Kevin, Box, Shadow, and Joe were huddled up.

"Yo, that's how Monica got sick?" Box asked.

"Man, I don't know what's been up with him lately," I said. "Where is he getting these black eyes from?"

"Yeah, well, that's Squirt's problem," Kevin announced. "Not ours. You should have smashed that fool for putting the junk in your bag, though."

After Kevin's cheery proclamation, there was a moment of silence amongst our cluster. As I looked around the room at my teammates laughing and joking, nobody really stretching out like we were supposed to be doing, I felt that it would be a perfect opportunity for me to tell everyone how important the team was to me. The death of Keko's men's group member was a blatant reminder of how quickly life could be snubbed out.

The mere thought of talking about things like faith and love and hope made my stomach unsettled. I didn't have butterflies; I had condors. *What would they think if I started in with all that lovie-dovie stuff?*

I looked over at the wrestling room entrance. Maybe Coach would come in, so I wouldn't have to go through with what my heart was urging me to do. But he didn't come in, which frustrated me even more because we'd been waiting nearly fifteen minutes already and Coach was never late.

I stood up slowly, eyes glued to the door, still hoping to be rescued. *Nothing.* Kevin, Shadow, and a few others looked up at me. I could feel my body temperature rise.

"Something on your mind, dog?" Shadow asked.

I gulped out a "Yes." It felt like I was seconds from wetting myself.

"One of my dad's homies was shot and killed the other day."

At once all the side conversations stopped. Everyone looked up at me.

"We're not promised tomorrow, fellas, especially here in Chicago. God loves y'all, man. And so do I."

The words felt foreign on my lips. I had never told another male that I loved them before.

My eyes lingered at the door again, but then I realized, Coach wasn't going to save me. It was meant for me to have that conversation at that moment.

"You all don't know, but I joined the track team last year only because my mother asked me to. I hated it. I love to run, but I hated everything else, the practices, the drills, the meets. So when she passed away over the summer, it was easy for me to quit. But what I just recently found out was my mom couldn't run track herself cuz she got pregnant with me in high school. It was her dream to go to college and run track. Once I found this out, I joined again to honor her. But now, I have my own purpose for running, for everything I do. My faith in Jesus is my purpose. I wanna be a better man, a better brother, better teammate, better homie. From now on, I wanna please God in everything I do. Just wanted y'all to know that."

There I was, standing amid my peers, bleeding from my heart to them holding nothing back. And the most amazing part, they listened. No one rolled their eyes or zoned me out. They all listened.

As soon as I finished, it felt like the courage I had seconds ago seeped into a puddle on the floor. *Maybe I did wet myself?* I sat back down on the mat avoiding eye contact. I knew they were all still staring at me for I could feel the heat from their eyes piercing the back of my noggin.

"BJ, man," Eddie-Ed began as he stood up. "I feel you, dog. See, God made me the best beatboxer at Mendel for a reason, a purpose."

Ed's stupid comment broke the ice permanently. It was the laugh that we all needed to breathe again.

"Why y'all laughing? I'm serious."

"But you not the best, fool—Box is," Kevin interjected.

"Can he prove it?"

With that, Eddie-Ed began producing some treble-like beats that I had to admit, were sounding pretty good. He eased his way over toward Box, beatboxing the entire way. Excitement flooded the wrestling room. We all stood up anticipating the inevitable. Everyone, that is, except Box. He didn't move a muscle. He just laid there on the mat looking totally uninterested.

The entire team followed Eddie-Ed over to Box, forming a circle around him.

Box looked up at Kev then over to me.

I smirked down at him, "Handle yo bizness."

Mendel's reigning Beatboxing King slowly rose to his feet. The team erupted with cheers. *It was on!* The long-awaited, highly anticipated battle for the number one spot at Mendel was finally about to go down.

Ed and Box squared off. . .*fight*. . .*fight*. . .*fight!*

Ed spit his last beat, then waited. Box began circling his prey because that's what sharks do. King Box maneuvered instinctively, eyeing Ed up and down, emotionless, unmoved by this would-be challenger.

The crowd hushed as it was now the king's turn. Beatbox battles were just like MC freestyle battles. Each person had a fair chance to go. One person goes first, then the other person. But unlike MC battles, where each rapper usually gets a verse apiece then a winner's determined, with beatbox battles, the competitors go back and forth for several minutes until someone either runs out of beats or concedes.

Box began as he always did before he took a sucker out. He would get this little bob-and-weave thing going with his head, like he's dancing to the music inside of his own brain before it's expelled from his mouth. I'd always thought that was ingenious because it built anticipation. It usually got a few people bobbing along with him before they've heard one beat, brilliant.

I looked around and saw several people doing just that, dancing, bobbing along with Box with huge smiles on their faces eagerly waiting. Heck, even I started smiling.'

"Sic 'em boy, sic 'em," I blurted out.

Box warmed up his lips with a simple bass roll. Then he added his patented breathing sounds that reminded me of taking quick sips from a straw that had a hole in it or like sipping hot tea from a cup. This, Box openly admits, he does to pay homage to the human beatbox from The Fat Boys, one of our favorite groups. A lot of beatboxing was stealing anyway. A person would hear something that another beatbox artist did and put his own twist to it, adding his own little flavor. It was masterful how Box blended beats into each other, one after the other, again and again.

Box abruptly stopped, and Ed didn't waste any time. He came back with this choppy beat that sounded like a transformer scratch while using the cross-fader. It was dope. A few of the fellas started nodding their heads along to Ed, really getting into it. But not us. Even though what Ed was bringing sounded fresh, I couldn't root against my boy. That just wasn't happening. The whole track team could have been digging what Ed was doing, but me and Kev wouldn't budge an inch.

Box checked out the crowd dancing to Ed's beats. I could tell he did not like that at all. Playtime was over. It was time to get busy. Box hopped right in with more bass, which was smart because there had always been a slight echo in the wrestling room. So when Box went to his bass drumbeat the echo amplified it.

"OK, OK, lemme go in my bag of tricks," Eddie-Ed said. "Check it."

Ed covered his mouth with his hands, creating his own echo. I had no clue what he was doing behind those ashy knuckles, but again, it sounded pretty dope. It was almost like he was doing some weird duck call.

Box seemed to be getting annoyed that Ed hadn't admitted defeat yet. It was clear to me that Box would have to go deep into his arsenal because Ed was actually hanging with him. Box was so used to beating down competition with one or two rounds, he rarely, if ever, had to do his more creative styles. But that was about to change.

Box pushed his glasses up on his face, getting ready for round three. Box jumped in rudely switching to a combination of different bass and treble beats.

Now it was Ed's turn to interrupt, but Box didn't stop. They both continued beatboxing at the same time making a blend of live musicality the likes I had never heard before. Neither of them backed down, both coming in and out, dropping the beat then picking it back up, smoothly transitioning from staccato beats to the bass we all loved.

Until, in the end, my dog had to set himself apart. Box inhaled deeply then let out a cacophony of sound that discombobulated little Eddie so much that he had to stop and just listen. In fact, we all stopped. Though it was totally groove worthy, we stopped dancing in order to appreciate the music that was coming out of my man's mouth. Box kept going and going and going. Some guys even closed their eyes, becoming one with the melody.

I watched Ed closely. He was dumbfounded. He stood there shaking his head in disbelief, wondering, I imagine, if Box was man or machine? That's when I knew Ed had conceded. It was like Box took every beat that he's ever known and compacted it into a thirty-second compilation, ending with the all-too famous "huh-huh-huh-huh" that Buff made as his signature beat.

We were all silent for a split second, then—jubilation! Guys jumped up and down, others rolled on the floor laughing.

"That was dope!"

"Yeah, Box, you did your thing."

"Box is still the champ."

I went over and dapped my man up, giving him a hug.

Kevin started singing Queen's hit, "*Doon-doon-doon*, another one bites the dust."

I joined in, "*Doon-doon-doon*, another one bites the dust."

Then everybody: "And another one gone and another one gone, another one bites the dust."

It was unanimous, *another one gone.* King Box stood in the middle of the room, smiling, hands on his hips, relishing another successful defense of his title while his subjects pulled and clawed at him. It was great!

As we celebrated Box's victory, Squirt finally showed up. He announced that Coach wanted everyone to meet him downstairs. Shadow and Hawk ran over to Squirt, filling him in on how Box just annihilated Ed in the beat-box battle of the century. Squirt was livid, jumping from person to person, "Who won? Box won? Deg, I missed it? Was it dope?"

It was undeniable. Box was still the best. And when Squirt went over to ask Eddie-Ed himself, Ed answered humbly and correctly, "Box is the King of Mendel."

CHAPTER 17

SPECIAL OLYMPICS

/

High off the battle, we stampeded downstairs to find Coach outside by the bus waiting for us. Coach announced that we were going to Chicago State University. This news made us even more pumped. We rarely ever had the opportunity to practice on a real track, so whenever Coach Abrams could hook it up for us to go to one of the local universities, it was a special treat. We all jetted to our lockers, grabbed our track jackets and were back in record time.

On the ride over to Chicago State several of the guys were still yapping about Box and Ed's epic battle. And Squirt was still sulking that he missed it.

Every now and again, Squirt would glance back at me and Kevin with a sour look on his grill. I supposed he figured I ratted him out to the rest of the crew about his delinquent extracurricular activities. That might explain why he seemed to be talking to everyone except Kevin, Box, and me.

We pulled into Chicago State's parking lot. Everyone began grabbing their gear but that's when Coach told us he had a surprise for us. He confessed that we weren't there to practice. Instead, we were honored guests to attend a track meet for some sixth, seventh, and eighth graders who were preparing for the Special Olympics.

Before we stepped off the bus, Coach made it clear what his expectations were.

"You are here to cheer, support, and encourage these athletes. After the meet, I want all of you to mingle around, introduce yourself to the kids, their parents, and coaches. A lot of these parents are supporters of our track team. So be sure to thank them for their support. Is that clear?"

"Yes sir," we all replied.

When Coach said that, I saw Squirt snickering and laughing with a couple of the guys. Right then and there I knew he was gearing up for one of his classic-clown performances.

"Everyone put your jackets on," Quan instructed. "Let's go."

Kevin and I were last to get off. Once I stepped foot on the asphalt, I heard, "Pssst."

"What was that?" I asked Kev.

"That fool's hiding around the corner, calling you." Kevin pointed.

Sure enough, Squirt was crouched down, hiding behind the front bumper of the bus.

I shook my head. "A'ight, save me a spot. Lemme see what he wants," I said, dismissing Kevin. We dapped, and he caught up with the rest of the team.

Squirt came from behind the bus and pried his fingers between the rubber posts of the bus door pulling it open. We both hopped back on.

"Yo, I know it's been a minute since we talked but I need that thang from you."

"What?" I asked incredulously. "Dude, I don't have that anymore."

"What you mean you don't have it?"

"My old man flushed it down the toilet."

"Aww man, don't tell me that!"

Squirt flopped down on one of the seats, putting his face in his hands.

"You lucky he didn't call Five-O," I said.

"Shoot, I rather he did. Being in jail is better than being dead. Deg man, you know we gotta pay him back, right?"

"Who?"

"My supplier?"

"I mean, 'we-who'? I ain't gotta pay nuttin' back. Nobody told you to put that junk in my book bag."

Squirt looked at me, angrier than I'd ever seen him before. He popped up, pushed past me, and stormed out the bus's double doors.

I took a quick moment to process what just happened then I left as well.

When I came around the corner into the outdoor track stadium, the stands were packed with family and friends there to watch their loved ones participate in the meet. I finally spotted the team. It was so many of us we took up a whole section from top to bottom. Coach was standing on the ground in front of our section.

He looked at me oddly, "Where have you been?"

"Huh? Oh, I was, uh—"

"Never mind," he cut me off. "Whenever someone begins with 'huh,' whatever's next is a lie. Go sit down somewhere."

Squirt and a few other team members were sitting near the bottom of the bleachers. So I made my way to the top to sit with Box, Kevin, Shadow, Joe, and Quan.

Just as I sat down the announcer came over the loudspeaker, "Ladies and Gentlemen before we continue with today's meet, please help me welcome the Mendel Monarch Track Team—"

"Hey, stand up. Everybody, stand up," Quan instructed.

"They're on a winning streak of five meets in a row," the announcer continued. "Let's give them a hand."

We all stood up and waved to the crowd. The audience cheered and clapped and whistled. We looked like an actual team with everyone wearing the same jackets and we felt like rock stars with everyone clapping for us.

After waving to the crowd, we all sat back down. A man walked up to Coach handing him a stopwatch. Though we were there as honored guests, Coach was there to work as a guest official.

"Behave yourselves." Speaking louder, looking up at us, pointing, he said, "You captains are in charge."

I was hoping and praying that the fellas would be on their best behavior. And by "fellas," I meant Squirt.

"Hey Coach, can we take these jackets off now?" Squirt asked. "It's getting hot."

"Yeah, go ahead," Coach answered as he walked off to join the other officials.

Squirt and Hawk collected everyone's jackets and ran them back to the bus.

It was a gorgeous sparkling day out. As I gazed around at all the smiling faces in the stands, I immediately spotted some faces that weren't happy but appeared a bit worried, other's looked hopeful. Maybe everyone just wanted their little athlete to do well at the meet.

The day moved steadily along even though after every event there was a five-minute celebration at the finish line with contestants, teammates, and coaches. As I watched throughout the day, I noticed there was one little boy who came in last place every event he participated in, yet he never gave up.

Unfortunately, I wasn't the only person who noticed him. After a while, this little boy became the target for Squirt's boneheaded jokes. Although we were sitting several feet above Squirt, I could still hear the jokes he was making about the Special Olympian.

Just then, the last event of the day, the 400 meter was about to begin. I leaned over and asked one of the parents if she knew what the little boy's name was. The lady thought for a moment, then asked her husband. He said he thought the boy's name was Adam. As the runners got ready to line up, I suddenly became nervous like I was about to run a race. I wanted my new friend, Adam, to win so badly. That's when I heard Squirt revving up his comedy act.

"Yo, why does that dopey-looking kid always come in last place? I got five bucks he comes in last again."

"Which one?" Red asked.

"Which one?" Squirt laughed. "The one who's come in last place ever since we got here. Yo, if he was a twin, he would've come out third, behind the placenta. If he runs backwards, it'll be yesterday."

Unbelievably, Squirt started singing the Beatles classic to drive home the point of his inappropriate comment. I couldn't understand why several of the guys were laughing and egging him on. I looked at Box to see if he was hearing this.

"Let it go, dog," Box said, shaking his head.

I looked at Kevin. Without looking back at me, he said, "Don't look at me. You the captain."

Kevin was right. What was I going to do about this? A spark burned in my belly. As many times as Squirt had been punked, I felt he should have been the last person to tease anyone. I bogarted my way past my other teammates, barely balancing myself on the narrow aluminum bleachers. I took Squirt by the shoulder and yanked him around to face me. He glared upward at me as I was standing a step just above him in the bleachers.

Once he saw it was me, he pulled away, then shoved me hard.

"Don't grab me!"

I was peeved. Instantly, my head began to ache like I had just popped a blood vessel. I became dizzy and light-headed then I blacked out. At least I thought I blacked out. I was told later that I *snapped out*.

The next thing I knew Box, Shadow, and a few other guys from the team were pulling me off Squirt. Somehow, we got lodged between some steps of the bleachers.

Box told me later that I shoved Squirt so hard that we both went flying down the stands with me landing on top of him. The fellas quickly separated us. Apparently, it ended just as fast as it started because only a few parents and a handful of guys from the team saw what actually happened. Many of them thought I fell, and Squirt was unlucky enough to be in the way.

Box walked me down to the pavement, while Shadow went back to join Kevin and the others. Squirt was still in the stands yelling, scowling, and trying to get at me, but Red and a few others held him back. I looked at him like, *C'mon dog, quit selling woof tickets.* Squirt knows he didn't want none.

Just then the starter gun sounded. An announcement blared over the loudspeaker, "C'mon folks, let's give 'em a hand. It's the last race of the day. Stand to your feet!"

The majority of the crowd clamored to their feet, obeying the announcer's encouragement. Shoot, he didn't have to tell me twice. I instantly forgot Squirt existed and whipped around to watch my little buddy.

The runners trekked around the first 100 meters at a moderate pace. Down the back 100-meter stretch, some of the competitors began to make their move. And Adam was right in the mix.

Box and I were already at the fence that bordered the track area. I leaned over the gate, yelling, screaming for my number one guy.

"C'mon, Adam," I screamed.

But my lone voice just wasn't enough. Then I remembered. I have an army behind me. I tapped Box, "C'mon, let's get it up."

I looked back at Kevin, Shadow, and the others. I waved frantically for them to come join us.

"Let's go," Shadow yelped.

Kevin, Joe, Quan, and Shadow came rumbling down the stands to join us. But that still wasn't enough. As the racers came into the straightaway, I saw that Adam was beginning to lose steam. He was straining as hard as he could to keep up with the other sprinters.

I went over to the whole team, "Eh, everybody, let's get it up. Right now. Everybody!"

All the fellas, even Squirt, stood and started cheering for the athletes.

As I went back to the gate, Kevin began to chant "Adam, Adam, Adam."

We all joined in, "Add-am, Add-am, Add-am." We were leaning over the gate at about the 50-meter mark as the runners were approaching us fast.

I did a quick head count to see what position Adam was in. He had slowly dropped from fourth place, to fifth, then to sixth place.

"C'mon, Adam," I yelled over the continuous "Adam" chants from my teammates.

"Don't give up. Adam. Don't give up," I encouraged him. "Refuse to lose."

The first-place runner zoomed by us on his way to the finish line. The other sprinters were approaching the line as well.

Then I saw it. I saw Adam's face, more than that, his eyes. As he got closer and closer to us, I watched him cut his eyes over to his personal cheering section. He wasn't just listening to us, he heard us. A light switch flipped on. Our rooting was giving him energy, power.

Adam's scrawny arms began to pump harder. His knobby knees began to lift higher. Somehow, our cheers were bringing something out of him. As Adam got closer his eyes were glued on us the entire way.

I turned to the fellas, "Let's do 'Reach Back.'"

I turned to the whole team, "Do 'Reach Back.' Everybody, 'Reach Back.'"

The team behind us repeated the chorus, "Reach back. Reach back. Reach back."

Adam shifted his focus from us back to the runners just ahead of him.

"Look, he's reaching back," said Kevin.

"Don't quit. Don't quit, Adam!" I shouted.

And he didn't. Adam dug into his reserved strength. A moment ago, he was done. But when he heard us cheering him on, well, that's all he needed.

Adam moved back into sixth place and quickly gained on the fifth-place guy. By that time, I was nearly hoarse.

"Reach back! Refuse to lose, Adam! Reach back!"

Adam's frail body shook as he kicked it to yet another gear catapulting him into fifth place.

"Yes. . .go. . .go!" I hollered.

Ten meters from the line, Adam went into overdrive, arms flailing, his running form, a hot mess. But his momentum alone carried him into fourth place as he crossed the finish line. And I was 100% sure that if he had fifteen more meters, he would have grabbed third.

When Adam crossed that line, the announcer erupted. The parents and coaches erupted. The other competitors erupted. Our whole team erupted. And Adam, collapsed from either sheer exhaustion or the weight of that huge smile plastered on his grill. The rest of the kids ran over piling on top of Adam as he lay gasping on the ground.

Shadow looked at me. I looked at Shadow. We both looked at Kevin, Kevin looked at Box. Simultaneously, we all hopped the fence and bum-rushed the track causing a domino effect of nearly everyone in the stands to flood the track seconds behind us. The pandemonium was like a Cinderella team upsetting the number one seed at the Final Four. We mixed in with the crowd, congratulating all the contestants on a job well done.

I walked purposefully through the mob looking for my speed demon. Clusters of Mendel track members were hobnobbing with parents and kids per Coach Abram's instructions.

After several minutes of searching for the little guy who tugged at my heartstrings, I spotted Coach Abrams to my left and asked him if he saw the little kid that everybody piled on. Coach said he hadn't, but I better find him quickly because the bus was leaving in five minutes.

I had to find him. I had to find Adam. I hunted desperately through the crowd, but it seemed like it was too late. Groves of people were collecting their sweaty children, along with their sweaty sweats, and walking toward the parking lot to head home.

Just when I had given up hope someone touched my shoulder from behind.

"Thank you for what you and your teammates did for my son," said a woman with tears in her eyes.

"Oh, you're Adam's mom?"

"Yes. How did you get him to run like that?"

"I. . .I don't think we did that much," I said, blushing.

"You're wrong," she interrupted. "My son has come in last place in every single event. At every single meet."

Tears began to flow again from Adam's mom as she continued, "My husband, Adam's sisters, and I come and cheer for him, but he's never responded like that to us. The only reason we continue to let him do this is because he loves to run."

"Yeah, I know the feeling. We just cheered for him, that's all."

"Well, thank you for *just cheering*. Would you like to meet him?"

"Of course," I responded eagerly. I didn't know why it felt like I was about to meet Jody Watley or somebody.

She took me over to her family who was standing by the bleachers. Adam's two older sisters were college students at Illinois State University.

"I'm Becky, by the way. And this is my husband, Steve. And our daughters Molly and April. And this is Adam."

I said hello to each of them and politely stuck out my hand. I was caught off guard when they all took turns giving me gentle bear hugs instead, thanking me for what I did. Everyone except Adam, that is. He just looked at me.

"Nice to meet you, Adam."

"Say hello, Adam," Steve urged.

"Hel-lo," Adam said matter-of-factly.

I congratulated him on a great race. Yet he didn't seem too interested in his new admirer. I was a bit surprised at how little Adam spoke in comparison to the other kids I heard yapping around me. It wasn't that he couldn't speak. He just chose not to, kind of like Joe.

Becky explained that it takes Adam awhile to warm up around strangers. I chatted with the Holland family for about fifteen minutes. They shared with me the joys and difficulties of having a son with autism.

They inquired about me and the track team and my studies at Mendel. Adam's sisters plugged how great a school ISU was and that I should consider going there. I was certain that the team bus was going to leave me behind, but I wouldn't have missed meeting Adam and his family for the world.

The Holland's and I said our goodbyes and that's when something most unexpected happened. I overheard Adam tell his father, "Dad, I refused to lose."

I turned around and watched the Hollands walk toward the opposite exit. Adam was holding his father's hand. Steve told him, "You sure did son. I'm so proud of you."

Although Adam wasn't particularly thankful or interested that I was there, when I heard him talk to his dad, I knew that we made an impact on him.

/

WATCH YOUR BACK

I sprinted through the parking lot overjoyed to find Mendel's lone bus sitting with the engine running. I climbed onboard and thanked our driver for not leaving me. He promptly replied, "You can thank your Coach for that."

Coach Abrams was standing in the aisle a few feet away addressing the team.

I scooted pass him and headed to the back to find a seat. Naturally, I had to endure a few hazes from the guys.

"It's about time."

"What took you so long?"

"I would have left you."

"Yeah, yeah, yeah. My bad, my bad," I said sitting down in the back next to Kevin.

"Now that we're all here, I guess I can continue," Coach snidely remarked. "I hope everybody paid close attention. Encouraging and helping others who can't return the favor is a valuable life skill to have. Remember that."

"Great job fellas," Hawk blurted out.

The team started clapping and hooting.

"No, wait, before you break your arm patting yourselves on the back," Coach interrupted. "A few parents brought a disturbing matter to my attention. BJ, care to elaborate?"

"Why does he get to go first?" Squirt objected immediately.

"Because as a captain I hold him fully responsible for any foolishness. You'll get your turn to speak, Antwan. BJ?"

I hesitated. I didn't want to get anybody into trouble. I looked over at Squirt. He glared back at me.

"Man, just tell him, BJ," encouraged Kevin.

"Shut up, Kevin!" Squirt shot back. "You don't know what happened. You were at the top of the bleachers—"

"Coach," Shadow interrupted, "Squirt was making fun of some of the athletes, and BJ set him straight, that's all."

"How bout I set you straight?"

"You can try," Shadow replied.

Squirt and Shadow both went after each other but several of the guys got up to hold them back.

"Antwan is that true?" Coach Abrams asked.

"Yeah, but I wasn't the only one. There was a bunch of us laughing."

"OK, who else?"

"Man, I ain't no snitch like some people," he glared at Shadow.

"Antwan? Last chance."

Squirt folded his arms and didn't say a word. Coach waited for like half a second before continuing, "All right, you're suspended. Two weeks. You can practice and come to the meets with us, but you will not be participating."

"That ain't fair, Coach! I'm not the only one who was laughing!" Squirt shouted.

"Let's go," Coach told the driver.

The bus driver put the bus in gear and took off.

"Yo, stop the bus! I quit this whack team."

The driver slammed on the brakes with no objections from Coach Abrams.

"Gimme my jacket White boy."

Shadow looked to the front toward Coach.

Coach stood again and motioned to Shadow, "Give it to him. It's his."

Shadow rummaged carelessly through the jackets that were piled at the back of the bus. He threw the jacket forward and several guys passed it on up to Squirt.

Squirt snatched the track jacket and huffed to the front of the bus. He stopped on the stairs and turned around, "BJ, watch your back."

"Boy, who you threatening? You couldn't bust a blackhead. Get outta here," Kevin sneered.

Several of the fellas laughed. Coach told everyone to shut up. Squirt got off the bus and the driver hit the gas.

I watched Squirt from the window as we drove away. Squirt threw his jacket to the ground angrily, then kicked it for good measure.

I was about to yell up to the driver to stop, but I thought better of it. After all the trouble Squirt's caused, I don't know why my heart still went out to him. I didn't mean to lose my temper and tackle him in the bleachers. Squirt was just frustrated because of his situation. I told Kev that I should have never embarrassed him like that. Kevin told me not to worry about Squirt's empty threats. I honestly wasn't worried about the threat. I was more concerned that right there on that bus an eleven-year friendship might have just come to an end.

/

INVITATIONAL MEET

It was no surprise that Squirt ditched school the next few days. Usually when Squirt had a temper tantrum it took about a week for him to calm down and get over whatever he was mad about. But admittedly this was a little more than a temper tantrum. I knew he felt betrayed by me. In my mind, I had only been trying to help him. Robbing old ladies, selling drugs, making fun of disabled kids; when was it going to end? Squirt had been on a downward spiral for a while now. Somebody had to say something.

I walked down the thin bus aisle looking for a seat. Several of the fellas laughed aloud and made silly remarks to me because I was wearing Squirt's teeny-tiny jacket. As far as Coach was concerned, our track jackets were part of our uniform. And I wasn't running extra 100-meter sprints for being out of uniform for anybody.

"Yeah, yeah, laugh it up," I said as I continued down the lane.

Shadow waved me over to sit with him.

"Dude," he began, "why on earth are you wearing Squirt's track jacket?"

"Because somebody—I wonder who—passed up the wrong jacket the other day. Dog, learn how to read."

"Oh," Shadow laughed. "My bad, dog. Anyway, finish telling me."

Shadow wanted me to finish telling him the story I began at lunch about how annoyed I was with Vanessa and the stupid upcoming prom. I picked up the story by telling him I knew more than I ever wanted to know about women's shoes. I had gone over to Vanessa's after getting back from the Special Olympics meet because she was dying to show me the shoes that she picked out to wear with her prom dress. Vanessa was psyched I asked her to go to prom. I went with her the week before to pick out the dress and for some girl reason she wanted me to see the shoes and dress together.

"Wait a minute, isn't it bad luck or something?" Shadow asked.

"Nah dude, you thinking about weddings," I told him.

"Oh, yeah, you're right. But it's still cool to see she's so excited about prom," Shadow suggested.

"I guess. But I told her that she didn't have to include me in every detail."

"Uh-oh, how'd she take that?"

"Man, she lectured me for like twenty minutes straight. 'Why don't you appreciate me? I'm doing this for you. I just want to look good for *your* prom.' Blah blah, blah blah."

Shadow laughed mercilessly.

"So, I spent the rest of the night trying to convince her that I was just as stoked as she was about that stupid dance. What guy in his right mind is truly excited about prom?"

"For real," Shadow agreed.

Our bumpy bus ride ended in front of Downers Grove South for an invitational meet. All of us looked forward to invitational track meets. Championship and invitational meets were the only few track meets where ribbons and medals were handed out for placing. Namely, medals for first through third place and ribbons for fourth through sixth place. No one really cared much about the ribbons though. It was all about that gold, silver, and bronze, baby.

I earned several first and second place medals at invitational meets during my junior year. I remember how Mom used to stare at them. She would make me put them on and just smile. Then she would place the medals around her neck and strut around the house, stopping at every mirror along the way. It was like Mom thought the medals were the evidence of one's hard work. Invitational and championship meets were special to me because of medals.

Bang! Out the gate Derrick and Red placed one and two in the 110-meter high hurdles. Joe, as expected, placed first in the 100 meter, and we dominated the first relay of the day, the 4x800 meter. It had been an extremely long Saturday meet. The most exciting one since indoor Catholic league and just as close. St. Paul Academy was in first with 103 points. We were in second with 98 points.

Between events Hawk made his way over to me as I was stretching out for my final two broad jumps.

"Yo, did you hear the news?" Hawk asked as he gave me dap.

"No, what?"

"Coach has a couple of colleagues of his in the stands. I hear they're assistant track coaches for a couple prestigious universities."

"Really? Where are they sitting?"

Hawk turned his back and sneakily pointed to Coach's friends near the top of the stands. "And they've been here the whole meet?" I asked Hawk.

"Quan said they've come the last two meets."

Just then, Coach headed our way.

"Mr. Hawk, could you excuse us please?"

"Sure thing, Coach," Hawk said. "Kill it, dog."

He gave me dap again and left me alone with Coach.

"So how do you feel?" Coach asked.

"Pretty good."

"That's good, good." Coach knelt next to me. "I wasn't going to tell you this but, you're mature enough to handle the situation."

"Hawk just told me. You have some recruiter friends of yours up in the stands."

"Yes, that's true, but that's not what I wanted to tell you."

"Why not?" I asked.

"This is an important meet, and I didn't want you to lose focus, getting all nervous, getting your hopes up. They're here as a courtesy to me. Their programs are already locked but they said if you're any good they'll ask their network of coaches if any scholarships are still out there. Now, can I talk to you about what I came over here for please?"

I nodded. "Sure, sup Coach?"

"I'm confident we'll get first place in the mile relay. So by my calculations, it comes down to what you do in this long jump. You need to take first or second place for us to win today's meet."

I learned quickly that most meets involved pressure on top of pressure. One point here, two points there, dropped baton mishaps, baton passed outside of the passing zone disqualifications, false start eliminations, foul jumps—*forget about it*.

None of that mattered now. My team needed me, and I couldn't let them down.

The gun fired in the distance. Coach gave me a reaffirming nod then walked away, placing his attention on the mile relay race.

Just then I heard the head event judge for the long jump call the last two schools over, Mendel and St. Paul Academy. I took a deep breath and psyched myself up to go head-to-head with Victor's boy, Bruce.

The judge announced that Mendel was up first. I ambled the approach looking down for the tape mark that I left on the ground from my previous jump. I didn't know why I was looking for that mark, considering I was disqualified for overstepping the board that first jump.

"Mendel, we're ready for you," said the judge.

I waved my hand to acknowledge the judge then closed my eyes, taking one last deep breath. When I opened my eyes, I saw Shadow down at the end of the runway. He gave me a thumbs-up and smiled, still sweating after completing the first leg of the mile relay.

I nodded back and began my approach. I methodically built up my speed down the runway like a plane on an airstrip. The closer I got, the faster I went. I hit the launch board and soared crashing into the sand until I tumbled to a stop. I looked back eyeballing the line judge. A dark ominous cloud seemed to appear over the track and field as the judge held up a red flag signifying that I had fouled again.

I wanted to bury myself in the very sand I sat in. I think I'd still be sitting in that sand if it weren't for Shadow.

"C'mon, dog, get up," Shadow said, helping me out of the *quicksand* pit. We walked back toward the beginning of the approach together, neither of us saying a word. Bruce zoomed by us to attempt his final jump.

We watched as Bruce hit the board and flew. It was a good jump. The measurer hurried over to the pit before Bruce could even crawl out of it. He stretched his measuring tape and yelled, "19-3," meaning nineteen feet and three inches. By that time, everyone in the stadium knew it was between Mendel and St. Paul for first place. Other teams that hadn't a chance of placing were already packing their things and heading to the parking lot. I didn't mind that in the least. Everybody could have left as far as I was concerned. But with the arena now a little emptier, I was able to spot scattered recruiters standing at attention. . .watching me.

Bruce was greeted by practically his whole team when he climbed out of the sandpit. Victor, Bruce, and a few others looked my direction and began laughing and pointing. Normally, being taunted would fire me up. But at that point, I didn't really care about Victor or his teammates. I couldn't mess up in front of these recruiters.

Shadow tapped me on the shoulder, "Look." I turned around to see Joe crossing the finish line first, just as Coach predicted. We won the mile relay.

"Mendel, you're up," the judge stated. "Last and final jump."

Shadow watched as I stepped onto the approach. I looked over to the stands again, spotting Coach's friends who could make my dream of going to college, reality.

"Dog, what are you looking at?" Shadow asked.

I motioned with my head.

"Those recruiters?"

"Yeah, Coach asked them to come. I can't mess this up. It's too important."

"I feel you, dog, but you won't mess up. You're gonna do it because it is important. BJ, you're right there. You barely missed the board. Look, I know I'm just a sophomore, but I've been doing this event since grade school. Can I give you some advice?"

"Yeah, yeah."

"Don't build up your speed like you did that last jump. Start off sprinting. Just go!"

"All right."

"You got this, dog."

I looked into my teammate's eyes, and we gave each other dap. *Who knew Shadow would be the one to give me the pep talk I needed?*

A hush fell over the few remaining teams in the place. All eyes were on me as I sprinted down the runway. I ran as fast and as hard as I could. I was going so fast that a gentle breeze enveloped my body as I ran. I didn't hear my heartbeat like Mom described, but I did finally, *finally* feel the joy of doing something I loved. And I loved the competition, being in the moment. It was do or die time.

Before I knew it, the launch board was just a few steps away. I hit it perfectly. No red flags this time. I floated through the air for what seemed like minutes. My spikes sunk into the sand. I bounced out of the pit and eagerly awaited my measurement.

The measurer hurried over to the sand. Shadow, Quan, Kevin, and a few more fellas ran down to join me by the sandpit.

The measurer stood, "21-1."

"Yeah, dog! You did it!" Quan squealed.

Twenty-one feet and one inch, just enough for second place and to seal another team victory, pushing our winning streak to six in a row.

I couldn't believe it. We'd won the meet. I let out a sigh of relief accompanied with a chuckle. I tried not to, but I couldn't help but look to the stands once more. I saw the recruiters nodding.

I joined the rest of the guys jumping up and down like we'd won a state championship meet. Nope, it was even better. We had beaten St. Paul Academy one more time.

CHAPTER 18

PROM NIGHT

/

Senior prom was created for women by women. I'm convinced of it. It was totally a chick thing. Getting dressed up to take pictures, mingle with friends, eat forty-dollar-a-plate food, and attempt to dance in formal wear, a guy would never think of that. I mean, we couldn't get loose in those penguin suits. Guys went to prom for one reason, to prove that they had game enough to pull a date. That was why my boys and I went. In our minds, there was nothing more embarrassing than to miss prom because of not having a date.

I wondered what was taking Vanessa so long. Unfortunately, Vanessa's mom had to work so Auntie Emma had Vanessa come over, so she could help her get ready. They'd been locked away upstairs at Auntie Emma's for more than three hours. I was dressed and ready for pictures two hours ago. *What on earth was she doing?* Mr. James got tired of me pacing back and forth so he had me sit down.

Mr. James joined me on the living room sofa. He told me that historically, men have always been able to get ready for special events faster than women. He said to always let a woman go into the bathroom first when getting ready, because men could go in after them, get ready and still beat them out the door. I chuckled at his attempts to be this old, wise sage that claimed to understand women. Heck, even I knew that women were the one mystery that men would never unravel.

Just then, Spud bust through the front door.

"They're on the way down now."

"It's about time," I replied.

We both stood up. I went over to give myself one last glance in the dining room mirror. Mr. James followed. He brushed off my tux jacket with his hand then straightened my bow tie. He snapped one more solo picture then we marched outside onto the front porch.

It was gorgeous out. We were a month in to daylight savings, so though it was evening time, the sun was still blazing in all its magnificence. Come to find out, Corliss and Carver were having there proms too. So it seemed like everybody and their mama was outside awaiting the fashion show, ready to take pictures.

The block was jammed packed with friends and families lined up in front of respective houses. I was a bit curious myself to see how other people were stepping out. Yet I doubted if anyone would be as smooth as Vanessa and I were.

My boy Stanley was on his porch with his arm draped around his chubby date. They were in classic white and red. I gave him a quick head nod. He pointed at me and shouted back, "What up, Beej?"

I saw that Ce-Ce was looking fine in her mauve dress. I met her lame boyfriend, Luther, a couple of times.

Nicky was taking pictures with her date in front of their limo in her fuchsia ensemble. Somehow, she talked the poor sap she was dating into wearing fuchsia as well. Ordinarily, I wouldn't have a clue what colors my home-girls were wearing. But I learned pretty quick because Vanessa dragged me to so many dress shops looking at different prom dresses with very specific color names: fuchsia, mauve, taupe, cream, and what did she finally pick? Purple. I suppose I should be grateful that it wasn't violet.

As Mr. James, Monica, and I were waiting on the porch a black car with tinted windows rolled up slowly and parked across the street in front of our house.

I recognized the car immediately. It was David's ride. The engine shut off, but no one got out of the car. I looked at Mr. James who had his eyes glued to the vehicle. I wondered what was going through his mind knowing that he and David had beef a few weeks ago.

Just then, Auntie Emma's front door opened and out came Vanessa along with Auntie Em.

Mr. James and I kept our eyes glued on the car, so much so, that Auntie Emma said something to me, but it didn't register.

Finally, Auntie Emma slapped me on the back of my head.

"Oww, what's up Auntie?"

"I said, doesn't Vanessa look beautiful?"

"Yeah, she straight."

This time Vanessa punched me in the arm. "You said you liked this dress. You helped pick it out."

"I do like it."

Just then, Vanessa noticed why I was so distracted. She yelled, "Y'all fools, come over here!"

Mr. James and I were both surprised that David didn't hop out the whip, but Victor. Yes, and of course, Bruce got out the passenger's side. Vanessa quickly explained to me, since Mrs. Colby couldn't be there to see Vanessa off, she ordered Victor to come over and take pictures for her.

"Don't worry about him, babe," she said. "Mama told him to be on his best behavior."

Vanessa turned her attention back to Victor and Bruce as they reached the sidewalk. Victor with camera in hand.

"Vic, take some pictures for Mama," Vanessa ordered.

Victor began snapping pictures of Vanessa and I while we posed on the porch. That's when Auntie Emma chimed in, "No, come up here and take 'em."

Victor reluctantly climbed the stairs while Bruce watched from the ground. It had to burn Vic that his archnemesis was dating his sister. Auntie Emma and Mr. James coached Vanessa and me on different poses. Mr. James joined in taking pictures as well from the porch.

After we took a few final snapshots with Monica, I told everyone that it was time for us to leave. We said our goodbyes and headed to the car. Mr. James tossed me the keys to the whip he rented for us, a black 1986 Cadillac Seville. It was sweet.

When Vanessa, Victor, and I reached the sidewalk, he felt it necessary to warn me to be careful with his little sister. Vanessa told him to shut up, but I politely nodded to his request, or I should say, his demand. Vanessa was only a year younger than Victor, but he still felt it mandatory to play the big brother roll.

As we walked past, Bruce glared at me, sizing me up. Apparently, he was playing the friend-of-the-big-brother role. They both mean-mugged me like I owed them money, but I paid them no mind. Oddly enough, Victor had no money woes anyway. On the way to prom, Vanessa confirmed the rumors that Victor was selling drugs and that he was moving up the ladder very quickly; he had a little crew of three or four guys serving for him already. *What a cliché.*

/

JACK YOUR BODY

Our prom was at the ritzy Palmer House Hotel downtown. Turned out we weren't late after all. In fact, we were one of the few couples that were there on time. I guess everybody wanted to make a big flashy entrance. That never interested me. I didn't have to be the life of the party or the big wig in the room. Besides, that night wasn't about us guys anyway. The women clamored over one another talking about how pretty each of them looked and what a great dress they were wearing and blah, blah, blah.

There were professional photographers camped at the hotel entrances snapping shots of couples as they pranced in. There was another photographer set up at the far end of the lobby. Each couple had a choice of three different backgrounds to choose from for their picture.

One backdrop was of a bright-orange sunset with palm trees. The other was a kind of midnight-blue type of feel. It had moonlight and sandy beaches in front of an ocean for the background. The last one was just a regular set up using the hotel decor from the lobby, plastic plants on either side of a couch. I didn't see anybody pick that scenery.

At first, Vanessa wanted the sunset backdrop but then later decided that maybe the vibrant orange would clash with our purple, so we did the midnight sandy beach backdrop instead. After taking our couples picture which, thankfully, was already paid for in our fee, we loitered in the lobby a bit to watch people as they entered. We made small talk with a few other couples and checked out the different outfits that people were wearing. We acted as the fashion police, giving props for worthy attire and appropriately dogging others if they were wearing something whack.

When Kevin and Sharonda finally got there, we decided to go inside the ballroom to find our seats. My boy Clifton was part of the prom committee and he hooked it up so that all my crew and our dates could sit at the same table. Kevin quipped that he hoped Clifton put us close to the dance floor.

Vanessa and Sharonda went the to the ladies' room, while Kev and I browsed the huge ballroom for our table. We occasionally stopped to holler at various people we knew. Everybody found it necessary to introduce their dates around to show that they actually did have girl-friends or at the very least a date for that night.

After searching a little longer, Kevin found our table. Clifton came through like gangbusters. We were the center table about ten feet away from the dance floor. I thought to myself that was good because we didn't want to miss any of the action. Sitting close to the dance floor would increase our chances to see most of our friends and their dates.

When Kevin found our table, he waved me over to check out the name plates. I quickly dismissed myself from Derrick and his date. When I got there, I saw that we were table number four. The name place setting had me and Vanessa; Kevin and Sharonda; *Samuel* and his date, Tiffany, Sharonda's cousin. Someone had drawn a line through "Samuel" and handwrote, "Box." It was probably Clifton. And the last two places were for *Antwan* and his mystery guest.

Kevin wanted to get rid of Squirt's name plate and have Derrick or Quan come over to our table, but I was able to talk him out of it. All we needed was Squirt to show up late and start beefing because we removed his nameplate.

Although, I did wonder if Squirt was even going to show up to prom. The Special Olympics track meet was a few weeks ago and Squirt and I hadn't said one word to each other since. Matter of fact, we hadn't seen him around school much.

I went to his house the other day to bury the hatchet and return his track jacket, but he wasn't home. I ended up giving Squirt's jacket to his mom, but she couldn't find mine in that pigpen Squirt calls a bedroom. I know that Box tried to talk with him a couple days after the Special Olympics, but he said Squirt just blew him off.

I tried to forget about it. If Squirt showed up to prom, he showed up. If he didn't, he didn't. I wasn't about to sit up and think about him all night when I was with the finest girl in the building. It was prom night and I wanted to have a good time, a great time.

The girls finally returned from the restroom and Box showed up with Tiffany a few minutes later. The night was going well. Surprisingly, the food turned out to be excellent. We all joked that the meal was actually good enough to be forty dollars a plate. We had an appetizer of salad and rolls. The entrée included the choice of some tender, juicy slices of roast beef or chicken penne, with garlic mashed potatoes or rice pilaf and steamed green beans or broccoli. Dessert consisted of an assortment of pies: lemon meringue, French silk, apple, blueberry, and of course, sweet potato. Clifton probably had something to do with that as well.

The faculty had just finished crowning the prom king and queen and introducing the rest of the prom court. None of us won any such distinctions but we didn't care. Although, I think Sharonda wanted some of that limelight. She kept asking Kevin why he didn't get nominated for prom king.

Now that all the boring speeches and other official activities were over, it was time to get our boogie on. Mendel's dances were legendary for being a guaranteed good time. Nobody ever wanted to miss a Mendel set. Jocks were always in attendance, hip-hop heads were definitely in the house, fly guys and fly girls never left the dance floor, even the nerds made their appearance to hold up the walls or sit in the bleachers. Whenever there was a Mendel party, rowdy teens, and occasionally, one or two early twentysomethings, faithfully congregated at 250 East 111th Street to dance until they were sweaty messes. Nothing mattered but the music.

Although, there were many kinds of music that could describe the culture at Mendel, there was only one that dominated, house music. Sure, we loved hip-hop and anything by James Brown, but house music was the heartbeat of Mendel, and everyone in the entire city knew it.

There were three or four guys that regularly deejayed the house parties at Mendel. But Jermaine was the coldest of them all. He was what we called "deep house." He wore the baggie pants, the shiny black patent leather shoes, and rocked the high-top fade. House music was pretty much his life. He ate, slept, and breathed house music, and it showed in his deejay performance.

The Palmer House deejay turned up the sounds. The records played were a beacon to our ears drawing us deeper into the *House*. We decided that it was time to join our brothers and sisters in the sweatbox, allowing our bodies to become slaves to the rhythm within. We had no idea where the prom committee hired the deejay from, but he was fresh. I mean, he was doper than Jermaine. He was mixing and cross-fading all the latest jams and even throwing in some oldies.

The dance floor was so packed there was barely room to groove. We were all having a great time. After about a half hour of dancing, Kev and Box took a break and sat back down at the table. But I was full of energy that night. I just kept dancing with Vanessa, Sharonda, and Tiffany without them. It wasn't uncommon for groups of people to dance together as opposed to just the traditional boy-girl combo. It was all about having a good time with your friends. And the way I felt, I planned on dancing the entire night.

At least that was my plan until Clifton tapped me on the shoulder. He leaned in close, so I could hear him over the thumping bass. He told me Squirt was asking for me, and that he was in the lobby arguing with the hotel manager and a few of the chaperones. *What now?* I thought, I told Clifton that I would be right there.

I didn't want to alarm Vanessa, so I told her that I was going to the restroom. I kissed her on the cheek and slid through the crowd. I didn't tell Kevin or Box either because I didn't know how they'd react, especially Kevin.

/

IN TOO DEEP

When I got to the lobby, sure enough, Squirt, all five foot two inches of him was in the face of the hotel manager and my homeroom teacher, Mr. Perez. Immediately, I knew something was off. Squirt was dressed in jeans, a T-shirt, gym shoes, and his Mendel track jacket that I gave to his mother. I said to myself, *Something just ain't right.*

I hurried over and asked what was going on.

"Good, BJ, would you tell these simps that I paid for prom."

"Yeah, Mr. Perez, Antwan paid. Matter of fact, his nameplate is at our table inside the ballroom."

"I've explained to him that's not the issue, BJ," Mr. Perez began. "Mr. Benson's. . .status at Mendel is in question. Therefore, he is not allowed to participate in any Mendel functions, and unfortunately that means prom. We'll kindly refund his money."

"Dog, you're suspended?"

"Man, I am a student, I just missed a few weeks because I was sick. All I gotta do is serve a Saturday JUG and I'm straight."

Wow! I knew we hadn't seen Squirt around, but I had no clue it was because he was suspended.

"If I'm suspended, why didn't I get anything in the mail? That's cuz my mama smoothed everything out with Principal Cooper already."

"Look, I never received any such message from Principal Cooper, so I'm sorry Mr. Benson, I cannot let you into prom."

Mr. Perez turned to the hotel manager, "If he causes any more problems call 911 and have him escorted off the premises."

I knew once Squirt heard that he would be tempted to act out, so I swiftly pulled him aside to try to calm him down. I told the hotel manager that we would just talk quietly in the lobby. Mr. Perez and the manager agreed that was OK and left me alone with my seething partner.

As I spoke with Squirt off to the side, I noticed something was amiss. My intentions were to calm him down, but strangely he didn't seem agitated anymore. He seemed nervous. I mean, like, *really* nervous.

"Dude, what's going on with you?" I asked.

"What?"

"C'mon, dog. We both know you're not here for prom. You're in jeans and your track jacket and you don't even have a date. Squirt, what's up? Talk to me, dog."

Squirt sighed as if he had the weight of the world on his shoulders. He looked around nervously, then carefully showed me a gun in his waistband.

"Dog, what you got that for?"

"I'm in big trouble man. If I don't pay this guy his money. . .I think he's gonna kill me."

"Who?"

"I can't tell you who he is."

"Squirt, listen to me, man. Whatever you're planning to do, don't do it."

"Then help me get the money for the stuff your old man threw away. It's your fault I'm even in this mess."

I hesitated, I thought maybe I could talk him out of the stick-up-kid mess, but now, I see he's too entrenched. If I refused to help him, I knew he would go out there and rob someone. What's worse, now he has a gun.

"Listen, my old man would know what to do. We're having a barbecue tomorrow."

"A barbecue?"

"Come over tomorrow. Let's talk to him; see what he says."

He scoffed at the idea as he turned to walk away.

"Squirt!" I reached out grabbing his arm.

He yanked away from me and pushed his way through the revolving doors.

Just then Kevin came up behind me, "Yo, Vanessa sent me out here to look for you. I hope that wasn't Squirt you were talking to."

I nodded.

"What he want?"

"Nothing. Let's get back inside."

Kevin and I returned to the ballroom to our dates. But my thoughts were haunted, wondering if that was the last time I'd see Squirt alive.

CHAPTER 19

BACKYARD BARBECUE

/

After Little Jay got killed, Mr. James said that he was going public with his men's group. He said things had to change in the hood so there would be no more secret meetings. Unbeknownst to me, Mr. James had already been talking to several prominent hardworking men and women from the community about what ideas they might have to change and improve Roseland.

He invited all of them for a barbecue mainly to allow these fabulous people to meet one another and discuss ideas. Mr. James knew that for any of his groups to have long term success, he would eventually need community support.

So for the entire day, our backyard became grand central station funneling teems of people in and out for the free barbecue. It seemed as if Keko invited the entire neighborhood. There were a few people I hadn't seen before but some I did recognize. There were several community leaders, aldermen, councilmen, church leaders, not to mention several active and ex-gangbangers. Even a contingency of the Chicago PD came through to show support and grab a plate of free food.

Keko took care of all the meat, while Auntie Emma whipped up baked beans, potato salad, and spaghetti. Vanessa was there making herself useful helping Auntie Emma organize food on the long picnic table.

People were eating, mingling, laughing—having a great time. We stayed in the backyard so long that the sun began going down. But that didn't stop the party. Keko turned on the floodlight in the yard and he continued to grill. He had burgers, ribs, and hot links smoking up the backyard, cooking well into the evening.

It was a beautiful evening. Monica and Leslie, one of the shorties from the MIT group, ran around the backyard playing tag with a few other neighborhood kids. Mr. James held many conversations with people from his group along with their wives and girlfriends over by the grill. I had some of the guys and girls from my school show up too. They blended right in mingling with Keko's guests.

Time passed, and there were less people remaining at the all-day party. Auntie Emma had me bring out a few card tables so people could play spades and bid whist. Then, Mr. James pulled out a speaker from the basement and played his James Brown collection. That's when the barbecue turned into a steppers set.

Vanessa and I sat on the back steps watching all the old-timers step to James Brown.

"Should we show these old folks how it's done?" I asked Vanessa.

"Oh let's," she replied grabbing my hand.

As we joined the action, dancing on the concrete patio in my parent's backyard, a flood of memories hit me. I suddenly remembered the backyard cookouts that Mama and Keko used to have back in the day before Monica was even born. They would have friends over and dance the night away to James Brown, The Temptations, Smokey, Aretha, and other R&B greats.

I looked over at Keko and Auntie Emma cutting a rug. I had forgotten that Mr. James knew how to step so well. Monica ran out and joined Auntie Emma and Mr. James. He picked her up into his arms and twirled her around as he stepped. It reminded me of how my mother used to scoop me up into her arms and dance with me.

The entire day was surreal—to see rival gang members dancing in my backyard laughing and eating together, along with police, blue-collar moms and dads, local church leaders, and city officials. . .everyone having a great time. People came and went throughout the day and night and there wasn't a hint of violence.

I didn't want the night to end. And I could tell, neither did Mr. James. I watched as he and Auntie Emma stood off to the side, arm in arm looking at the peaceful gathering in our yard.

The floodlight continued to illuminate. Now, even less people were in the yard as James Brown crooned softly. I took a swig from my Pepsi when I noticed Mr. James staring at me.

"What?" I asked, almost spilling on myself.

"I'm proud of you, son," Mr. James began. "Maintaining your grades while being a student-athlete, still on time to graduate in a week. And Vanessa? She's a great girl. Kathy would be proud."

"Thanks."

"Listen, the ground is soft enough now. Why don't we have your mother's headstone put in, just me and you? We can bring the girls up later."

"Yeah, I'd like that."

Keko and I dapped and hugged it out. I walked over and joined Vanessa sitting on the steps. As I approached, she wore the cheesiest smile ever.

"No, no, no Vee. Van, stop it."

"Awww, that was so adorable," Vanessa cooed.

"What's adorable?" Monica asked as she bumbled down the steps sitting between me and Vanessa.

"Your dad and BJ just hugged."

Monica giggled then thankfully brought the attention to herself, where she felt it always should be.

"Vanessa, guess what?"

"What's that, love?"

"We're going to Santa's Village."

"Really? Wow, I'm so jealous. I wish I was going to Santa's Village."

Spud giggled uncontrollably again. Auntie Emma came to the edge of the steps hovering over us.

"Little girl, time for bed. Let's hit it."

"Nooo, I wanna stay up with Vanessa and BJ."

"Monica, I could read you a bedtime story. Would you like that?" asked Vanessa.

Without saying a word, Monica snatched Vanessa by the arm, yanking her up the stairs. Vanessa stuck her head out the door, "Hey, when I'm done, can we read more of your mom's journals?"

"Sure," I said.

Vanessa left, and I headed upstairs to the dark quiet place. But before going to the attic, I turned around once more to watch Keko, impacting lives. He was holding conversation with two rival gang members and their significant others. Mr. James was speaking to them about how these two young Black men had more in common than they had differences.

"We can't keep killing each other just because we live a few miles in the opposite direction," he told them. I never understood how or why Mr. James commanded so much respect, but the guys were listening intently, nodding their heads in the affirmative as Keko spoke truth and life into them.

Mrs. Morales told me once that I needed a plan for my life. I knew my short-term plan was to get into college. Yet as I watched Keko, my dad, in that backyard, I finally knew what my long-term plan would be, to impact lives just like him.

/

THE SECRET'S OUT

I hurried inside to prep the usual "library" setup: chairs, lamp, diaries. I remembered to grab the more recent journal so Vanessa wouldn't know I'd been reading without her. As I waited patiently, I allowed my mind to drift.

Soon would be the anniversary of my mom's passing. I never thought I could make it to this milestone without a nervous breakdown. *Maybe God was looking out for me all along.* I mean, I adjusted to life without Mom, finally had the workings of a great relationship with my father, and survived Squirt's attempts to involve me in his constant drama, and semi-avoided beef with Victor and David. I also had an awesome girlfriend and would be graduating in one week. The only thing missing was confirmation from Coach on if his buddies found an available scholarship.

The creaking stairs alerted me of my welcomed guest. Vanessa ambled diagonally across the floor like she'd just been in a fight and lost.

"Whew, your baby sister is—"

"Exhausting," I completed the sentence for her.

"Yes, Lord," Vanessa chuckled, agreeing. "I finished one story, and then she wanted another one and another one. And she asks so many questions. That girl's gonna be a lawyer."

Vanessa sat down next to me and promptly took my hand.

"Why'd you have that look on your face when I came in?"

"What look?" I asked.

"I don't know, like. . .peaceful."

I smiled brightly, "I am."

"Hmm, tell me more."

"Just the nostalgia of tonight. The barbecue, the music, all the laughter, it reminds me what this house was like when Mom was alive. And it kind of felt like she was here."

Vanessa held my hand to her cheek briefly, then kissed it.

"So where did we leave off?" She grabbed the journal from my other hand. She flipped the pages and stopped and began to read.

May 4, 1985

Dear Lord,

I wonder if I should tell BJ that Keko will be getting out soon. Maybe, I'll just tell him after my surgery. I'm glad that Keko has been around from the beginning. At least BJ has some good memories.

Vanessa paused slightly to turn the page and to clear her throat.

"Excuse me."

May 20, 1985

Dear Lord,

BJ's father sent flowers to the hospital—

"Aww, that's so sweet," Vanessa interjected.

I gave her a playful glare.

"OK, sorry, sorry."

> *I told the nurse to throw the flowers away. If Keko knew BJ's father sent me flowers, Keko would...*

Vanessa hesitated. She looked up at me, confused. But I was more confused than she was. I rudely snatched the journal away from her and read.

> *If Keko knew BJ's father sent me flowers, Keko would explode.*

I lowered the diary. I wanted to keep reading but there was no more. The mystery stopped there. It just ended. That was it. Mom didn't write anymore. And from the looks of it, that was the last entry. The rest of the journal pages were blank, all the way to the back cover.

I threw the journal aside and dashed over to the grocery bag. Vanessa's face filled with horror as she watched me ransack the bag. I grabbed several of the previous journals, ripping frantically through them looking for answers, but I knew from the dates, that was the most recent entry, the last entry before her surgery. *Deg! Vanessa was right. I should have begun from the most recent journals.*

"You...you were adopted?" Vanessa asked gently. "And nobody told you? You didn't know?"

I looked over at my girlfriend who was on the verge of tears. Steadily her tender face disappeared behind my clouded thoughts. I was beyond seeing red; I saw burgundy. *Were Mr. James and Auntie Emma ever going to tell me? Were they going to carry this secret with them to their graves like my mother did?*

I threw down the notebook of lies and darted toward the attic door.

Vanessa in hot pursuit. She called after me as we rumbled down the back-porch steps.

"BJ try to calm down first."

Later for calming down. In my mind, they had no excuse for keeping something that important from me.

I leaned out of the second-floor window to see if Mr. James was still in the backyard playing Gandhi. He wasn't. I kept going down the steps until I reached the first floor.

/

WHO AM I

I busted through the kitchen back door. Mr. James was just coming out of the bathroom. He had on his CTA uniform. Vanessa stumbled in seconds later.

"I was just about to come upstairs to grab you two. I got called in to do the night shift. Monica's already asleep. Vanessa, you wanna ride home?"

"No, no thank you. BJ, I'm gonna go."

I shook my head, "No." I didn't take my eyes off *Mr. James.*

"Something the matter?" he inquired.

"Funny you should ask."

"BJ?" Vanessa cautioned with her tone.

"Anything special about my birth I should know? Anything at all?"

"Son," Mr. James laughed uncomfortably, "I'd love to sit down and share details of your birth but I'm on my way to work. Vanessa, sure you don't need a ride?"

"Yes, I'm positive, Mr. James. Thank you."

"OK, I see you're in a rush, I'll make it quick. Who did I look like when I was born?"

"Who did you look like?" he asked confused.

"Yeah, ya know, did y'all say 'aww, he looks just like Kathy'? Or did someone say, 'aww, he looks like his real daddy'?"

Mr. James looked as if he saw Mama's ghost at the stove cooking grits. Seventeen years of lies unraveled in a matter of minutes.

"BJ, son. . .I uh—"

"Apparently, I'm *not* your son! Man, y'all lied to me my entire life!"

I rushed over to dear old Dad and rammed him into the kitchen wall as hard as I could. I tried to split the back of his head on the wall tiles. But just like the rest of my life had always gone wrong, Monica came running out of her room.

"BJ, what are you doing to Daddy?"

"We don't know if he's your daddy!"

I meant it, but I *didn't* mean it. Instantly, Monica turned into a weepy mess.

"What, why did BJ say that?" she frantically asked Vanessa.

"Get her outta here!" I yelled at Vanessa.

"I'm trying!" Van yelled back. "Shush, Monica, it's OK; it's all right."

I shot Vanessa a look. It was not all right. I didn't know if it would ever be all right again.

She picked Monica up, but Spud wasn't having it. Monica flailed and kicked her in the shin until Vanessa placed her back on the floor. Monica darted out the back door.

"Go after her!" I screamed.

"No, you need to calm down," Vanessa fired back.

Vanessa pulled me away from Mr. James. She plopped me into one of the kitchen chairs and sat on my lap.

"OK, fine. I'm cool; I'm cool. C'mon *big, bad Keko*. Tell me the truth, 'Mr. Reformed Christian Man.' I'm listening."

Mr. James took a deep breath, "Yes, it's true."

All the breath left me. Even though I read it in my own mother's journal, deep inside I didn't want it to be true.

"I did adopt you. BJ, how did you find out?"

"I'm doing the questioning."

"You don't want to tell me? Fine. I'm going to work. Bye, Vanessa."

Mr. James picked up his car keys from the kitchen table and walked toward the front door.

What? It wasn't supposed to be happening like this. He was supposed to be on his hands and knees groveling for my forgiveness, not walking away like he and my mother hadn't done anything wrong. I snapped. I pushed Vanessa aside and went after him. I caught up to him in the dining room and tackled him.

We flew across the dining room table onto the floor.

"BJ, stop," Vanessa pleaded.

I tried to hold him steady, so I could get in a good *pop*. But he was just too strong. Mr. James stood up with little effort at all. I might as well have been a twin-sized bed sheet on the back of a brontosaurus on a windy day. I slid right off him as soon as he stood.

I threw some combinations at him, jabs, crosses, hooks. Mr. James barely noticed, evading the punches easily.

"Good. Good series of combos," he nodded in approval. "You still telegraphing a little bit though."

His boxing advice infuriated me. I charged him again. Mr. James lifted me into the air and pinned me on the dining room table.

Just then, Monica stormed into the room with Auntie Emma, "Keko, no!"

Keko backed away, "I'm not gonna hurt him."

"What's going on in here!? Monica, go to your room!" Auntie Emma spouted.

Spud promptly obeyed, shutting the door behind her.

Keko turned and continued to the front door. But I wasn't done yet. I chased him down again, but Vanessa tackled me onto our movie sofa and sat on top of me again.

"Would somebody please tell me what the hell is going on?" Auntie Emma screamed. "Heck, I meant *heck* is going on. Oops, sorry, Lord," she said looking up at the ceiling like the sky was gonna fall because she cursed.

"Nah, it's cool. You know what? You can go to the cemetery by yourself, dog. I want nothing to do with her or you."

"BJ?" Auntie Emma exclaimed.

"OK, I'll have the headstone done after my shift. I know what you're trying to do, BJ. It's not gonna work. Love you, son. I'll see you when I get back from work."

Mr. James exited, gently closing the door behind him.

"Keko! Ke. . .Brandon, what's going on?"

"I'll tell you, Auntie. Yo, babe, let me up."

Vanessa reluctantly slid off my lap and sat next to me. I sat on the edge of the sofa, leaning forward, glaring with cruel intentions at, in my mind, one of the coconspirators of my ruined life.

"Why hadn't y'all told me I'm adopted? That's what's going on."

"Oh Lord. How did you find that out?"

"Never mind how I found out!" I snapped.

"Boy, you may be adopted but I will still slap the taste out yo mouth. You hear me?"

"You're right, Auntie. You're not the one I should be talking to."

I grabbed Vanessa by the hand and headed for the front door.

"Where you think you're going?" Auntie Emma asked.

"To find my real daddy. C'mon, babe."

I pulled Vanessa to the front door, but she yanked back in protest. "BJ, stop. Stop!"

"Wait a minute," Auntie Emma said confused. "Keko done already dealt with him. Why are you looking for that man?"

"Why wouldn't I look for him? I want a relationship with my real father."

"Why on earth would you want a relationship with the man that raped your mother?"

I had no words. Vanessa spoke, but it was more of an autistic parroting, "Oh my gosh. . .Oh my gosh. . .Oh my gosh. . ." She sank slowly into the recliner beside the front door.

My knees were as stable as wet spaghetti noodles. I slinked over to the sofa again to sit before I collapsed. The reality of what was said began to echo through my mind.

"My, my mother was. . .ra. . .raped."

"Hold on. Wait a minute, honey? I thought you kn—"

"Oh my gosh. . .Oh my—"

"Vanessa! Shut up!" Auntie Emma barked.

Vanessa covered her mouth with both hands. Auntie Emma rushed over and joined me on the sofa. She took a calming breath before inquiring, "BJ, sweetheart, if Keko didn't tell you, how did you—"

"Upstairs. . .we, I found Mom's journals. And we—"

"You all found Kathy's diary? In the attic? And she wrote about what happened?"

Instantly, I could see the journal pages in my mind. The word "incident" jumps off the page now. I had guessed right. *I* was the incident but not in the way I had imagined. Then like a bad nightmare, flashes of my mother's horrific ordeal filled my mind. Depictions of her screaming, hitting, fighting, clawing.

Heat rushed into my cheeks. I flopped on the couch wailing, kicking, punching the air. I turned and buried my face in the sofa cushion hollering as loud as I could until my throat burned. I felt so sorry for my mother. I also felt sorry for me.

My whole life had been a hideous lie. *If I wasn't "Brandon James Jr.," who was I?* This deep family secret of my identity tore at my very being. And I felt incredibly guilty that my prideful, self-absorption robbed me from properly mourning the tragedy that happened to my dear mother. It wounded me to the soul as if she had died all over again. Yet my family's betrayal was a refrigerator magnet clinging to my heart. I felt like all the classic characters we read about in literature class: Julius Caesar and Brutus; Othello and Iago; even Jesus and Judas—all back stabbed by people they loved and trusted.

Even my name was the height of deception. How could I be "Brandon James Jr." when I had no biological ties to the man whatsoever? I finally got ahold of myself and sat up again. Vanessa came and sat on the other side, sandwiching me with Auntie Emma.

As she gently rubbed my back, I suddenly remembered something.

I looked at the woman whom I'd called "Auntie" my entire life sitting next to me. I wiped the remaining tears from my eyes and asked her, "What did you mean Keko already dealt with him?"

/

THE INCIDENT

Auntie Emma exhaled as she got up and paced the floor. It was time that I knew the truth about my birth. It had been a long time since Auntie Emma had told me a story about the olden days when she and Mr. James were part of the Gangster Disciples in their early adulthood. Yet the story she was about to tell was weightier than any other, this was my life.

Auntie Emma began to speak, slowly and purposefully, she sat on the edge of Mr. James' recliner. I had almost forgotten the crazed look she would get on her face, like the memories of those times were dragging her back into a terrible nightmare.

Vanessa gripped my hand bracing herself for the most death-defying roller-coaster ride. Rightfully so, Auntie Emma's stories about the past could get graphic. Auntie Emma told us a little background of the time when the "incident" occurred.

She stated that the rivalry between the Folk Nation and the People Nation was reaching an apex because of the brutality of one man, Mr. James. From the beginning, Keko was a well-known enforcer. He had a reputation of being able to outbox anyone in a fight. It was because of their reputation of being all-out brawlers that he and Lights-Out both moved up the gang ranks so rapidly.

Auntie Emma stated that one day Mr. James got jumped by three Vice Lords as he was taking a shortcut home through an alley. Although he was outnumbered, Mr. James beat them so badly they each had to go to the hospital. Auntie Emma said she always felt this prompted the revenge attack on my mother.

"The day of the incident. . .the rape," Auntie Emma explained, "Kathy walked to a local corner store. She saw a Vice Lord named Skip there, but she wasn't too worried. Ya see, Skip and your mother grew up together. They knew each other way before either one was in the gang life. Anyway, when Kathy left the store, Skip was outside waiting on her and attacked her from behind. He dragged her into a nearby alley. After. . .it was done, Kathy ran home and told me and Keko right away."

"What did y'all do?" Vanessa asked.

"Like we always did back then, retaliate. Keko and I hopped in the car and went looking for him. We hit every spot we could think of, nothing. Then, on our way back home, we finally spotted a group of about seven of them hanging out on a street corner and Skip was with them."

"What happened?" Vanessa eagerly asked again.

"I slammed on the brakes. We both hopped out and started spraying. Once they heard the first shot, everybody scattered. I dropped two of them on the spot, *boom-boom*. Keko shot another. Skip took off down an alley. We chased him, cornered him. He knew why we were there."

Suddenly, Auntie Emma went silent, gazing off into the distance. I knew she was back in that alley. Her face began to twitch, her eyes saddened, she swallowed, then continued.

"We had Skip at gunpoint. He dropped to his knees and started begging. I mean, he *begged* for his life. I remember thinking something was wrong because Keko hadn't fired yet. Keko *never* hesitated.

"I looked over at him. And his hand was shaking, like he was trying to pull the trigger but forgot how. This made me nervous because we were sitting ducks. The guys that escaped earlier could've been strapping up and on their way back. I told myself, 'I have to do this.' So I stepped to Skip, but Keko waved me off, 'No. I got this.'

"I moved back. Keko walked over to Skip, told him to stand up. Skip did. Keko said, 'Shooting you is too easy.' He turned and gave me his gun, 'I'ma beat you down with my bare hands.' But when Keko turned back to face Skip, he had his gun pointed right at my brother's forehead."

Auntie Emma stood, acting out the rest of the story.

"I circled to the side of Skip, screaming for him to put his gun down. Ooh, I promise I was this close to blasting him. I had my gat pointed right at his temple. I told him again, 'Let him go Skip or I'ma drop you.' Then out of nowhere, police sirens.

"Skip looked back and forth between us. I still had a bead on him. I was just waiting for him to lower his pistol. He finally took a step back and said, 'They made me do it. Tell Kathy I'm sorry.' He lowered his gun then he took off running. Just as I was about to pop that fool,

Keko grabbed me, told me we had to get out of there. So we started running back to the car. I looked back down the alley and saw Skip scaling a fence. That was the last time we saw him until you and Keko bumped into him at the store."

So that's why the attack happened. I lowered my head instantly remembering the encounter that seemed a bit hazy so many years ago. I had convinced myself all these years I was blinded by the sunlight glaring off the door because I didn't want to believe my eyes. I didn't want to believe my dad was so ruthless to beat someone into a bloody pulp over, what I thought was an accidental bump to the shoulder. I mean he beat that man until his hands were swollen and heavy. Bystanders tried, but no one could stop him. I couldn't even watch the whole thing.

"That body slam ended up paralyzing Skip," Auntie Emma added, sitting back down on the recliner. "That's why Keko was gone for so long. That and some added time for fighting while in jail."

"Really? Paralyzed?" Vanessa questioned, shocked.

"Yep, he's a paraplegic now. Lives somewhere in Iowa, I hear."

"Wow, this is unreal," Vanessa exclaimed.

"Baby, you were too traumatized to give any details about it then," Auntie Em began. "And Keko's never said a word. I mean, I guess he didn't have to. I know why he did what he did. But I've always wondered, did they say anything to each other?"

I exhaled sharply.

"It all happened so fast. Um, I remember this Skip guy held the door for me, so I went out first. Then, I heard Skip say, 'my bad.' That's why I thought they bumped shoulders passing by one another. When I turned around, they were already squared off, eyes locked, and. . ."

I hesitated. My breath became shallow. After all these years I never remembered Keko saying a word. I just recollected Keko grabbing the guy, throwing him to the ground then beating the crap out of him.

"What did Keko say?" Vanessa asked.

"He said, '*You?*'"

Like a person recognizing someone after nine long years. Like a man who's dreamed of vengeance every single day because of the rape of his woman. *You*, like a man who's waited patiently to get his hands on his ultimate foe.

"*Hmm*," Auntie Emma grunted, scooting back in her chair.

"What is it?" I asked.

"BJ, baby, Skip didn't say 'my bad' because they bumped shoulders. He was apologizing about Kathy."

It was hard to process everything my auntie had told us. The entire night was absolutely draining. We all sat there quietly until I asked Auntie Emma if she wouldn't mind making Vanessa and I some Hot Chocolate.

She smiled softly. "Sure."

While Auntie was walking to the kitchen, I asked Vanessa a small favor as well.

"Babe, could you peek in on Monica for me. I wanna make sure she was asleep and not ear-hustling this whole time."

"Of course, babe. I should probably call my mom, too, so she'll know where I am."

"Yeah, yeah, use the phone in the kitchen."

Before checking on Monica, Vanessa gave me a hug and a kiss.

I waited until both Vanessa and Auntie Emma were out of sight, then I tiptoed to the front door. I didn't know where I was going. I just knew I had to be alone for a while. I snuck out gently closing the door behind me.

CHAPTER 20

A LISTENING EAR

/

My mind was an empty slate of nothingness. After leaving the house, I walked aimlessly around the South Side for hours, which was not the smartest thing to do in the middle of the night. But after the news I received earlier, I didn't care if somebody came up behind me with a gun and smoked *me*. I wouldn't have felt a thing. My body was completely numb.

Eventually, I found myself riding on a bus. I think there were maybe three or four other people on it. I don't remember how many were male or female, their faces were complete blobs to me. I got off the bus at the Ninety-Fifth Street terminal. Instinctively, I got onto the L and just rode.

After riding for a while, I finally figured out where my subconscious was actively leading me. As the 'L' train pulled to a stop on Sixty-Third, I became keenly aware that I had to snap out of my inattentive state. Englewood was the one neighborhood in Chicago that rivaled Roseland for its heightened crime, dangerousness, and all-around toughness. There were probably ninety-year-old grandmas that would slap spit from a kid's mouth for back talking in Englewood.

I hopped off the L and went up the stairs to the street level. I hung a quick left heading east. I decided to walk instead of grabbing another bus. I knew it was risky, but I was hoping that I would be OK. My goal was to get in and out without being mugged. For some reason, guys can tell when someone isn't from their hood.

There were several project buildings in the area that me and my friends had heard about but didn't know too many people who lived there. Box had a cousin who lived in "the Wood" and that's how I knew the little that I did about the neighborhood. In Chicago, the projects were notorious for having a bad rep, like black holes—meaning you may be able to get in, but you might not come out. Box's cousin always warned us to never come there without him. Rumors of hardcore violence were always associated with the housing projects which kept the lore of terror alive and outsiders away.

So for me to go to Englewood in the middle of the night to talk with Coach showed how desperate I truly was.

I stood at the Vista Garden security double doors, browsing for Coach's name. Found it. I rang the bell like a madman.

An angry, sleepy voice blared over the speaker.

"Do you know what time it is?"

"Coach, it's me, BJ. I need to talk to you."

"BJ, what are you. . ."

The buzzer sounded. I flung the door open and went inside.

I wasted no time verbally exploding all over Coach when he let me inside his place. I gave him the rundown of the last several hours. After gathering his composure, he apologized for all the horrible things that happened to me, then out of the blue, gave me a hug.

I couldn't help but break down into a slobbering mess once the weight of it hit me again. Not to mention the fact that I finally had someone besides Vanessa to sympathize with me. His acknowledgement and apology for what I had gone through meant more to me than he would ever know.

We talked for several hours about my mother, Mr. James, and Auntie Emma's role in keeping the secret from me. As usual, Coach was instrumental in getting me to see things from the family's angle and the delicacy of the situation. We spoke for so long and I was so exhausted, I ended up falling asleep on Coach's sofa. I drifted in and out of sleep throughout the rest of the night. Each time I woke, I'd be a little startled by the unfamiliar surroundings of Coach's apartment. I noticed that he had even put a blanket over me. I curled up in the blanket and went back to sleep.

The next morning I was awakened by the glimmering light of sunshine glaring through Coach's living room window. I sat up on the edge of the couch. I could hear Coach in the shower getting ready for work. Fortunately, the seniors were all done with classes for the rest of the week. I just had to show up at the end of each school day for practices for our final meet, the Outdoor Catholic League Championship which was Saturday, and then graduation, Sunday.

As I sat, waiting for Coach to come out of the bathroom, I began to process the things he and I discussed. Although my life was a shambles, I was still alive to live it, thanks to the sacrifice of two people. Just then enormous gratitude warmed my heart. It no longer mattered to me that my life was a lie. It no longer mattered to me that they didn't tell me the whole sordid story before. It only mattered that I was alive. *I was alive.* And I was by all accounts, remarkably, unconditionally, loved.

In that moment, I knew what I had to do. I folded Coach Abrams' comforter and placed it neatly on his sofa. I grabbed my shoes and snuck out the door. Over that school year, I depended on Coach a lot for advice. Yet his most valued asset to me that night was just listening.

/

MY HERO

I hopped off the bus at 127th Street at Burr Oak Cemetery. I scaled the gate and began the task of trying to locate my mother's burial plot. I was a little disoriented as to the exact spot. I hadn't been there since the funeral. Maybe it was guilt that kept me away for so long. One thing for certain, it would be way easier to find the plot if Keko were standing next to it as the groundskeepers put in the tombstone. I was sure Keko kept his word. So all I had to do was find him.

As I approached the general area of where I thought her gravesite might be, my eyes scanned all the different plots. Reading the various names etched into stone, I allowed my mind to wonder what type of people they were, jobs they had, impact they left, and if they knew God before they died. I felt it was tragic that most people only thought of God when somebody died or was about to die. I understood I used to be one of those people. Yet in the last month and a half or so since accepting God in my life, I thought of Him often. I had only read the Book of John, but I was so curious now and couldn't wait to know more.

I spotted a huge gray tombstone to my left and wondered, *Could it be?* I didn't see Keko or any of the grounds crew, but the freshly disturbed earth gave me confidence that I could be in the right spot. I walked with purpose eager to see if it were true. When I came around the front of the stone a shudder went through my body. I was extremely glad Keko didn't let my foolishness keep him from planting Mom's gravestone.

The cold slab of rock looked back at me. It had lost its dazzle from when I last saw it under our Christmas tree lights. At that moment, I remembered gray was Mama's favorite color. I didn't know why. *Who in the world likes gray?* I chuckled to myself. Mom would also be proud to know that we buried her in the same cemetery as Emmett Till.

A flood of emotions attacked me as I allowed my eyes to dance across my mother's name, Kathryn Jean James. I ran my fingertips up the side of the stone, then across the top, and down the front, careful to outline each letter of her first, middle, and last name.

"Hey, Ma. I know. . .I know what happened to you. Thank you for wanting me."

I couldn't hold the tears any longer. I clutched and kissed Mom's tombstone over and over again. Sliding down to the grass, I melted, holding onto her stone for dear life.

When I grew tired of hugging the cold stone, I turned around and leaned against "Mom" in the somberness of the cemetery allowing its quiet presence to soothe me. I closed my eyes noticing the tender wind across my nose. Chills went down my spine. It had to be my mother's fingertips comforting me one last time. I smiled and listened to the wind as I thought of my own life in light of how my parents lived theirs.

My mom kept me despite certain ridicule and a twenty-four-hour-a-day reminder of her brutal attack from someone she thought was a friend. She loved me with all she had. Never once did I feel unwanted or unloved. Sometimes I felt she loved me too hard. I'm sure she feared Keko would leave her. But he didn't, instead he placed a ring on her finger, gave me his name, and raised me as his own.

My *real* dad, Brandon "Keko" James Sr., showed me every day what it looked like to be a man. Not only me but so many other guys from our hood too. The last thing I remember thinking before falling asleep against Mom's tombstone was, *God is so wonderful.* It was only while sitting in a graveyard that I finally understood true love is *sacrificial.*

/

SQUIRT STRIKES AGAIN

It was eerily quiet when I returned home. I put my keys in my pocket and strolled into the kitchen. *Did they vow to move if I ever found out the family secret?* After spending several hours at the cemetery having a heart-to-heart with Mom, I needed to make things right with Keko again and tell him I was sorry for the way I acted and that I forgave him and understood why he wasn't in my life when I was younger.

Since no one was home, I figured I'd fix myself something to eat, that's when I saw Auntie Emma's note on the fridge.

> *Hey Baby,*
>
> *We're gone to take this girl and her little friend to Santa's Village. There's food in the oven. Have fun at practice. Love you.*
>
> *Auntie Em*

Ahh, practice! I had totally forgotten. I checked the time and dashed to my room to change into my practice gear. I got dressed in record time and as I was leaving, the phone rang. I picked up the receiver and heard crying.

"Van. . .Vanessa, baby slow down. I can't understand you."

Vanessa cleared her throat, attempting to calm herself, she began again, "I said my mother was mugged. I think it was Squirt."

"Are you sure?"

"No, not one-hundred percent, but the person was wearing a Mendel track jacket. Who else could it be?"

"OK, baby, um—"

"She was able to tear it off him. Victor and Bruce were just here. She said they took the jacket and ran out of the hospital."

Vanessa began crying again and I couldn't understand a word. I cut her off several times, explaining I was on my way. As soon as I hung up, I picked up the receiver to call Kevin and Box. As I was dialing, I remembered again, *practice*. Shoot, by now they're already at school.

I rumbled out the front door, down the steps and sprinted as fast as I could. There was an uneasy tug in my heart. If it was Squirt, and likely it was, I still couldn't let him get beatdown by Victor and his crew.

When I made it to Roseland Community Hospital, I zoomed down the hall and out of the corner of my eye I saw Vanessa sleeping in the family and visitors lounge.

"Babe, Vee. It's me," I said, gently shaking her awake.

Vanessa wiped her eyes, stretched, and sat up.

"How is she?"

"How do you think she is?" Vanessa snipped. "She got beat with a tree branch."

An instant wave of relief consumed me. At least Squirt didn't use the gun he flashed to me at prom. Although, I don't believe Vanessa would have considered it good news that her mom could have been pistol whipped instead.

"Vanessa, babe, I'm so sorry."

I reached out to hug my girlfriend. Vanessa shoved me away rudely.

"Did you talk to Squirt?"

"I don't know where he—"

"No, I'm not talking about today. I asked you weeks ago to talk some sense into Squirt about all this gang-banging and robbing people."

"Vanessa, I tried—"

"No, you didn't! No, you did not. Because if you had, my mother wouldn't be laying up in a hospital bed right now."

I knew I wasn't going to convince Vanessa while she was so upset about her mother. I didn't want to frustrate her even more, so I got up and just told her that I'd call her later.

I went into the hall heading for the exit. Vanessa was right behind me.

"BJ, wait," she grabbed me by the arm. "What are you gonna do?"

I sighed, "I'ma find Squirt. Try to get to the bottom of this."

"BJ, don't let Vic and his boys hurt Squirt, OK? And promise me you won't get into any fights either."

"No babe, I won't fight anybody," I reassured her then turned to leave.

"Oh, BJ," she called after me. "Please be careful. My cousin David is with them."

It just got real.

CHAPTER 21

THE CHASE

/

I ran down the hill toward Mendel. Squirt lived on Indiana which was just a few blocks away from school. I knew it was a long shot, but I figured I'd try him there first.

I knocked on the door and Squirt's mom answered. She said Squirt wasn't there and that some boys she didn't know already came by looking for him. Ms. Benson confessed that she had kicked Squirt out of the house about two weeks ago for getting expelled from Mendel.

Ms. Benson asked me what was going on that everyone was looking for him. I didn't want to worry her, so I lied. I felt guilty about lying but I didn't want her to think he was in danger because she put him out on the street. Squirt was in danger because of Squirt, not because she kicked his butt out. I told her that everything was fine and that if he did come home to please tell him that I was looking for him.

Since I was so close to the school, I decided to let the rest of the guys in on what was happening. I knew this would be kind of tricky though. I was supposed to be there anyway for practice, but this was more important. Squirt's life was at stake.

I crept to the parking lot behind the school weaving in and out of parked cars making my way to the weight room window. I peeked through the window and saw most of the team inside lifting. I finally saw Shadow and Box over by the bench press.

I waved my hand frantically trying to get their attention without drawing looks from the whole crew. My efforts were rewarded as Shadow reclined back to do his set. He spotted me and sat back up. I immediately put my finger to my lips to *shush* him and pointed to Box then the weight room door. Shadow nodded and stood up to talk to Box.

I went back to the parking lot and camped out behind Coach's car until they came outside. It wasn't long before Shadow, Box, and Kevin joined me.

"Yo, you pick this week to ditch practice? Where you been?" Kevin inquired.

"Ya know, Coach is close to benching you for Catholic league, right?" Shadow added.

"Yo, we gotta find Squirt right now," I said.

"Why, what's up?" asked Box.

"This fool might have robbed Vanessa's mom. Victor and his crew are looking for him."

"Oh wow, they gonna put a serious hurting on him, dog, guaranteed," Box concluded.

"Not if we can find him first. C'mon."

I started to lead the way, weaving through cars again, but Kevin grabbed me and brought me back.

"BJ, slow up. Squirt made his choice. If he wants to gangbang, sell drugs, and rob people, I say, let him get what's coming to him."

"Nah, dude, he needs our help."

"He doesn't want our help," Kevin replied. "He doesn't want to be our friend anymore. I mean, BJ, this cat planted crack in your book bag, which could've got you kicked out of school, your baby sister almost died from it, and now he jacks your girlfriend's mom? And you still forgive this fool? Why?"

"Cuz he's our boy, that's why! Kev, we're no better."

"What are you talking about?"

"We're not perfect. We hurt God every day and He still forgives us."

"Oh, my goodness! Get outta here with that 'turn-the-other-cheek' mess, man!"

Kevin and I stalemated.

Shadow and Box didn't know what to do. They looked back and forth at Kevin and I as we glared at each other, neither of us backing down. I had made up my mind. I couldn't let Squirt self-destruct without doing everything possible to help.

"So you're willing to get beatdown or die? For Squirt?" Kevin asked.

"I am."

Kevin shook his head and walked away. I let Box and Shadow know if they decided to come that I would be searching the retail shops on Michigan Avenue. The longer I stood there trying to convince them to help, the closer Vic and his goons were to finding Squirt.

Michigan Avenue was sort of our retail store district. Spanning several blocks on either side of the street were retail clothing shops, shoe stores, convenience stores, jewelry shops, and hole-in-the-wall restaurants that served some of the greasiest, tastiest grub in the neighborhood. Since Squirt spent some of his wad on the new Jordans last time, I figured it was as good a place as any to start.

I hit up all the food shops and retail stores that I knew Squirt frequented but couldn't find him. Time was running out. I knew that Victor and his boys were still out there looking, so I had to keep looking too.

As I walked by one of Monica's favorite goodie spots, I saw Squirt out the corner of my eye. A sigh of relief exploded through my mouth as I entered the Old-Fashioned Donut Shop. Squirt was in line eyeing this "honey" with glasses and pigtails in front of him.

"Yo, I've been looking all over for you."

"Why you looking for me? Hold up, Beej." Squirt turns to the shop worker, "Yeah, lemme get a dozen, six chocolate, six glazed, matter fact, put some sprinkles on three of them chocolate."

I waited impatiently while he ordered and paid for his donuts, then pulled him to the back wall. The donuts were made to order, fresh on the spot, so I had about seven minutes to talk some sense into Squirt.

"Look, I know you robbed Mrs. Colby today."

"Who?"

"You know who, Mrs. Colby? Vanessa and Victor's mom?"

Horror filled Squirt's eyes.

"What's the matter with you?" I asked.

"That was Victor's mom?" Squirt inquired through a frightened whisper.

"Yes man. Look, we gotta go. Victor and 'em are looking for you. The safest place for you right now is the police station."

I walked to the door, but Squirt wasn't behind me. When I turned around, I knew something was wrong. He was shell-shocked, paralyzed. Sweat began to accumulate on his forehead.

"What's wrong with—" I gasped when it finally dawned on me. "It's Victor, isn't it? Your supplier? He's the one who gave you the black eye."

Squirt didn't say a word. He just moaned like a five-year-old with an upset stomach.

"Ohhh Squirt, you idiot! You mean to tell me, you robbed Victor's mom. . .to pay back money you owe Victor? Have you any idea what he's going to do to you?"

"Obviously, I didn't know it was his mother, now, did I? Oh man, what am I gonna do? BJ, dog, you gotta help me. Please!"

"OK, OK, um. . .I'll go outside to see if the coast is clear. If it is, you run, all the way home, dog. Don't look back. You probably should get outta town for a while too."

"BJ, thanks man. . .and I'm sorry for everything."

"It's gonna be OK, dog," I said. I gave him dap then left.

The donut shop's door hadn't even fully closed behind me before I was standing face-to-face with Victor and Bruce as they were entering the store.

Their eyes widened. Bruce grabbed me and shoved me hard against the wall of the entranceway. Victor approached holding a brown paper grocery bag. He started to open it. Just then the girl Squirt was eyeing came out swinging the shop's door wide open.

"Get yo 'Skeezah' butt back in there," Bruce ordered.

The girl gasped backing away, reentering the shop. As the door was closing, I could see Squirt at the counter getting his last meal. Bruce looked over as well, just as the door was closing.

His forehead wrinkled with recognition. I could see it in his eyes, in his facial expression.

"Yo, ain't that Squirt—"

Before he could finish his rhetorical question, I pushed Bruce as hard as I could and sprinted out of the shop's entryway.

Victor and Bruce took off after me as I blazed a path down the semi-crowded sidewalk of meandering shoppers. Two other St. Paul Academy guys stepped out of a jewelry store ahead of me. Before I knew it, I was upon them. There was nothing I could do but attempt some slick Walter Payton jukes and hope I was as good as I thought.

I cut, stopped, spun, then cut again. The St. Paul guys stumbled over themselves trying to nab me. I looked back and there was an extra bonus as they almost took out Victor and Bruce too. When I turned to continue running, I was stunned at what I saw, driving down the street was Keko and Auntie Emma coming back from Santa's Village.

They looked right at me, petrified. I shook my head *no*, warning them not to get involved. I sped around a corner ducking behind a building. I was hoping like crazy Keko kept driving. Monica and her little friend, Leslie were in the back seat. I didn't want to put the entire family at risk.

In and out. In and out, breathe, breathe, I coached myself. Well, I had certainly done my job of getting them off Squirt's scent. My one source of comfort was knowing I had beaten all these guys running track. If I played it smart there should be no way they could catch me.

I was nearly done catching my breath. As Mrs. Morales would say, I needed a plan. *Mendel? I'll head back down the hill to Mendel.* Kevin and the rest of the guys should just be finishing up with practice. There was no way if Kevin saw me being chased that he wouldn't help. If I could just make it to Mendel, I'd be fine.

I eased my way from behind the building, peeking out to make sure the coast was clear. I walked briskly to the traffic light. I hid myself beside a husky couple, who in my opinion, were being overly affectionate feeding each other from a giant bag of Doritos. *Ugh, I'll never look at fingers or a Dorito the same again.*

I needed to cross the street now. I glanced at the light, still red. That's when I noticed the sensual crunching of chips had stopped. I looked over and the girl was tugging on her boyfriend's arm. She pointed, so I looked to see what her problem was. Turned out her problem was my problem. Victor, Bruce, and the other two St. Paul guys were closing fast.

I couldn't wait for the safety of a green traffic light any longer. I shoved the overweight lovers toward Victor and his boys and darted into the street. Oncoming traffic headed for me in both directions. I was in a real-life game of *Frogger*. Cars honked. Tires screeched. I narrowly escaped being splattered by a pathfinder.

I sprinted down the massive hill full speed. In retrospect, I don't know why I abandoned my original plan of heading to Mendel. I guess because I was getting tired, and the alley was right there. Funny, it was so close to my school, but I had never been in that alley before. If I had, I would have known it was a dead end.

I punched the palm of my hand in frustration. I quickly turned to run out of the dead-end death trap, but it was too late. Victor and his boys spotted me as they were running by.

/

LOOKING FOR ME

We all took a second to recover. My eyes connected with each of theirs as we took in deep breaths of garbage scented air.

"A'ight. . .y'all caught me," I said between wheezing breaths. "But I swear, I don't know where he is."

Which was true. I didn't know where Squirt was. By now, he should have left the donut shop and could be at any number of places. I was just relieved it was all over. I still felt bad for Mrs. Colby, but I would work on Squirt to do the right thing and turn himself in.

"Where who is?" Victor asked quizzically.

"We found who we're looking for," Bruce stated.

"What?" I answered back confused.

I didn't understand. Victor stepped forward unzipping his jacket. He pulled out the brown paper bag he had earlier at the donut shop. I watched closely. It's never good when someone pulled out a bag on you. And I was right. Victor opened the grocery bag pulling out an article of clothing. Everything became crystal clear to me at that moment. It was a wrinkled, shiny-blue Mendel track jacket, *my Mendel track jacket.* The one Ms. Benson couldn't find when I returned Squirt's jacket to his house.

I never considered that it was my own jacket that Vanessa's mother ripped off Squirt's back. It all made sense.

Victor and his boys slowly approached me. I backed away.

"Listen, Vic. Man you guys got this all wrong. It wasn't me."

They continued to ease toward me. I backed even farther away until hitting the building behind me, which was what I wanted. This way I could keep all my attackers in front of me.

Victor carefully placed my track jacket on the urine-soaked ground. I was not going to talk my way out of this one. I assumed a fighter's stance and waited for the first sucker. If Victor thought I made quick work of him in front of his house, that was nothing compared to what I was about to do in that alley. And if all else failed, I'd do just enough to create an opening then make a break for it. That was my plan at least, but it didn't work out that way.

Instead, the heart-change I had experienced reared its beautifully divined head. Love is sacrificial. I had seen this in both my parents, in my auntie, even my coach. I had recently learned it from Jesus himself, "Greater love has no one than this that he lay down his life for his friends." *Was I ready to live this life lesson, personally?* I thought back to when I last saw Squirt in that donut shop. The genuine fear he had in his eyes about Victor. This was likely the same fear that compelled him to leave me as the scapegoat for his dirty work.

Kevin had asked me if I was willing to get beatdown or die for Squirt. I answered his hypothetical question rather flippantly at the time. I told Kevin, yes, I would do it because Squirt was our boy. I'd be the pawn on life's chessboard because of the love I had for him. Squirt was the lowdown, dirty, conniving friend I would trade places with because it was once done for me by Jesus. *I was ready.*

I unclenched my fists. I tried to mentally, and physically prepare myself for what was about to happen. The only problem was I knew how to fight. My dad taught me. I knew how to defend myself. Even if the person's skills were more advanced than mine, I still knew how to avoid being hurt.

Yet something within urged me not to defend myself, not even with blocks or ducking. For my actions to be a true sacrifice for the love of my friend, I had to do this the hard way. I told myself, *Take it. Take if for Squirt.* Fear gripped me for the first time since Mom's purse was snatched from me when I was nine years old. I had never felt the full brunt of a dead-on punch before. I didn't even know if I could take a good, solid, clean punch.

Rightfully so, Victor was the first to get it going, then Bruce, then after that, I didn't know who was hitting me. Each punch felt uniquely different. I never knew punches came in such variety. There were sharp pains, blunt, thud-like pains, some punches stung, feeling more like slaps than anything else and some oddly enough felt like Monica was hitting me.

The punches accumulated, and my energy oozed from my body. My resolve told me to stand, to take it, but I just couldn't. That was it. I raised my hands and arms blocking the assault as best I could.

My knees buckled. I fought desperately to stand, grasping at the wall behind me and even clutching at the next person in line to throw blows.

Squirt wasn't the only reason I wanted to stay on my feet. I secretly feared the most vicious thing someone could do to a downed opponent. It was one of the reasons why I trained so hard in boxing, because I never wanted it to happen to me, getting "stomped." Growing up in Chicago, I'd seen countless guys get stomped to bloody pulps. Yet never in my wildest dreams did I ever think it would happen to me. A severe traumatic brain injury was not the way I wanted to go out. With that swirling around in my head, I held on a little longer than I should have.

Eventually my legs gave way beneath me. I knew what would be coming in a few moments. And they knew it too. Victor's boys rooted for it, in fact.

I continued to cover my face and head pulling my knees into a perfect fetal position. At that point, it made me feel as if I should have helped those people I saw getting stomped in the past. The experience of it was as painfully traumatizing as it looked when I'd seen it happen to others.

The only way I felt I could survive was to look up and onward to the heavenly place promised to me because I believed. I told myself, *Hold on, it will be over soon.*

One of the other guys must have felt the same way. I heard someone tell Vic, "Let's get outta here before somebody comes."

Hmph, he couldn't have suggested that sooner.

I watched as several pairs of blood-spattered sneakers ran away. I tried to talk myself up some, "Ok, relax, breathe. It's over."

I waited for the feeling to come back into my body, although maybe I should have been grateful for the numbing throb I had going on. I told myself not to move until I knew they were gone for sure. But the urine smelling ground was sickening. I conjured up an ounce of energy to prop myself up against the wall behind me.

A couple deep breaths and I was resting peacefully. Yet that didn't last long, I heard footsteps approaching. It was probably Keko coming back for me after dropping Auntie Em and the kids off. Or maybe it was Kevin, Box, and Shadow. I guess their conscience got the best of them and they came to check on their boy. I looked up. But the sun was blinding. I couldn't make out the person looming over me until he crouched down to get a better gander at me. *Oh no. Not him.*

/

LOVE IS SACRIFICIAL

David and I locked eyes.

"Day-yum!" David exclaimed slowly. "Vic finally got you back, huh?"

My heart was racing. I knew David's reputation, yet maybe seeing me all busted up, he'd have some sympathy for me. God, I hope so. I couldn't defend myself if I tried.

"Don't worry," he said. "I ain't gonna hurt you, dog. Besides, I know you ain't rob my auntie. This was just Victor's lame excuse to get revenge for you kicking his butt."

Suddenly, car tires screeched to a halt. Running footsteps approached us. I heard a familiar voice that brought joyful tears to my eyes.

"BJ, BJ," Keko called out.

I turned. He was at the alleyway entrance but seemed hesitant in approaching. *Doesn't he see my face?* I thought. *What was he waiting for? Take me to the hospital, man.*

David rose quickly, throwing his hands back like Keko was the police.

"Eh, it wasn't me," David chuckled. "I found him like this."

As David examined Keko's worried expression, the snickering stopped. I could see his wheels turning. Mine began to turn also. Was this the first time David had seen my dad since he pulled that gun on him? And why was Keko acting all skittish when before he just about placed his eyeball in David's gun barrel. The oddness of it all made me uneasy.

Keko called my name again, gently, lovingly with a compassionate gaze to match. But still he wouldn't come any closer. David took a couple of steps back, forehead wrinkled like a detective on the verge of uncovering a vital clue.

"Wait...Keko, what you doing here? How y'all know each other?" David questioned, pointing at me.

Again, I thought, *That's an odd question*. I looked up at David, then at Keko, back to David.

David looked down at me, then back to Keko. The game of Russian roulette head-swivel didn't last long before David solved the mystery.

"Wait a minute. Is this. . .Is he your kid? 'BJ' stands for Brandon Jr., don't it?"

Oh snap! I finally understood. David only knew me as Vanessa's boyfriend, not as Keko's son.

"David, we can talk about this," Keko said calmly, now easing toward us carefully.

"This is the 'abomination' you should've killed."

Looking directly at Keko, David drew his gun from his waistband and pointed it. . .*at me*!

"David, put the gun down—"

"It's bad enough you let your queen get raped, but you raised the kid of the Vice Lord that did it? You even named the kid after you?"

"David, listen to me—"

"You're right Keko. I can't kill you—"

"David, Dav—"

"But I can kill him."

I began to hyperventilate. I pressed my back so firmly against the brick wall, I could feel the individual stones cutting into my lats. Even Monica could shoot a fly off my nose at that range.

David glared at me. I looked deeply into Vanessa's cousin's eyes. His brown pupils burned with anger, hatred, disgust, and at that very moment, I wanted to know why young Black men hated each other? What started it all? Did anybody truly know why, by in large, young men with the same socioeconomical background, same poverty struggles, same school systems, stereotyped with the same negative disdain, and possessing the same skin color hated each other so much? And why did so many innocent people have to die because of it? Kids and elderly people hit by stray bullets. Gangs shooting into crowds of people hoping to hit their target but truly not caring if they don't, as long as they hit someone. And I was next.

How could David's feelings about me change in a matter of moments. He had just pardoned me a minute ago. He even tried to befriend me in the cereal aisle a while back. *Why didn't I let him? I should have laughed at his stupid Lucky Charms joke.* If I had, would he still want me six feet under? Would he still be standing three feet away from me with his gat pointed right at my face?

"Goodnight, Mendel man," David said, shaking his head, almost with a hint of remorse, as if the decision to pull the trigger was beyond his control.

"David, no! Don't!" Keko yelled.

I looked over and saw my dad charging like a bull. My heart skipped. David's resolve wasn't rattled in the least. Keko got closer and closer. At the last second, David calmly swung his pistol in Keko's direction. Yet I knew Keko would not stop charging because that's what bulls do.

David steadied his burner center-mast on the only father I'd ever known. What happened next, is still a bit foggy. I can only describe it as adrenaline, pure adrenaline. Energy surged through my flesh. I bounced up like a pogo stick and threw myself between David and Keko.

Pop, pop, pop, pop. Shots rang out. I went limp in Keko's arms as he swung me around. I heard four shots, but I think only two of them hit me. Immediately my back began to burn where the bullets entered. I mean, really burn. The intensified pain made me forget all about the beating I just took. Extreme heat radiated filling my entire torso, I couldn't escape it.

Keko flopped back onto his bum, lowering me across his lap. I felt his massive biceps hugging me. I looked up at him. My eye lids, heavy, but I fought to keep them opened. Tears streamed down Keko's face. His mouth, wide, like he was yawning. *Was he crying?* It irked me that I couldn't hear for some reason

"It's OK, Dad. Dad, it's OK," I said through sputtered breath.

Looking over Keko's shoulder I saw David walking away casually. It bothered me; he didn't even have the decency to run after blasting me.

Keko rocked me back and forth, and I remember the indescribable feeling of being loved then the pain was gone. That's when I became aware that life was leaving my sweaty, blood-drenched body. Keko had disappeared. So had the urine-saturated alley. My eye lids flickered wanting to shut out the wonderful light that had engulfed me. But I struggled to keep them opened, longing to identify the shadowy figure who was approaching me.

Her walk familiar. Her smile captivating. Her hand reached out to mine and I could see my hand stretching to meet hers. I wondered, was this the out-of-body experience that people described when you die?

"BJ, baby, what are you doing here?" my mother asked, quizzically. "It's not your time."

As I placed my hand into hers an unseen force tugged me away gently. I wanted to stay with her, but I couldn't. Something wouldn't allow me.

"Mom. Mom!"

"It's not your time."

Another voice, unwelcomed and gravelly, "Clear!"

Beep. Beep. Beep.

My eyes shot open unaffected by the dull emergency room lighting. A doctor gawked at the heart-rate monitor.

"He's back. Get him prepped!"

Intense tingling reintroduced itself to my bullet-riddled body. *My legs. What was wrong with my legs?* The prickling sensation I had throughout my body had disappeared but stayed in my legs. I tried to say something to the doc, but the throbbing pain made me forget I could speak.

Several nurses and orderlies scrambled unplugging tubes and hoses.

They whisked my gurney past Auntie Emma and Keko who were in the hallway. Before I blacked out, I heard the doctor tell them, "There's a bullet near his spinal cord. We have to operate now. Do I have your consent?"

"Yes, go, go, go," Keko said hurriedly.

The doctor took off running after his team who were zooming me down the hall to surgery.

I drifted back into unconsciousness thinking about how Auntie Em once told me I would never understand the sacrifice Keko made for our family. She was wrong. I understand what both my parents did for me. My mother did the unthinkable. She loved me when most would have considered me unlovable trash. My dad taught me how to stand up for myself and for others. He taught me how to forgive. I will never forget these lessons. But most of all, I understand love is sacrificial and comes at great cost.

Hours later, I woke up in the recovery room. Everything looked kind of blurry, but *new* at the same time. I scanned the room. I saw Auntie Emma's purse and jacket on the chair in the corner. A couple of half-eaten chicken wings and coleslaw in Styrofoam platters were on the counter. *I hope they brought me some chicken; I was starved.* I wondered how long I'd been out of it.

From my room, I could see Keko and Auntie Em talking with Dr. Sawyer in the hallway. I couldn't hear them, but their conversation seemed intense. I wish Auntie Emma knew I was awake and doing OK.

Hunger pangs punched me in the gut again. I couldn't take the smell anymore, I was gonna eat somebody's chicken. I peeled the warm blankets back and tried to get out of bed, but I couldn't.

I looked back down the hallway. Auntie Emma was crying hysterically. Keko put his arm around her, but then I noticed, his other arm was in a sling. Keko must've been shot too. Just then he looked in my direction. We locked eyes. My father's face contorted as he fought back his own tears. He turned away. I grabbed the blankets and flung them to the floor, looking down at my legs, I wondered, *What had my own sacrifice cost me?*

CHAPTER 22

AWAKENING

/

Was it real? I know the shooting was real. I could still feel the pain from the bullets and the surgery. But was *heaven* real? I heard her voice, saw her face, touched her hand, but was it. . .real?

"Oh no, no, no," Vanessa's voice rang out.

I turned my head inch by inch until I saw Vanessa and Kevin standing in the doorway. I didn't know why my neck was stiff. I didn't get punched in the neck. My swollen face and lips throbbed rhythmically with every pulse beat.

Positioned upright in the bed, "for comfort" the nurses explained, my torso was wrapped with gauzed stuffing like a mummy. Turned out I was shot three times. Thankfully, no bones or vital organs were hit. The first bullet they removed during surgery was lodged near my spine, though it was impeded slightly by first going through Dad's arm. The other two bullets pierced my side, in and out, when Dad swung me around. I guess as I was trying to protect him, he was protecting me.

Vanessa and Kevin approached wearing mixed emotions on their faces. Vanessa struggled to fight back tears; Kevin brooded.

"Brandon, I'm so sorry," she choked out. "How are you feeling?"

Kevin was more to the point.

"Who did this to you, dog?"

Loopy off pain medications, I felt as though I was in a slow-mo version of good cop, bad cop.

"Doesn't matter," I managed to eke through my puffy, split lips.

"Doesn't matter!" Kevin echoed. "Auntie Em told me you can't walk."

"Kevin stop it. Leave him alone," Vanessa interjected.

Kevin scowled at her clenching his teeth so hard I imagined the dentin and enamel turning into powdered grit inside his mouth.

"Was it your brother and his friends?"

Vanessa looked like a witness on the stand about to crack. Tears flowed and her body trembled.

"Mm-Mmm, let it go," I groaned.

Kevin looked at me then back to Vanessa. He left the room without saying another word.

I motioned with my hand for Vanessa to come closer. She wiped her eyes as she came right to the edge of the bed with care. Vee eased my hand into hers, looking deeply into my eyes.

"I never meant for this to happen, BJ," she cried. "If I would have known—"

I shook my head *no*. It wasn't Vanessa's fault, and I didn't want her to feel guilty about her brother's actions. As much physical pain and mental anguish I was in, I didn't want Vanessa trying to carry my burdens. Yet, I knew the weight of the world was on her shoulders. Her brother and his boys beat me up, then her gangbanging cousin tried to finish me off. Vanessa told me that the police were on the lookout for David, which made me think of another fugitive.

"Squirt?"

"No one's seen him either," Vanessa replied.

I felt bad for Vanessa and Mrs. Colby. It's likely that Squirt took my advice and got out of town. Deep inside, I was sure Victor knew I didn't rob he and Vanessa's mom. And, if Victor was ever to find out the truth, Squirt would be in the hospital beside me or the morgue.

"I'm gonna tell Mama what he did to you," Van continued.

"What will that accomplish?"

"I don't know. I just...I feel like I should do something or Vic's just gonna keep on bullying people like he always has. I hate my brother for what he did to you—"

Vanessa and I felt it at the same moment. We weren't alone. I looked at the doorway entrance. Vanessa followed my gaze.

Kevin heard every word. He nodded angrily and stormed off. I called after him, but he didn't return. Kevin and I had been best friends for a long time, and I can attest with full assurance his little head nod with that vicious glare meant he wanted revenge. Immediately, Vanessa started crying again. When would this nightmare end, I wondered?

Over the next few days, I didn't receive many visitors except family. Dr. Sawyer said my body had gone through severe trauma and I needed to rest. *Rest*, like I could. If I wasn't in pain from the assault and shooting, my mind was on repeat, obsessing whether I'd be permanently paralyzed or whether David would try to finish the job one day.

I laid in bed awake. My room door creaked open, and squeaky shoes made their way across the frigid floor. I watched my favorite nurse pour fresh, ice-cold agua into my adult sippy cup on the tray table.

"Hey Nurse Sharon," I said with my dry, cracked voice. My swollen face and lips had subsided, and I was beginning to sound and look like my regular self.

She turned around surprised to see me still awake.

"BJ!" she scolded through a whisper. "It is two thirty in the morning, why aren't you asleep? Thirsty?"

She motioned with the cup.

I nodded *yes*.

Nurse Sharon leaned over holding the thick straw to my parched lips. I took several excited sips promptly dribbling all over myself. Not to worry, Nurse Sharon cleaned me up before the chilled water could even reach my chin. Nurse Sharon had taken care of my mother, my sister, and now she was taking care of me.

"Can't sleep?" she asked. "Is it the pain?"

I nodded again.

"I'll get you something." Nurse Sharon began walking to the door.

"No, it's not time yet. My next dose is at three o'clock."

"I'm impressed," she said, walking back. She took a seat in the chair next to my bed. "Most people jump at the chance to get more narcotics."

"One overdose was enough for this family," I laughed in discomfort.

I looked at Nurse Sharon and smiled. I had always liked her for the kind way she treated my mother. I wish there were more nurses in the profession like her. That's why I knew she would shoot me straight.

"Nurse Sharon. . .do you think I'll ever walk again?"

"There's a possibility, BJ. The surgery went well. You're young and healthy and strong. Let's see how the test results look tomorrow and go from there, OK?"

"But. . .what if I can't—"

I couldn't even get the words out before I began to cry.

"Stop it," Nurse Sharon said, sliding to the edge of her seat. "Look at me. Wipe those tears."

I must not have done a good enough job because she reached over and wiped the tears for me.

"I've seen a lot of miraculous things happen while I've worked here. And it's had nothing to do with the surgeons or nurses or the specialists they fly in and out of here. I've seen cancer just go away. I've seen holes in hearts disappear. I have seen huge, inoperable tumors one day, shrink down all on its own to operable size a week later. Miracles are just that, BJ, miracles—divine, inexplicable occurrences that can happen to anyone of us. You hear me?"

"Yes ma'am," I answered sharply.

"Have faith, BJ. Allow your body time to heal. And let God do what He's gonna do."

Nurse Sharon gave me time to compose myself as the tears wouldn't stop. It seemed every time I wiped one, two more would fall. I reached over slowly for my cup and took a few more swigs.

"It's been quite the year for your family, hasn't it?" she quipped.

"Yeah, no kidding," I said, finally settling down, pulling the sheets to my chin.

"It's coming up soon. How you holding up?"

At first, I didn't know what she was talking about, then it hit me. I looked over at Nurse Sharon. Even in the dimly lit room I could see her eyes, warm, tender, the same eyes I saw last year. It would be a year ago this month that my mother passed away.

And since then it's been a cascade of disappointment and drama in my life: Dad being released from jail the same day Mom died, finding out Squirt's a thief and drug dealer, Monica overdosing on his drugs, discovering my mom was raped and in a gang, finding out the man I believed was my father wasn't, having no scholarship, having one of my closest friends betray me, getting beatdown, shot, and now less than 24 hours away from learning if I will ever walk again. That was my past year. I couldn't lie to her. I wasn't holding up well at all. I was exhausted.

"Well, one thing I know," Nurse Sharon said. "Your mother, Kathy Jean James, was extremely proud of you. So find comfort in that."

"She was?" I asked quizzically.

"Yessss, child, we couldn't get Kathy to stop talking about her son, BJ. BJ this and BJ that."

I laughed softly as Nurse Sharon went on and on about my mother. The longer she talked, the more my eye lids felt like weights. I allowed them to shut succumbing to my cloudy haze of slumber. I could feel the smile on my face. There was no better lullaby than to hear stories about my mom.

Just as Nurse Sharon said good night, I heard the phone ring.

Nurse Sharon answered quickly and rather annoyed, "Hello, this is Brandon's room. . .no, no it's almost three in the morning, he's sleeping now. Well, you'll have to call back another time. I'll give him the message. Bye."

Nurse Sharon's squeaky shoes headed toward the door.

"Who was it?" I mumbled.

"Somebody named 'Squirt,'" she said, closing the door behind her.

/

WALK-RUN-FLY

After Squirt called, I stayed awake the next five hours ruminating about where he might be, would he call again, how did he hear I was in the hospital, if he was sorry for selling me out. The thoughts in my head were replaced by voices, conversations all around me, disturbing my much-needed rest. It would have felt like a dream if I didn't know every single, cackling voice in the room: Monica, Dad, Auntie Emma, Vanessa, Shadow, Box, and Kev. That's when I felt a nudge on my shoulder.

"BJ, baby," Auntie Emma said softly. "You got company."

I pried my eyes open and saw blurred visions of the fellas donned in their track uniforms chatting it up with Vanessa, Monica, and Dad. Then I realized, today was outdoor Catholic league.

"Y'all on your way to the meet?" I asked, still trying to wake up.

Everyone laughed as each of the fellas came over giving me dap and a careful hug.

"Look at this dude, man," Shadow said. "Go back to sleep."

"The meet's over, BJ," Box added. "We came right over afterwards. It's three o'clock in the afternoon, dog."

"Man, it is? Where's Coach?"

"He had to make a run," Shadow explained. "He'll swing by later."

"OK. Well. . .did we win?"

"Did we win?" Box repeated. "Monica, show him."

Spud looked at Box and nodded. She skipped over and opened the door. I grimaced in pain as I attempted to sit up more.

Quan entered with the Outdoor Catholic League Championship trophy and sat it on the tray table besides me. Then, he removed the gold, first place team medal from his neck.

"Careful, careful," Auntie Emma urged.

"Yes ma'am," Quan answered, gently placing the medaled ribbon around my neck.

Quan gave me dap, then stepped aside as Hawk entered the room. He took off his medal and placed it around my neck, then Joe entered and did the same thing, then Red, then Eddie-Ed, Derrick, Mark, and so did every member of the team with Shadow, Box, and Kevin going last. It was like a receiving line at a wedding. And I was as glad as the bride and groom. The medals were heavy and clanky and shiny and they aggravated my back, but I didn't care. I cherished every one of them as the guys told me they dedicated the meet to me. I know the hard work we put in as a team and winning a sizeable meet like Catholic league was no small feat.

After the impromptu medal ceremony, the team hung around for a while. All of them couldn't fit inside the room so some stood just outside the open doorway. I was happy for the company. It kept me distracted from obsessing over what was coming. At any moment, Dr. Sawyer would enter the room with news that will change my life forever. But for now, the vibe in the room was upbeat. Everyone seemed to be in good spirits except one person, who was isolated from the pack staring out the window, Kevin. I caught him and Vanessa a couple of times exchanging dirty looks.

"Yo, Kev!" I waved him over. Kevin squeezed through the group to my bedside joining Shadow and Box.

"Hey, y'all mind if I talk with Kev alone?" I asked.

They looked at one another then conceded to my request. It was a long shot, but I figured with everyone distracted with their own side conversations, it would be safe to gauge Kevin's intention with this Victor thing.

"So, Kev tell me about the meet? Did anything. . .interesting happen?"

Kevin gave me a wry look.

"We don't need to talk about that now," he said.

"I get that. Just wondering if something was said at the meet. Or, if you had intentions to—"

"Oh, Victor's gonna see me," Kev interrupted. "Please believe that."

I looked across the room and Vanessa was watching us like a hawk.

"I don't get you BJ," Kevin continued, leaning in. "This is serious and you're up in here sniggling and giggling with everybody like you don't have a care in the world."

Vanessa had seen enough. Though she couldn't hear our conversation, I was certain she felt, by Kevin's demeanor, he was being too hard on me. Van made her way through the crowd toward us. I saw the look in her eyes and my heart fluttered more than when David pulled his gun on me.

"Oh, here she comes," Kevin sneered. "What—"

Just before Vanessa could respond, I heard the unmistakable booming voice of Dr. Sawyer.

"What is going on in here?"

He parted through the track crowd, Nurse Sharon following close behind. Kevin and Vanessa went to neutral corners.

"Nurse Sharon how were all these kids allowed up here? Get them out of here now."

"Yes sir," Nurse Sharon answered softly.

"Wait, please, Dr. Sawyer, these are BJ's teammates," Keko said. "They're just here to support him."

"I understand Mr. James, but I'm here to discuss the test results with the family."

"They are my family," I said proudly.

"Fine, five more minutes," Dr. Sawyer conceded reluctantly. "But those medals have to go. That's too much strain on your back, Nurse Sharon."

Nurse Sharon maneuvered through the crowd. Box and Shadow helped her remove my prized possessions.

"OK, Mr. and Ms. James, the bullet I removed doesn't appear to have caused permanent damage."

Dr. Sawyer held up my X-rays and continued his surgical spiel to Auntie Emma and Dad as if I wasn't even there. Eventually, I zoned out allowing my mind to wander until he got to the important part. I began to reminisce about all the times as a kid running, jumping, skating with my mom. The times we raced each other and laughed till our stomachs ached as we crossed imaginary finish lines. I wondered would I be able to have fun like this with Monica again. Would I be able to race my own kids someday? I didn't care about the technical terminology of my damaged *this or that*. I only had one question.

"Look, Dr. Sawyer, all I wanna know is will I walk again?" I interrupted.

Dr. Sawyer gasped slightly. I'm sure he didn't like for a *kid* to talk to him like that. It was evident from the way

Nurse Sharon looked at me no one ever spoke to him in that manner.

"I was coming to that," he said. "The nerves appear to be uninjured and technically should be capable of sending signals to your leg muscles. Your back muscles are still inflamed so they're interrupting those signals through the spine. We'll know more as they heal. But, for now, my professional prognosis is with time, hard work, rehab consisting of physical and occupational therapy, there's no reason you shouldn't make a full recovery."

I closed my eyes and said, "Thank you."

Dr. Sawyer replied, "You're welcome" but I wasn't talking to him. Sure, I was grateful the surgery was a success yet at that moment I was thanking God.

My teammates cheered so loud I felt like I was at one of our track meets. Guys were high-fiving and dapping each other. Auntie Emma and Keko thanked Dr. Sawyer on his way out, then made their way to the bed with Monica and hugged me. Though it was the news I wanted, I still couldn't believe it. I sat there in awe with my mouth opened.

Just then Nurse Sharon bellowed, "All right, Mendel track champs, it's time to go. C'mon everybody, out-out-out. BJ needs to rest."

The guys said their goodbyes and began trickling out. It was still surreal to me. I think I experienced sorrow, hope, doubt, gladness, fear, and shouting-from-the-mountain-top joy all at the same time. I was so excited about the news I felt I could fly.

Evening had rolled around. Vanessa, Auntie Emma, and Monica kissed me and said their goodbyes an hour earlier. Keko decided to hang out with me and the few fellas who remained: Box, Shadow, Kevin, Quan, and Joe.

Kevin appeared to be doing a little better since Dr. Sawyer's news, but I still wanted to finish our conversation. While the other guys were preoccupied with side chatter, I called Kevin to my bedside again with a slight head nod.

"Sup, Beej?"

"Yo, you heard what the doctor said, right? I'm gonna be straight."

"Yeah, I heard him, but you don't get it."

"What don't I get?"

Kevin looked me in my eyes.

"You came to me for help, and I turned my back on you cuz I was mad at Squirt. Beej, if I would have come with you, maybe you wouldn't have gotten shot."

"Kevin, stop it," I said. "It's not your fault that I got shot."

"He's right, Kevin," Keko chimed in.

I looked over at the guys and they all were listening to me and Kevin's conversation. I wish I could make Kevin understand that my experience in that alley was something that I had to go through, for my own growth. Not Keko or Kevin or anyone else could have taken the pain that was meant for me to bear.

"The important thing is that BJ's alive," Keko said coming over to the bed.

"I'm with you, Dad," I agreed. "A'ight man," I looked at Kevin.

Kevin gave me dap and verbally said *OK*, but I could tell in his eyes that he had no intention of letting this go. I had no choice but to fake a laugh, so the others wouldn't know something was going on with me and Kevin.

"Now, would somebody finally tell me about this meet?"

"I got you BJ," said Box.

"Man, you ain't no good storyteller," Quan interjected. "I'll tell it—"

"No, let me tell it!" Shadow shouted.

"Let's all tell it," Kevin interrupted. "Quan, you go first. Set the stage."

/

BLUE SMOKE RISES

It was appropriate for Quan to start. He was the history buff. The information man. Next to Squirt, he was the most animated storyteller I knew. Quan took the center of the room like a performing arts student giving an opening monologue.

Quan started with the team meeting they had on the bus. He said they arrived at St. Paul Academy's track about twenty minutes early and Coach was adamant the team remembered me and how much I wanted to be there. I wasn't surprised at all to hear Coach used what happened to me as motivation.

Quan said, "Coach told us after we win Catholic league, we're gonna march into that hospital thirty deep, give BJ the trophy and wrap our medals around his neck."

"My man, Coach," I said. "Tell me about—"

"Whoa, slow down, we got this," Kevin stopped me. "Go ahead, Q."

"The entire meet can be boiled down to two teams and one event," Quan continued.

"St Paul Academy and the mile relay," I answered with sweaty palms.

"But the only difference was we had added motivation to see it through," Box said, standing taking Quan's spot.

"Thanks man," I said humbly.

"I'm not talking about you, dog."

Everyone laughed.

"No, I'm talking about this genius over here," Box said walking over to Kevin and patting him on the shoulder.

Box asked if I remembered that Kevin was supposed to come up with a pep squad chant for the mile relay. Honestly, I had forgotten all about it. But Kevin hadn't. Box explained that Kev came up with one last cheer specifically for the mile relay race and it was his best one yet. I asked them to let me hear it, but they told me to calm down and be quiet.

Quan stood again, "Beej, picture this, the stadium is packed out. It's so quiet you could hear the bees buzzing in the stands. We're tied with St. Paul for first place, so winner takes all. Since you had better things to do—"

"Shut up!" I laughed, shaking my head.

"Coach put Hawk in the relay. So this was the pecking order, Shadow took your spot at the first leg, I was second, Hawk third, and you-know-who sitting over there—*Superman* was cleanup," Quan pointed his thumb like a hitchhiker back at Joe.

I played along acting as if I was tearing through my hospital gown to show the capital letter *S* on my chest.

"But your boy, Shadow—" Quan began to laugh, which made everyone else bust up laughing except me and Keko.

"What happened?" I asked curiously.

"No, no, let me tell this part," Kevin pleaded as he stood.

I looked over at Shadow who was turning shades of red that I'd never seen before.

"It's funny now, but it wasn't funny then," Shadow quickly added.

"True that, true that," Kevin conceded. "But you have to admit, it was risky."

Shadow chuckled.

"So again, BJ, this is for all the marbles," Kevin resumed. "Stands are packed; it's quiet as a mouse. Shadow is down in the blocks; the gun fires. And Shadow doesn't move. He stays there. All the other runners are gone."

I looked at Shadow again, "What?" I laughed. "Did you freeze up?"

Shadow looked at me stone-faced, "No, I didn't freeze up. I was counting to three."

The room fell silent.

I inhaled sharply. My eyes widened. It was like a rush of electricity surged through my body once I realized what Shadow had done. Numerous times, I spoke of how my mom used to count to three before she would come back and smoke me in a foot race. To Coach's annoyance, I did it a couple of times in practice, fooling around. And I had even done it to Victor when we faced one another in the 4x200 relay. To hear what Shadow did during that juncture made it even more special to me.

Shadow walked over to the bed and gave me dap. Keko looked around at the rest of the guys confused.

"I don't understand. . .what happened?" Keko asked.

Box leaned over and explained, "Oh, Mr. James, Shadow dedicated his race to BJ. That's why he counted to three."

"Shadow, man, what were you thinking!" Kevin blurted out, prompting everyone to laugh again.

Shadow walked back to his spot by the door, pointing at Joe, he shrugged, "Superman. What?"

Joe joins the fun mimicking ripping his shirt to show the Superman letter *S*.

"BJ, don't be too impressed," Kev went on. "It was a half-hearted dedication. Quickest three-count ever, it was like one-two-three. Anyway, Shadow finally explodes out the blocks and no lie, he pushes so hard he snaps one of the block pedals."

"What? Will the real Superman stand up?" I whooped.

Kevin continued, "Wait, there's more. Shadow's booking down the track full out crying. Tears and slob everywhere, all you could see, tears, slob, and snot running down his beet-red face. His eyes were so puffy from crying, I have no clue how he saw Quan for the exchange."

Kevin had us laughing so hard my stomach and back were hurting. I was literally in stitches and didn't want to tear them. So I took several deep breaths to try to calm myself down.

"The best part though," Kevin wrapped up. "Shadow ran a 49.2 split, personal best."

"Nice," I said.

That's when Box stood and took over. With the deficit that Shadow intentionally placed on the entire relay, ground had to be made up and fast.

"So the whole team is in the bleachers. Kev has us stand up and we did this clap."

Box demonstrates right there inside the room. Two claps; one. Two claps; one.

> *Clap-Clap. Clap!*
> *Clap-Clap. Clap!*

Box continued, "Then we repeated over and over almost like a soft echo: 'Blue smoke. Blue smoke. Blue smoke' on the one beat."

That's when it happened. My hospital room began to morph into a school pep rally. The guys in the room took over clapping and softly chanting "blue smoke" as Box teleported us back to the track meet.

Box explained the clapping cadence continued over the "blue smoke" refrain while the other half of the team shouted,

> *The blue and white ma-chine.*
> *(Clap-Clap. Clap! Clap-Clap. Clap!))*
> *The blue and white ma-chine.*
> *(Clap-Clap. Clap! Clap-Clap. Clap!))*

Dad and I locked eyes with big smiles on our faces as Box explained that Shadow cruised down the track, arms and legs pumping like a steam engine locomotive. He got closer and closer to the two runners just ahead of him, climbing into sixth place. Just when he was about to hand the baton off to Quan, he yelled "blue smoke!"

I was shocked. We changed our baton pass signal from yelling *stick* to the name of Kevin's new chant. I loved it! But that wasn't the only *new* thing. Once the baton was passed off to Quan, Kevin initiated the next sequence of the cheer for the second leg, Box explained.

The guys promptly demonstrated in the room using deep baritone voices echoing behind Kevin's lead of "The Blue & White Ma-chine" with "Yeeeeah work it harder!" It was dope. The hand clapping never stopped. The soft undertone of "Blue-Smoke, Blue-Smoke," never stopped. It was a symphony of organized confusion that had me and Keko rocking. Well, as much as I could anyway.

> *The blue and white ma-chine.*
> *(Yeeeeeah work it harder!")*
> *The blue and white ma-chine.*
> *(Yeeeeeah work it harder!")*

That's when Quan hopped up, "OK, now it's my leg," he began. "Once we figured out that Shadow wasn't cra-zy and was dedicating the race to BJ, we locked into that Mendel pride, baby. Plus, me being a captain with you, I had to represent. I passed St. Ignatius which put us into fifth. Mt. Carmel was just ahead of me. Leo was in first, St. Paul was second, and Rita third.

"Hawk was waving me in, hopping up and down. I was coming in hot. All I remember is hearing Kev's pep squad in the stands move to the third-leg mix-drop."

The guys quickly restarted the rhythm section. This time when Kevin said, "The blue and white ma-chine," Box would immediately follow him, echoing the school colors. Then they would all join back in saying, "Yeeeee-ah, work it harder."

> *The blue (bluuuuue) and*
> *white (whiiiiite) ma-chine.*
> *Yeeeeeah, work it harder!*

> *The blue (bluuuuue) and*
> *white (whiiiiite) ma-chine.*
> *Yeeeeeah, work it harder!*

Kevin had outdone himself. If that chant didn't pump up our relay team, nothing would. This was the team we were destined to be, all of us, together as one. Running as one. Sounding as one. I was so pumped that I wanted to race even while sitting helplessly in that bed.

As much as I enjoyed hearing Kevin's work of art secondhand while sitting in my hospital room, I knew my dog Hawk loved the *live* version. Hawk was a music aficionado. I knew he loved running to our very own theme music. Every great team should have some.

"Hawk went from fourth place to third," Shadow hopped in to explain. "But by this time, St. Paul edged their way into first."

"Who was running third leg for them?" I asked.

"Bruce."

"Oh, that idiot," I replied.

"So St. Paul went into first, pushing Leo back to second place. While St. Rita snuck back up and was battling Hawk for third place. But Hawk did his thing, he held pat coming into the exchange."

I knew what was coming next. I looked over at Joe, sitting quietly by the windowsill. I smiled big. Joe nodded and smiled back.

Quan hopped back up, "BJ, you already know what time it is homeboy. It's winning time!"

Quan paced the room back and forth like a lion, getting us all hyped, he went over to Keko, "See, Mr. James, Mendel has the anchor of all anchors, we call him Superman, our very own thoroughbred, Joe. He was out the stable whinnying, neighing, hoofing at the track with his spikes. After my leg was over, I went to the infield to get dressed and there he was. BJ, I looked at the man and fire was in his eyes. *Blue smoke* was snorting from his nostrils. I'm getting goosebumps thinking about it."

Quan rolled up his sleeve to show us his goosebumps. He bounced around the room slapping "five" with Kevin, Shadow, and Joe. Quan was in rare form telling his animated recollection. *Man, I wished I was there*. Sitting in that bed watching my friends get excited telling me and my dad about a track meet, I realized I was no longer vicariously living out my mom's dream. I was living out my own. I loved track and lamented the fact that even though it was possible I would run again, I didn't have a collegiate scholarship to continue doing what I now knew I loved.

"BJ," Quan called, snapping me from my daydream. "You know how Joe's a quiet storm brewing before his events?"

"Yup, yup," I nodded and smiled in agreement.

"Not this time. Joe snapped! He was pacing like I am right now, talking smack to St. Paul's anchor—"

"Don't tell me, Victor?" I interrupted.

"Not just Victor! To all the anchors. Joe was screaming, 'It's over! I don't even know why y'all here! This is my race, it's a wrap! Go home!' So you know me, I had to put fuel on that fire, I was like, 'Yeah, Joe. Yeah. They don't want none, boy! They don't want none!' BJ, we almost got into a fight right there on the infield."

Joe laughed out loud, lowering his head, that's how I knew Quan was telling the truth. I was done. . .done. I would have paid money to be in that raucous.

Since Quan was hyperventilating, Box gently nudged him aside and finished the story. The final lap bell rang as Bruce passed the baton on to Victor. He took off, still in first place. The Leo anchor took off and Hawk stumbled in just after Rita, giving the baton to Joe in fourth place.

"Now's the time we've been waiting for," Box began. "Joe was running anchor leg and the entire team was primed for the final leg chant."

The blue (bluuuuue) and
white (whiiiiite) ma-chine.
Yeeeeeah, work it harder!

They choke on that blue
and white smoke.
Yeeeeeah, work it harder!
They choke on that blue
and white smoke
Yeeeeeah, work it harder!

"Dog, no exaggeration," Box continued. "In the first hundred meters, Joe passed the St. Rita dude and was gaining on Leo. Believe it or not, the Leo guy turned to see where Joe was. When I saw that, I knew it was a wrap. Joe sucked him up, quick, easy work. Now Joe had a full two hundred meters to suck up Victor."

"BJ," Shadow jumped in. "It was like watching a cartoon running the way Joe reeled in Victor. He hawked Victor worse than you did in the 4x200."

"Nah, BJ was more graceful than I was," Joe finally chimed in. "I was hurting that last hundred meters, but when I heard that crowd, man. . ."

Suddenly, Joe stopped talking and just shook his head. I looked around at the rest of the fellas who also looked like they'd seen a ghost.

"What happened?" Keko asked.

"I saw Joe was starting to fade that last hundred meters," Kevin explained. "The idea just popped in my head to go acapella on 'em. I turned around, looked up at the team waving my hands. I told the team to stop clapping. Just say, 'blue smoke, blue smoke, blue smoke.'"

"When we caught on, it seemed like those two words cut through all the spectator chatter," Box said.

"Bruh, the whole stadium, everybody, joined in," Joe explained. "Dude, picture the entire track and field stadium, full of spectators chanting 'blue smoke, blue smoke, blue smoke.' Then imagine how I must have felt being on that track, hearing my brothers and that crowd. No way I was losing to Victor. Got him at the line by seven tenths of a second."

The room fell silent again. I could feel the weight of the moment. We all looked around at one another locking eyes, content smirks on our faces, even Keko. Joe was the lone runner, but it took his team to bring him home. Joe ran a blistering 47.9 split to pull off the upset.

"Excuse me guys," a shift nurse said, poking her head inside the room. "Sorry, visiting hours are over."

"Thank you," Keko replied. "We're leaving now."

Just as the shift nurse left, I overheard her telling someone else in the hallway about the visiting hours. The all too familiar voice told her he would only be a minute. I looked at the doorway expectantly. Coach Abrams entered the room.

"Hey Coach. . .you made it. . .sup Coach," the fellas greeted.

"Hey, hey, you guys still here?" Coach replied. "Mr. James, how are you? How's the arm?"

Coach and Keko shook hands.

"It'll be fine, Coach. Thanks for asking."

Coach looked around the room and spotted the Championship Trophy on top of the tray table.

"Good, I see the team showed you the trophy. You know it's not yours, right?" Coach joked. "But you can keep the medals though."

Everyone laughed.

"Yeah, I know. Sounds like I missed a good one."

"It was an incredible win that's for sure. The team really rallied together."

The guys started gathering their belongings to leave as Coach came over to my bed. He placed his hand on my shoulder.

"How are you doing, BJ?"

"I'm doing all right, Coach. The pain isn't too bad thankfully."

"That's good to hear."

"There is more good news too. My paralysis is only temporary. The doctor said I should make a full recovery."

"So I've heard. Your auntie called, gave me the good news. That's part of why I'm so late visiting."

I looked at Dad then back to Coach Abrams, "How do you mean?"

Coach walked over to the other side of the room and picked up the Championship Trophy. He examined it carefully.

Dad and I traded looks again. The guys stood around watching and waiting as well.

"Coach Abrams, what's going on?" Keko asked.

Coach placed the trophy back on the tray table. He had a serious look about him.

"BJ, do you remember asking me to help you secure a scholarship?"

"Yeah."

"And I told you not to get your hopes up even though I had a couple colleagues of mine attend a few meets. Well, when I heard from your auntie that you would walk again, I went to my friend's house, and we made some calls on your behalf."

"What? Coach, wha. . .what are you saying?"

"I'm saying that we couldn't get you a scholarship for next year. You're gonna need about a year to rehab anyway. But my friend has a buddy who leaves one scholarship slot open every year just in case a stud becomes available. He's willing to look at you for the following year if you can be anywhere near the level you were."

"Are you serious!?"

"I told him you would be. I guarantee that."

Kevin and the rest of the guys rushed my bedside, hugging and giving me dap as if they forgot I was shot. Dad thanked Coach Abrams as they shook hands again.

Dad watched from afar and waved, "Congratulations. I'll see you tomorrow son."

"OK," I muttered back from under the pile of blue track uniforms.

He and Coach Abrams walked out together.

Box started shouting, "Blue smoke! Blue smoke!"

Soon all the fellas joined in, hopping around the room, crashing into one another like it was a mosh pit, yelling, "Blue smoke! Blue smoke! Blue smoke!"

Immediately, several hospital staff flooded the room barking orders for them to be quiet while escorting them out. They wouldn't be quiet, however. I could hear my Mendel teammates as they went down the hall, disturbing the entire floor, "Blue smoke! Blue smoke! Blue smoke!"

I sat there astonished, staring at our trophy I softly joined my brothers' fading refrain, "Blue smoke. Blue smoke. Blue smoke. Yeeeeeah, work it harder!"